The Book of Joshua I

TRUST

Books by Iris Bolling

THE HEART SERIES
Once You've Touched The Heart
The Heart of Him
Look Into My Heart
A Heart Divided
A Lost Heart
The Heart

NIGHT OF SEDUCTION SERIES
Night of Seduction/Heaven's Gate
The Pendleton Rule

GEMS & GENTS SERIES
Teach Me
The Book of Joshua I - Trust

Printed in the United States of America
ISBN-13: 978-0-9801066-9-5
ISBN-10: 0-9801066-9-9
Library of Congress Control Number: 2013914687
This is a work of fiction. Names, characters, places and
incidents are with the product of the author's imagination
or are used fictitiously, and any resemblance to actual
persons, living or dead, business establishments, events,
locales is entirely coincidental.

SIRI ENTERPRISES
RICHMOND, VIRGINIA
www.sirient.com

To Loretta R. Walls
Trust and Believe
A dream can become a reality

Chapter One
Africa

An explosion rocketed through the darkness of the midnight hour, filling the air with orange flames and black smoke. Men began shouting, pointing and running towards the area of the buildings that had erupted.

BOOM! Another explosion pierced the night, knocking some of the men off their feet, causing more confusion. Men dressed in brown, khaki, military uniforms with guns drawn rushed from other buildings toward the flames. Voices of shock and fear filled the once quiet night. The explosions were the perfect decoy for the covert action taking place ten miles away.

Dressed in black, with a ski mask covering his face, CIA Operative Absolute, watched as a third explosion burst into the night. Securing the thin binocular tool in his pocket, he closed his mind to the confusion and focused on the mission at hand. Crawling, belly down, from his hiding place in a ravine, he made his way to a large tree at the end of a fork in the gravel road. Fifty feet away, perched behind another tree, he pulled a slim palm size device from his pocket, aimed it at the root of the tree, then pushed a button. To a trained eye, the thick root was a latch. A well disguised latch, but a latch nonetheless.

The green light on his handheld device indicated the opening was clear of explosives. Patience was paramount to his mission. Remaining motionless, his senses alert, he listened for any sound or movement. In the jungle, or in a rural area, there were always night sounds. Eliminating the natural sounds of the critters that belonged, from the two-legged creatures who could take his life, was an art form. It was his best asset.

A light ruffling of gravel, proved his patience prudent, footsteps were approaching. This confirmed he was in the right place. That tree was the entrance to the tunnel that would lead him to the mansion.

Absolute's mission, sanctioned or not, was to extract the hostage inside the mansion without inciting an international war. This restriction made his mission more difficult. Hell, casualties were a way of life in his job. Keeping the countdown meant he had to be selective. He could not just kill anyone who was in his way. He hated that. The sound of another footstep cleared his mind of all thoughts. A smile formed on his face. Perhaps he could have a little fun after all.

Slowly, his six-four frame rose against the tree trunk. His normal weapons of choice would be air to land missiles, however, this situation called for a little, just a little, diplomacy. The missiles were out. As it stood, the explosives would have to be explained. He pulled the night vision glasses down to his eyes. From his pocket he took out a device that resembled a straw, placed it between his lips, and waited. A few moments later, a guard walked within ten feet of him. He pursed his lips and blew. A dart, filled with enough tranquilizer to drop an elephant, struck the guard in the side of his neck. He fell unceremoniously to the ground. Knowing the guard's partner would hear the sound and investigate, Absolute remained in his position. The other guard called out to his partner, then approached with his weapon ready to fire. He bent over his partner and soon found himself suffering the same fate as a tranquilizer dart struck him as well.

Only the sounds of nature, and the faint shouts from miles away filled the air. Absolute waited a few moments, listening for other guards. Once he was certain no other guards were in the area, he moved from his position.

Standing over the fallen men, he reached down and removed the miniature darts from their necks, leaving no trace of his presence. He simply removed the clips from their weapons, placing them in his army fatigues pants pocket, then continued with the mission.

Absolute was an expert on setting explosives, better still at finding and deactivating them. Crouching on the ground, he examined the tree trunk. A tiny light appeared on his monitor, indicating an electronic feed surrounding the tree. He pushed a button deactivating the feed. Satisfied the area was clear, he began tapping the ground with his booted foot. There was a hollow, five by five area at the base of the tree. Stooping, he ran his hand over the ground where he originally saw the latch. Different objects on the ground moved at his touch. A stone did not. Shining his penlight at the stone, he pushed it down, nothing happened. Pushing left, then right, still nothing happened. He continued to run his hand over a longer stretch of the ground. He discovered another stone that did not move. Following his previous motions did not reveal the results he desired. "Damn."

Thinking for minute, he stretched his long arms out to reach both stones, pushing simultaneously. His reward was the sound of the latch releasing. He looked at the crack of an opening and noticed what he'd thought was a twig, was a handle. Using his penlight, he checked the joints of the opening to ensure there would be no danger upon entering the underground facility. Believing it to be clear, he pulled the wood trap door that was covered with artificial turf up, revealing a stairway leading to the tunnel.

Before descending the stairs, he lay on his belly and examined them for any wiring. When he was certain they were clear, he walked slowly down the man-made steps checking for any security feature that would detect his presence. Nothing so far. Reaching up, he pulled the opening down, until it appeared to be closed. He stopped just before touching the last step and flashed his light around the dirt floor, searching for anything out of the norm. Nothing. Stepping down, he followed the neatly carved out walkway that curved the further he walked. Flashing his light, he strategically checked for any motion detectors or land mines that might be buried along the way. So far there were none.

The interior of the tunnel widened the further he walked. About one hundred feet in, the walkway changed from dirt to cement, the walls were now brick. He stopped. Another twenty feet ahead, there were glimpses of light. The corridor led to a fork, one to the East and another to the West. He turned west.

A few steps in he saw a detector in the ceiling with a red light indicating the alarm was activated. Slouching down, flush against the wall, he pushed a button on his handheld, waited a split second and watched as lights on the camera flashed three times, then turned solid red again. More buttons were pushed, a second later the red motion detector lights blinked, then disappeared. Whoever was watching the monitors on the other end, would see the area empty and undisturbed.

Continuing down the corridor, he came to a door. He tried turning the knob. It was locked. Locked doors meant nothing to him. There was always a way around them. You could go through, under, over or around them. Locked doors, never kept him from entering anything. Pulling out his lock pick set, he settled on his favorite, inserted it inside the lock, then listened for it to click. It did. Examining the door, he noticed another detector at the top. He simply deactivated it with his handheld, then slowly opened the door.

There were rooms on both sides of the hallway. Moving cautiously, but quickly down the corridor, he peered through the eight by ten window of the closed doors, checking the locks as he passed by. Each room had a bunk bed, sink and a toilet. *Cells*, he thought as he continued on. Using his night vision glasses, he could see that each of the rooms he passed was empty.

Up ahead he saw more steps, which he believed led to the lower level of the mansion. Silently, he walked past several more doors peeking inside. He stopped, stepped back and looked inside the room he'd just passed. It was different from the others he had peeked into. Unlike the others, which were single rooms, here he could see there were multiple furnished rooms. On carpeted floors there was a sofa, a table with books sitting next to a lamp, a kitchen table with two chairs next to a sink, a stove and a refrigerator. He moved to the next door, which was the connecting room. There was a full size bed in the middle of the room, a dresser, a closet, and an open door leading to a bathroom. What held his attention was the body on the bed.

Not believing for one minute his mission could be this easy, he moved back to the first door. Using his tools, he picked the lock, heard it click, then waited. Five seconds later, he was inside the room. Using his penlight, he checked for any traps as he quickly walked towards the bedroom. There was a slight movement inside the room. He stood back in the shadow of the bedroom door and waited.

A minute later he saw a small figure take a pensive step through the doorway and stop. The figure's back was to him, as it peered into the room with something in hand. Absolute clamped his hand over the person's mouth and inserted a dart into the neck. The small figure fell limp. He placed the body on the bed, and then used his penlight to take a good look.

Shining his penlight on the figure's face. He quickly looked down the body, then back up to the face. "You are not Princess Zsa Zsa," he said as he shined the light down the unconscious female body on the bed. The woman was not the sixteen-year-old sister, to his friend Prince LaVere' Ashro of Emure, who had been kidnapped from her home.

"Who are you?" With his hand held device he snapped a quick picture of the woman, then transmitted it to his handler, with one word, "*Identify.*"

The operative sat on the side of the bed with his head tilted to the side, his mind fighting the natural rise of his libido as he perused the woman's body. Saying she was beautiful would be an understatement. Her hair was in a thick French style braid, neatly pulled back from her angelic face. Long lashes, a perky nose, high cheekbones, and tantalizing lips completed a very alluring package. The rise and fall of her breasts was his first indication this was not a sixteen year old girl.

The silk pajama pants concealed the remainder of her body from him, however, there was no doubt, she was a well-endowed, full grown woman. He could tell from his body's reaction. The things he could do with her body. His device chirped with a message bringing his wandering mind back to the task at hand. He blinked at the identification. He sent a message back. *Contact the lead Senator in Foreign Relations.*

He glanced around the room wondering, *what are they doing, collecting women here, and if so, why?* Using his handheld device, he pushed a button activating the heat sensor. Holding it up, he walked through the rooms. The sensor, showed three bodies on the lower level of the complex, yet, there was only the two of them. He checked the wall to the left, where the device indicated the still body was located. Whoever it was, he knew the person was alive. He worked diligently knowing his diversion would allow only a limited amount of time to complete his task.

Running his gloved hand over the wall, he could not detect an opening, but he knew it was there. He stretched out on the floor, using his penlight to examine the baseboard. The opening could not be seen, but he felt the slightest change in the air. He ran his finger along the area where the wall met the floor and there it was, a crack. The opening was upward.

Sitting on the floor Indian style, with the device in his hand as if playing a video game, he pushed another button, a red line appeared. "Hmm, an electrical current." Following the flow of the electrical current on the device, he looked at the wall where it stopped. He tapped the baseboard with his hand. Nothing happened. He then stood, applying a bit more pressure on the baseboard with his foot. Bingo. The wall slid up, opening to an adjoining bedroom.

Inside a small figure sat up in the bed. Absolute ducked under the moving door, to silence the person before she could speak. The young girl began to squirm under his grasp. He whispered in her ear, "Zsa Zsa, I'm here to take you home."

The girl froze. He moved the night goggles from his eyes. He could see the frightened, uncertain look in the young girl's eyes. He put a finger up to his lips indicating for her to be quiet, and then he removed his hand.

Zsa Zsa held on, wrapping her small arms tightly around his neck. He could feel her body shaking with fear and relief as tears rolled down her cheeks. She spoke English with an accent. "Did my father send you?"

Zsa Zsa was holding him so tight, it took a moment for him to pull her arms down as she sat on the bed. He wiped tears from her eyes as he spoke. "Your brother LaVere' sent me. Listen, we don't have much time. I need you to be very quiet and stay behind me." He put a band on her wrist. "Never take this off."

Zsa Zsa nodded. "Okay," she replied as she slipped on her shoes.

He took the girl's hand as they walked into the other room. Absolute tapped the baseboard with his toe, and the wall retracted.

When they walked by the bed, Zsa Zsa gasped. "Is Akande dead?" the girl asked with a shaking voice.

Absolute looked down at the woman. "No. Let's go." He took Zsa Zsa's hand to walk towards the door, but the girl pulled back.

"We can't leave her," the girl cried out.

"Zsa Zsa, we have to go, now."

"She cared for me, I cannot leave her behind."

"Yes, you can and you will," Absolute said as he picked the girl up.

"No, no," Zsa Zsa cried out. "You don't understand. This is not her home. She was taken, just like me."

Exasperated, Absolute sat the girl on her feet. "You speak English. Therefore, I assume you know what the word quiet means."

"Never assume," Zsa Zsa said. "It makes an ass out of you and me."

The reply made him smile. "Where did you hear that?"

"From my friend in the United States."

With younger sisters, he had dealt with teenagers before. He knew not to dismiss what they had to say. Bending down on one knee, he looked into the girl's eyes. "Okay, what do you mean she was taken?"

"Akande, that's her name, she told me she was taken and placed here a short time ago. I don't know the entire story, but I can tell you, she cannot remain here. They will kill her once they learn I have escaped. If we do nothing more, then get her out of here, it should be enough to ensure her safety."

She may be young, Absolute thought, as he listened to her speak, *but her assessment of the situation was accurate*. He rose, walked into the other room and returned with the woman across his shoulder then looked down at Zsa Zsa. "No more talking until we are out of here, understood." He pulled his night vision glasses down.

"Understood," she nodded and followed him out the door. "It's dark."

Absolute turned to the girl frowning. She could not see the look in the dark, but he hoped the swiftness of his turn would give her the message. He took her hand, hooked her fingers through the belt loops of his pants, then held them there indicating for her to hold on.

Absolute enlisted in the military because his big brother had. During his time at Quantico, he was recruited for clandestine operations with the Central Intelligence Agency, or simply the CIA, and he never looked back. His trainer remains one of the best operatives at the United States' disposal. He drilled in him to be ready for all possible outcomes. Retreating the way he'd come, so many things could go wrong, he thought. Every scenario possible played through his mind. He was prepared for each of them. What he was not prepared for was his body's reaction to the woman he was carrying. He pushed that aside and thought of the more pressing issues.

His escape plan, for two, had to be altered. How would the woman react once she awakened? Would she be friend or foe? The thought of leaving her behind to die was not something his conscience would allow him to do. Neither of the captives were dressed properly for an escape. Their clothing could be spotted in the dark. The one over his shoulder did not have on shoes and the other was too young to understand the situation was dangerous.

Absolute stopped when they reached the outer door. He braced the woman on the ground against the wall, then pulled Zsa Zsa out beside him. Using his handheld device, he pushed a button. The red lights blinked three times, the beam was solid again.

"What did..."

He quickly put his hand over the girl's mouth. Turning his penlight on, he flashed it in her face, then put his finger to his lips indicating for her to be quiet.

Zsa Zsa nodded her head. "I do apologize."

An exasperated looked covered his face. He shook his head, knowing he had to hurry up and get them out of the area before the girl gave their location away. Quickly, he pulled out a thin cord, hooked one end to his pants and the other to a buttonhole on Zsa Zsa's pajama top. He stood, put the woman back over his shoulder, then walked the remaining distance to the steps leading out.

Reaching the trap door, he stopped, pulled out a long cord with a glass covering on the tip. He connected it to his hand held device. He inserted the end of the cord through the small crack of the door.

"What are you doing?"

"Shh," he said, then looked down at the monitor. The simple attachment turned his device into a mini monitor. The camera on the end allowed him to see what was outside. The scan only displayed a portion of the area. It was the area he could not see that concerned him. Instinct was his only resource in this situation.

Placing the woman on the step, he unhooked Zsa Zsa. "Stay," he whispered. Slowly he raised the door just enough to ease his body out to scan the area for any movement. Once completely out, he lowered the door, leaving it cracked. Walking the area, he surveyed it to ensure he could get the women to the low lying area he'd used for cover earlier. The two guards were still on the ground where he'd left them.

A sound from behind caused him to hit the ground, then look back. The door was open and Zsa Zsa was pulling the woman out.

"What in the hell?" He hurried back over. "Get down." Absolute pulled Zsa Zsa to the ground.

"A light came on behind us," Zsa Zsa explained.

Absolute quickly pulled the woman completely out, then closed the door. Putting the woman over his shoulder, he grabbed Zsa Zsa with the other arm and ran for cover. He slid feet first into the ravine where he'd left his equipment, pulling both with him. Not wasting any time, he pulled his black bag from its hidden location and pulled out black tape. Tearing a strip, he immediately put it over Zsa Zsa's mouth. She reached up to remove it. He gave her a look, which indicated not to try him. He then did the same to the woman, for he wasn't sure how much longer she would be out. From the bag, he pulled out a black shirt, giving it to Zsa Zsa to put on. He pulled the shirt he was wearing off, and put it on the woman laying on the ground. Taking a small package from the bag, he unfolded it and placed the harness around the woman then secured it around his back as if carrying a baby. From the bag, he pulled out a round device, aimed it at a nearby tree, then pushed a button. A rope snaked out and wrapped around the tree. He hooked the rope, securing it in place. He tied the rope around Zsa Zsa's waist, pulled a large hook from the bag then hooked her to him again. Placing the bag on his shoulder and the woman now secure on his back, he placed Zsa Zsa in front of him. They slowly descended the hill using the rope. He watched the girl turn and look down. The fear was clear on her face. "I have you." He tightened his hold around her waist and continued moving down.

Voices could now be heard above them. Taking a look down, they had about twenty feet left to go. Too far to drop down, with two additional people. Steady movement was the best course of action he decided and continued moving. There were ten feet left to go when he saw the first man look over the hill. He held Zsa Zsa in front of him and pushed their bodies flush against the hill. The darkness of the night should be enough to conceal them, but they had to move soon.

A man's call to another was all the motivation he needed to move again. The moment his foot touched the flat surface of the area, he unhooked Zsa Zsa. "Follow the path, when you get to the opening stop."

Tears flowed down the girl's face as she pulled the tape from her mouth. "It's dark."

Gunfire rang through the air. "Run," he demanded. "I'll find you."

Zsa Zsa did as instructed. Absolute quickly unhooked his connection from the rope. He unhooked the top clamp, pulled a thin device from his pocket, and touched the rope. A spark ignited and traveled upward. He ran into the woods, following the trail Zsa Zsa had taken. He came to the opening that led to the road but did not see Zsa Zsa. "Damn," he swore as he pulled out his hand held. He pushed a button, and a beep appeared on the screen, showing him where the girl was. He walked towards the road and froze. Two guards were standing near his vehicle with Zsa Zsa in their grasp. He stepped back, unhooked the harness and put the woman on the ground. He placed his bag under her head. He casually walked from the woods looking down at his device as if he was distracted.

"Stop," one guard called out pointing his weapon at him.

"Whoa, hold up," he put his hand up as if in surrender. "What's up, man? What's with the guns and stuff?" The other guard grabbed Zsa Zsa around her waist. "Hold up, that's my sister, man. What are you doing?" he called out as he continued to walk towards them. The guard's radio cut in, and as he reached to respond, Absolute ran, jumped, and kicked him in the chest. Then he pulled his knife from his belt and flipped it up, stabbing the guard holding Zsa Zsa in the neck. The movement was so fast the Zsa Zsa did not have time to scream before he grabbed her and put her in the backseat of the jeep.

"Stay down," he demanded.

Running into the woods, he grabbed the woman and his bag just as gunfire sounded through the air.

"Oh hell!" Absolute exclaimed as he quickly placed the woman in the back seat as well. He threw the bag in the front seat then jumped across it, into the driver's seat, turned the engine and floored the vehicle out of the hidden cove.

Pushing a button on the console of the vehicle, Absolute spoke. "Princess Zsa Zsa is secured."

Ned replied, "Are you at the drop site?"

"Ten minutes out."

"Acknowledged. Your transportation to Emure is waiting. The radar on the band is coming in clear. We can track the Princess now." He could hear his handler hitting buttons through the speakers. "An hour ago we received communication of several explosions in the region. You?" Ned, the handler asked.

"Diversion. No injuries."

"Any deaths?"

"Not mine," Absolute replied as he drove in the dark with his night vision ware the only light.

"I can report a successful mission without incident."

"Not exactly."

"Not exactly what, Absolute. What did you do?"

"The person you identified earlier was also extracted."

"Leave her."

"Not possible. We're on the move."

"Absolute, taking her will have international implications."

"I suggest you contact the lead Senator in Foreign Relations. Advise an international situation is at hand. I'm out." He pushed the button ending the conversation.

Glancing at Zsa Zsa in the back seat, he smiled. "I'm taking you home."

Chapter Two
Richmond, Virginia

"Why can't all of them go?" Shelly Knight's angry question resonated around the meeting room of the community center. "We made promises to these children. They did all that was asked of them and more. Now you want to tell them they can't go. That's going to leave a great impression on them about this world and our government. Jump through this hoop, stand this way, walk that way, talk this way." Shelly's friend Rochelle Delany, grabbed her arm trying to get her to be quiet, but Shelly pulled away. "I will not be quiet while our government officials, who we, by the way, put into office, scam our children." She squinted her eyes at the man who had enraged her so, Senator Royce Davenport, and then spoke directly to him. "I would have expected more from you, Senator. You know what these children are up against. Hell the scholarship is in your name for Christ's sake. And you are going to sit there and say nothing." She put her hands on her hips. Never had anyone enraged her so deeply.

Senator Royce Davenport watched and listened, as the argument grew more intense. This was one of the reasons he stayed away from community meetings, time was wasted. It seemed nothing was ever accomplished. His brother Grayson normally handled the scholarship distribution to the various organizations he supported. One person appealed the decision of the board to the very top and demanded his presence. It would have been simple to delegate the authority to Grayson to make the final decision, but his brother insisted he take part in this particular meeting. Grayson feared negative publicity was sure to arise if he did not make an appearance—or so he said.

The woman contesting the board's decision was a looker. She was a thick, curvy sister who looked to be in her thirties, with short, naturally wavy hair that appeared to have been simply brushed back. At the nape of her neck the curls were flipping up indicating it was time for a cut. Then there was the teasing shade of her skin, it was hard to say if it was a natural brown, or if she had recently spent time in the sun, but it looked good on her. Maybe it was the contrasting, crisp white button down blouse, with two buttons open at the top, showing just enough cleavage to make a man curious. He would have never thought the conservatively dressed woman would be so feisty. Apparently she was as passionate about this situation as she was fine. If only he could see her legs, but since she was on the second row, those sitting in the front blocked his view. Clearing the unusual thoughts from his mind, Senator Royce Davenport looked up at the woman who was now speaking.

"Ms. Knight, please watch your tone and refrain from insulting our guest. Senator Davenport was kind enough to take time out of his busy schedule to meet with us today and I will not stand for your insolence." Tammy Richardson, head of the Board of Trustees at the Royce C. Davenport Community Center and one of the richest matriarchs of the community, demanded as she pushed her weaved curls over her shoulder. "Now," she said as she used the program bulletin to fan herself, "we are doing all we can to help those children. It certainly is better to assist a few than none at all."

"How can you possibly consider sending fifteen children, when twenty met the requirement? All twenty should be allowed to attend the camp. If we had put a limit on the number at the very beginning of this contest, then I would not have an argument. But we did not; we can't come in now and put in limitations. If all twenty qualified, then all twenty should be allowed to go." Shelly continued with her argument.

"We don't have the money for all twenty. We only have the funds to cover fifteen." William Casey, the treasurer stated. "Some of the children will have to be eliminated."

"I refuse to accept that. What is the message we are sending the children we turn away? Hmm, follow all the rules, but sorry you still don't measure up. I don't like that message. And how do we select who goes and who doesn't? The same old, those that have the right connections with the right families will be selected while others that are less fortunate and need this trip more will be left behind."

Tammy rose from her seat. "Ms. Knight, how dare you insinuate this board is biased."

"It's not an insinuation Tammy, it's a fact!" Shelly charged back.

Royce looked at Grayson and gave the nod to end the meeting. Grayson stood and addressed the audience and the ten board members. "Ladies and gentlemen, please, let's keep this cordial." He waited until things quieted down a bit, then looked over at Rochelle, who pulled Shelly down into her seat. "The purpose of this meeting was to allow Senator Davenport an opportunity to hear both sides of the debate before rendering his decision. I believe both sides have had ample opportunity to state their positions on this matter. It is only courteous to allow the Senator to say a few words." Grayson turned to his brother, "Royce."

Shelly took her seat and looked down at her shaking hands, for she did not want to hear what the man was going to say. She knew the Richardson family were huge contributors to the Senator's campaign, and it was doubtful that he would go against them. She thought he was a good man. If he heard firsthand what she believed to be an injustice, he might do the right thing. Sitting there shaking her head, she vowed she would find a way to get every child that qualified on that bus.

As Royce's six-one, two hundred and ten pound frame stood, the room seemed to get smaller. His very presence was overwhelming, along with his looks and charisma that had women from North and South vying for his attention. As a single U.S. Senator representing the state of Virginia, he was sought after by all women, Black, White, Asian—it really didn't matter. They all wanted an opportunity to be seen on his arm. If the media was any indication, he spread himself around for all to enjoy. Just last weekend, he was in a magazine with some starlet from Hollywood. He was equally as popular amongst his colleagues in Washington. They sought after him to get his support on bills as if he was the President in waiting. They respected his opinion just that much. However, tonight he was going to have to disappoint someone and that did not please him. The woman with the

almond colored eyes had a compelling argument. The
stipulations should have been clarified in the
beginning. Nonetheless, the funds were not available.

"I want to thank each of you for taking an interest
in the well-being of our children. From what I have
witnessed tonight, I know the children of this
community have people who truly care about them.
That's more than what many disadvantaged children
around the world can say. To the matter at hand." He
sighed. "Before coming here tonight I stopped to
speak with Mr. Casey and to take a look at the books.
The bottom line is clear; the funds needed are just not
there to include all of the children. Therefore, a
decision has to be made on how to eliminate five." He
watched as the woman, who made the argument to
have all of the children attend the camp, stood and
walked out of the room. He made a mental note to
find and speak with her once the meeting was over.

Twenty minutes later as the meeting dispersed,
Rochelle found Shelly in the lobby of the community
center pacing back and forth. The two had grown up
together in a foster home. As loving as Cephus and
Virginia Brown were, they could not afford certain
things. The two girls were constantly left out of social
events and shunned while growing up. So she
understood why Shelly was reacting angrily to the
injustice of the situation. Their past life was haunting
her and she did not want to see another child go
through what they endured.

"Shelly," Rochelle sympathized, "Are you all
right?"

"No," Shelly replied with fresh tears in her eyes.
"How am I going to tell those children they can't go?
How am I supposed to do that?"

Rochelle pulled out a tissue and wiped away the
tears that streamed down her friend's face. "I know

it's going to be hard. At least you have a little time before a decision will be made."

"What do you mean? The next full meeting is this Saturday." Shelly sniffed.

"Senator Davenport wants to be the one to make the decision and since he can't come back until the middle of the month, no child will be notified."

"Well, at least he's good for something." She took the tissue from Rochelle. "Man, was I wrong about him." She said while shaking her head. "I always thought past all the media crap and gave him credit for being about something. Humph, he certainly proved me wrong."

"He's a politician, you can't expect but so much."

"I don't' know why, but I expected more from him." She looked up at Rochelle with a little hope in her eyes. "I was thinking, if I give up my trip to New York, I could pay for two of the children. That only leaves three for me to find money to pay for their trips."

"Shelly, you can't do that. You have been planning that trip for years. You can't give that up." Rochelle implored. "When we were little all you ever talked about doing was going to New York and staying at the Waldorf-Astoria like Eddie Murphy in *Coming to America*. It's taken you five years and two jobs to save that money. You can't just give your dream away."

"It was a fairytale, Rochelle. I'm thirty-five years old. It's time to live in the real world. These kids will never recover from the disappointment. You know that. Hell, I've face disappointment all my life. It's nothing new."

"Shelly," Rochelle had begun to argue with her, when Tammy walked out of the meeting room and approached them.

"I hope you are satisfied, Shelly Knight. Senator Davenport has taken the decision out of our hands. You've given him reason to doubt our ability to run the center. Now, what are your precious children going to do if he takes it all away?"

"What?" Shelly asked shocked at the thought.

"He did not say that Tammy," Rochelle gave Tammy the look of death if she said one more word. She turned back to Shelly, "He just wants to ensure the decisions the board members are making are fair." She looked back at Tammy to emphasize the meaning.

"That wasn't my interpretation," Tammy said and stomped off.

Both Royce and Grayson Davenport walked out of the room still surrounded by a few admirers and before Rochelle could stop her, Shelly was in the Senator's face.

"How could you threaten to take away the center?" Shelly attacked, "It's the only thing the children in the neighborhood have to look forward to. Would you have them hang out on the corner and fight their way through the drug dealers? Senator Davenport, I must say you have certainly disappointed me. I truly believed in you. With all you've done to help those less fortunate than yourself, I don't understand how you can even threaten to close the center down." She turned to walk away and stopped. Looking directly at Royce, she simply said, "I just don't know if I can continue to support you after this," she turned and walked away.

Rochelle watched her, shocked. She then turned back to Grayson and the Senator. "I have never seen her this upset," she exhaled. "Senator, Tammy Richardson misrepresented what you said to make Shelly feel guilty. Please accept my apology for her behavior."

Royce was too stunned to speak for a moment. He did not know the woman, had never set eyes on her before tonight, but for some reason her last statement cut him deep. He never liked excessively emotional women, so why did what this one had to say matter. Now, he was angry. Damn angry that she spoke to him in that manner. Didn't she know who he was? No one talked to him like that, no one! "You cannot apologize for her actions. She must now deal with the consequences." Royce stomped off leaving Rochelle and Grayson both staring at his back.

"Oh hell," Grayson said.

Rochelle turned to look up at the man worried. "What is he going to do?" she asked.

Grayson did not want to give the woman an answer for two reasons. One, he could never get Royce to see reason when it came to women. Two, he had no idea what actions his brother might take. "Don't worry, I'll calm him down. You work on Shelly." He walked out the door.

Grayson opened the back door to the limo and climbed inside. The driver pulled off once the door closed. "Well, that was a spirited meeting."

Royce turned to his brother with a dubious look. "You think. Who in the hell is she?" he yelled. Before Grayson could speak, Royce continued to vent. "Did you hear what she accused me of?" He turned away and looked out the window. "She had the nerve to be disappointed in me. Who gives a damn who she is disappointed with? Does she know I control the center and will take it down if I see fit?" Grayson began to speak, but was cut off—again. "She said it twice—did you hear her?" He jerked back around facing his brother. "You know she said it twice. That she was disappointed in me. Her words were: 'I would have expected more from you Senator.' Who is she to expect anything from me?" His fist hit the side of the door. "Pull over!" he demanded. The limo driver pulled over and parked near the lake at Maymont Park in Richmond's West End. Royce pushed the door open and stormed out.

Grayson remained seated for a minute, inhaled, then joined his brother by the lake. For a good fifteen minutes they just stood there, not a word passing between them. Then just like children they both began to laugh, for the situation was really not that serious and they both knew it.

"Believe it or not, tonight was the first time she has ever spoken up at a meeting," Grayson laughed. "Man, did she come out with a bang. All directed at you."

After calming down, Royce thoughtfully exhaled. "Well, she is certainly passionate about the children."

"That she is. She left a corporate position making six figures to teach in the high school."

"What?"

Grayson nodded his head affirmatively, "Yes, she did. Now she works two jobs and heads up the teen initiatives at the center. The two week camping trip was her idea. It was a way to get the teens to get their grades up and abstain from sex. She is the first one here every afternoon and the last to leave at night. Her dedication is commendable."

"What's her story?" Royce asked.

"I'm not sure. According to Tammy, Shelly Knight and Rochelle Delany were foster children, didn't quite fit into her world, as she put it."

"Hmm, not many people can fit into Tammy's world, except you." Royce displayed a devilish smile. "She just loves touching you."

Grayson gave his older brother a look that would drop most men. "Don't even play like that."

"I'm just messing with your head." Royce replied as the two looked out over the water. "Dad would have loved the center. You did a good job of pulling it all together."

"It was your name that opened the right doors and wallets. We have good programs with dedicated people."

"Some were for the right reasons and others, not so much." Royce held his head down in thought. "She's right you know."

"I know. I just don't know what to do about it. That's why I called you. Shelly isn't just thinking of the children, but their families as well. In the short time we've been open she has put a light into eyes that were dull before. Those families believe it when she says something is possible. I hate like hell to disappoint her."

Royce raised an eyebrow. "Are you involved with her?"

"Shelly? No. She is fine though with those thick legs, but not me. Now—Rochelle is another story."

"Man, Rochelle Delany will break you in two." Royce chuckled as he began walking back to the limo.

"I think I'd like that. Rough."

Royce looked at his younger brother who was almost a twin in his likeness and laughed as they entered the limo. "You would." The two laughed as Royce's cell phone chimed. He listened as the caller spoke. "Send me the Intel." He turned to his brother. "I have to get back to Washington."

"Man, you always pull that national security excuse when you don't want to deal with things."

Royce looked at his brother and smirked. "You want to be Senator for a while?"

"Hell no," Grayson knocked on the glass partition between them and the driver. "You're forty-four years old with gray hair, that's not for me." The limo pulled away from the curb.

A black town car was waiting at their mother's home when Royce and Grayson arrived. The Secret Service agent assigned when security alerts arise, stepped out of the back of the vehicle and opened the door for Royce.

"Senator Davenport," Agent Conrad McNally spoke. "There is an incident in Nigeria that needs your attention in Washington. A chopper is waiting to take you in."

"Thank you, Agent McNally. I'll be with you in one moment." He turned to his brother. "Let mother know, I'll call her later."

Grayson hugged his brother. This was his life. The country came first. "I'll handle it for you. Take care."

Royce entered the vehicle and within the hour he was at the Pentagon. Lieutenant General Mark McGary stood at attention as Senator Davenport walked through the door. "Fill me in, General."

"Senator Davenport, at twenty-one hundred hours our time, an operative entered Nigeria with the intent to extract Princess Zsa Zsa Adannaya Ashro, daughter of King Ahmed Ashro and sister to the current King Aswan Ashro, who was taken from her home two days ago. During the mission, he came across a woman identified as Akande Ariana Aubree, the niece of self-proclaimed King Tarik Tochi. Believing the woman was taken and held against her will, he extracted her as well."

"Our relationship with Tarik is tenuous to say the least," Royce stated as he looked over the file. He looked up at the monitor. "Are we tracking him?"

"Yes," the Lieutenant General used his pointer to indicate the location on the monitor. "He is currently en route to the drop site we set. The question is..."

"What do we do about the niece of the self-proclaimed King of Asmere?"

"No Intel. We have minutes to make the decision before the mission is jeopardized."

"Are communications open with the operative?"

"Yes sir."

"Let me speak with him."

The Lieutenant General nodded his head to one of the other military personnel in the room. The young officer pushed a button on the speaker in the center of the conference table. "Ned Gerhardt is on the line, Senator. He is the handler for the Operative, who is unavailable."

"What the hell do you mean, he is unavailable," Lieutenant General McGary yelled into the speaker.

Royce knew the name. Ned Gerhardt was the handler to a small group of CIA Operatives assigned to the Office of the President, used for delicate situations foreign and domestic. Royce had worked closely with one of the first agents assigned to Gerhardt nearly twenty years ago. Without ever having met the man, he trusted his judgment.

"Good evening, gentlemen. Senator Davenport, I'm forwarding documents to your phone for your eyes only. I'll give you the time it will take for Lieutenant General McGary to blow off steam for your response."

"Gerhardt, you do not address me as gentleman. I am a Lieutenant General in the United States military; you will address me as such. As for Absolute, you tell him to get his ass available."

Royce reviewed the information received on his phone as the Lieutenant General continued to layout his many accomplishments to the handler. Royce knew the CIA handler had probably placed the Lieutenant General on hold while he dealt with life and death situations. He couldn't care less why the Lieutenant General thought he was so important.

Joshua Lassiter was one of their top CIA operatives. The operative had over fifty successful missions behind him, with a hundred percent success rate. His decisions had been as extreme as his kill rate. His operative name, Absolute, was earned each time a mission was completed with precision and no trail leading to the United States. He is the best active agent in Gerhardt's arsenal. That statement was issued by Lassiter's training operative, Sylvester "Sly" Pendleton, the man Royce worked with twenty years ago. Each of the four operatives under Gerhardt's control, were weapons, human weapons. Any of them could take out an army with their specialized skills.

A message came through as the Senator was reading the file. It was from Absolute.

> *Senator Davenport, the woman extracted was being held against her will. While that is acceptable in this part of the world, it is against the American way. Your decision.*

The message brought memories of similar words he'd spoken in the very same region some twenty years ago. He still had the same beliefs, if not stronger. However, now, unlike then, he understood the need for diplomacy.

Royce looked up. "General," he said to quiet the man who in his opinion, was about to burst at the seams. "Gerhardt, give me your take on the situation."

"I trust my agent. The woman was rendered unconscious during the mission therefore unable to confirm the information provided by Princess Zsa Zsa."

"We are acting on the word of a sixteen year old," Royce speculated.

"Yes sir," Ned replied.

The situation caused Royce to take a moment as the eyes of the occupants in the room, the handler on the phone and the operative in Nigeria waited for his decision. Waiting for authorities to give him an order when he was a young lieutenant in the army, stationed in the region, caused the death of the rightful King of Asmere as well as that of his wife.

"Senator?" The Lieutenant General called out. "We do not want to cause an international incident on the word of a child."

Royce respected the General's take on the situation, however, he could not ignore the information provided. Certain region's beliefs on women were deplorable in his estimation. If he could, he would remove any woman who requested asylum, however it was not his country. "Return the child to her home. Request King Aswan's permission to bring the woman there until her situation is determined." Royce sat forward. "Impress upon the operative the importance of keeping this woman's location and existence covert. We do not want to incite a war between Asmere and Emure. If she requests asylum, grant it. Under no circumstances do we enter Asmere."

"Understood," Ned replied.

"I want daily updates on this situation. There is a time limit on the discovery of information Mr. Gerhardt. I want the operative out of that region." Royce nodded and the officer disconnected the call.

"Senator I'd like to clearly state my opposition to this action." Lieutenant General McGary stated.

"Duly noted. I will be sure to put it in my report to the President."

Chapter Three

It may have been the middle of the night in Emure, but you certainly could not tell it by the activity going on at the palace. They were celebrating the return of their beloved Princess Zsa Zsa. Every light in the palace was on. Every servant was working, either preparing food, rooms, or baths for the people about to enter. The royal family was waiting patiently on the veranda for the chopper to land.

"Mother, quickly Mother," Prince Raheem grabbed his mother's hand joining the family gathered on the veranda as the chopper began to descend.

Queen Nasheema walked swiftly, taking her middle son's hand. "Is she here? Have you placed eyes on her?" she asked with the urgency of a mother whose child has been missing for days.

"The helicopter is landing now." King Ahmed held his hand out for his wife. He wrapped his arm around her shoulders. "Once they land, she will be fine. You will see," he patted her shoulder to reassure her and himself as well.

A lone figure stepped off the chopper carrying a body in his arms. "It's Joshua," LaVere' lurched forward.

LaVere' and his brothers ran out to join the man walking towards them. LaVere' took his sister from Joshua as his eyes shined with unspilled tears. "Is she all right?"

"She's fine." Joshua released the girl. "I had to sedate her to stop her from talking."

The men released nervous laughter, for they were all emotionally drained. Their only sister was taken from the palace right from under their noses. While they were sharing a moment of relief at the return of their loved one, they also were grateful to Joshua yet weary of the next stage that must unfold. "We have often sought ways to silence her," Aswan, the current King of Emure joked, "Until now the means has escaped us. You must leave us with the drugs you use for the future. I am certain Zsa Zsa will have much to tell us upon her awakening."

"Of that, I am certain." Joshua stood watching the family gathering around the young girl. Not many of his missions turned out this way. He wanted to savor the moment.

Joshua Lassiter was attending his sister's wedding when their friend LaVere' received word of the kidnapping. Joshua, as a CIA operative, knew his expertise would be needed and did not hesitate to return to LaVere's home to assist in any way he could. Once they arrived and he was apprised of the delicacy of the situation, King Aswan and Prince LaVere' determined the best solution, to avoid a possible war between underground factions in Nigeria and Emure, was to turn this into a United States rescue mission. Since Joshua was an active agent, it was determined he would be the person to lead the operation.

Standing in the field, dressed in combat fatigues, legs apart, arms folded across his chest, Joshua, was a menacing sight, if he wasn't on your side.

LaVere' approached him knowing what he had accomplished was no small feat. He also knew there was more to come. "You have another package?"

"I do." Joshua's grin widened. "A woman."

LaVere' rolled his eyes. "Samuel tells me you find a woman on every mission. Why is that?"

Joshua shrugged his shoulders. "They find me, man. What am I supposed to do, leave them?"

"Yes," LaVere' replied. "You cannot bring every woman you meet home with you."

"Now see, that's where I feel the government should step down. If a woman wants a piece of this, she should have it. Why should we deny them when there's so much of me to go around? I feel it's my duty to share."

LaVere' turned towards the chopper, shaking his head. "One day a woman is going to bring you to your knees."

"Several have, and I can't begin to tell you how sweet they were."

Laughing LaVere' walked to the chopper. "Where is she?"

Joshua followed him. "Hey, it's not my fault Samuel, and Zack," his older brother and new brother-in-law, "have turned their backs on the female population by getting married." He picked the woman up in his arms as if she was a feather. "Somebody has to fulfill the demand for sexual healing." He looked at the woman, then grinned up at LaVere'. "She looks like an angel, doesn't she? Where can I take her?"

LaVere' just shook his head. "This way." They turned to walk away from the palace. "We have a cottage, we use for guests. You have unlimited use of the grounds and security for as long as you need."

"And the women?" Joshua raised an eyebrow.

"If they are willing." LaVere' chuckled.

Following a brick pathway, they came to what LaVere' referred to as a cottage.

The cottage was a two story, five bedroom, four bathroom, airy, luxury guest house, fit for a King.

"I've assigned security and staff to be available for you." LaVere' walked inside to ensure all was as he instructed. "There is a master suite upstairs to the right. I'm certain she will be comfortable there."

Joshua carried the woman upstairs where he was met by two servants. They were given orders to bathe the woman then make her comfortable. Two guards were placed at her door. Joshua showered and dressed then returned downstairs. He knew the family would have questions.

"Joshua, words cannot express my gratitude or that of my family for what you've done." LaVere' smiled. "Zsa Zsa is the heart of this family. The last few days have been hell with her gone."

He patted LaVere' on the back. "Unfortunately, we have another issue we have to deal with."

"The ransom demand?"

"No," Joshua said as he stood dressed in a gray Armani suit, crisp white dress shirt, gray and red tie, and Italian loafers. "We need to determine who is the inside person." He sat in a chair across from LaVere' and looked up. "What?," he questioned.

LaVere', who was at the wet bar pouring drinks, just stared at him. He glanced at his watch. "It's three o'clock in the morning. Are you expecting someone?"

"No," Joshua replied. "I have to look good at all times. My appearance is paramount to my mission in life."

LaVere' raised an eyebrow as he handed Joshua a drink. "I can't wait to hear this. What is your mission in life?"

"To grant as many women around the world as possible the pleasure of my body," Joshua replied as he accepted the drink. "It's the American way," Joshua replied as if the answer was a given. He crossed his legs as he sat back. "Tell me about the ransom demand." A few hours ago, LaVere' didn't think he would have anything to laugh about. Now, he could not contain himself. "The American way?"

"Yes, supply and demand. The women demand pleasure and I supply it."

"Samuel warned me about you, but I must confess, I did not believe he was serious.

"My game is serious." He took a drink. "Tell me about the ransom demand."

LaVere' knew both brothers. They were very different yet similar. Both were fearless leaders, extremely loyal and dedicated to their family. Samuel was settled, reserved, and mature, while Joshua was brash, uninhibited, and at times, immature. However, he would put his life in either of their hands, without question. "Now that Zsa Zsa is back, why the questions about the ransom?"

"To find the responsible party you have to follow the money. Or, at least know how the money was to be paid. Then follow that trail wherever it may lead."

LaVere' nodded. "The demand came to Raheem. He was given an account number to transfer the money to by midnight. The funds were to be transferred as American currency."

"Any idea who is behind the kidnapping?"

"No," LaVere' replied.

"It wasn't the people holding her," Joshua responded. "The people holding her did not care who she was. They only cared about the payment." He sat forward placing his glass on the table. "The place I infiltrated was a holding cell. It appears to be a kidnapping ring that acts as the go-between, to protect the mastermind. There are several operations in this region whose sole purpose is to take the person and hold them until the ransom is paid. Once they receive their split, the person is released or killed, which ever the mastermind instructs. The person behind the plan has no part in the implementation. I believe the woman upstairs, may have been taken from her home as well."

"When was she taken?"

"I can't say," Joshua replied. "What we need to determine is the woman's role in all of this. If she was taken, we will give her the option of returning. If she is a part of the operation, then she is subject to the laws of your country. If I'm correct, any act of violence against the royal family is considered treason. The penalty for treason is death."

"I can tell you now that my mother will not allow Aswan to take the woman's life if she cared for Zsa Zsa in any way."

"The woman's outcome is secondary and can be determined tomorrow. What needs your attention now, is who inside your home is a traitor."

"It is inconceivable to believe any member of the staff is capable of this. Every staff member is the descendant of servants. Their families are groomed for their positions from birth. It is an honor to be a part of the staff."

"Was it an honor for Jamal?" Joshua asked as he thought about the man who attempted to kill his sister-in-law Cynthia, who at the time was engaged to LaVere'.

LaVere' sighed, "This is true, however, many changes and security features have been put in place since that time."

"Yet, they were still able to come into the palace and take Zsa Zsa." Joshua nodded.

"Sadly, he is correct," King Aswan stated as he walked into the great-room. The men immediately rose at his entrance. He waved them down. "Sit, please," he said as he took a seat in the chair across from the sofa. A table was between him and Joshua. "My family, my country and I thank you for your actions on this day. You have our gratitude and bond from this moment on." He lowered his head, "I am ashamed to say, you are right. The gates to the palace could only be opened by someone inside." He looked up at LaVere'. "Since the birth of my son, I'm afraid I have been negligent in my duties. The security details have been left on Raheem's shoulders."

"Raheem is not to blame for this Aswan," Lavere' defended his brother.

"Please do not misunderstand, my brother. I do not hold Raheem responsible for this in anyway. It is my responsibility to protect this family and my country. I alone bear the burden of our mother's tears and our father's disappointment."

"Our mother's tears are now dry, King Aswan," LaVere' stated.

"I think you are more disappointed than your father, King Aswan." Joshua added. "This type of attack happens regularly. What you need to do now is ensure the people responsible are found. Others need to know, your countrymen are protected by you. Come after any one of them and the consequences will be death."

"How do we find the responsible parties? Zsa Zsa is now home and in her mother's arms. We do not have to pay the ransom."

"There are a few leads," Joshua stated. "I will find the responsible party and put them at your doorstep."

Chapter Four

It felt as if she was floating on a cloud. *The guard would be coming through soon to check on the girl,* she thought. Opening her eyes was the last thing she wanted to do, but she had no choice. Akande rolled over flinging one arm against her forehead. Suddenly she sat up, threw the sheet off and jumped out of the bed. Turning around, she looked from one item to another. *This is not the dungeon,* she thought as she swiped her hair from her face. Her eyes quickly looked around the room until she spotted him sitting in the chair near the door.

"Good morning."

Akande looked up to see a man dressed in a tan linen shirt, matching pants and sandals, with his legs crossed at the knee. She had never seen him before and had no idea if he was friend or foe. Looking around the room there was nothing she could use as a weapon. Glancing down, she noticed her clothes had been changed and she felt clean. She narrowed her eyes at him. At least in the dungeon, she knew who her captors were. Here...she did not know where here was. The unknown was a fear for her; therefore she did the only thing she could: Attack.

Joshua saw her intent before she took the first step. He jumped from the chair he was casually leaning in. Using his arm, he blocked her kick, which caused her to fall to the floor. Standing now, he watched as she took the battle stance with her feet apart, arms up, ready to attack. He almost laughed out loud seeing her take a battle stance against him. He thought she would stay down. He was wrong.

"So you know a little Tae Kwon Do?" He asked as he appeared to be lazily leaning against the wall. He'd learned a long time ago to never underestimate his opponent. He may appear to be relaxed, but he was alert and ready.

"Come near me and I will kill you."

Two strides and he was in the center of the room with his arms folded across his chest. He smiled. "Many women have tried, my sweet, and as you can see, I'm still standing."

"Who are you?"

"Joshua." He raised an eyebrow. "I know who you are. I don't understand your attitude at the moment. Most women are grateful when I rescue them." He looked perplexed for a moment. "Do you know each of your names begins with the letter A? Akande Ariana Aubree. Nice name, by the way. You know, we have this company at home called Triple A. Can I call you Triple A?" He turned to take a seat at the table, when she attempted to kick him from behind. He caught her legs in midair and held her upside down. "Now, why do you want to be this way? All I said was good morning."

When she composed herself, in the upside down position, she curled her hand to make a fist, pulled back and swang.

He jumped back. "Oh no, baby, not the jewels." He flipped her onto the bed, as if she was nothing more than a flea. Taking the silk scarf from the chair, he tied her feet and hands together behind her back. She lay on her stomach like a seesaw. He pulled a chair to the foot of the bed, where she could see him, and sat.

"I'm going to forgive you, for I understand you may be a little confused at the moment. However, you take another swing at my jewels and I'm going to knock you out. Are we clear?" He smiled, as daggers appeared to be shooting from her eyes. He wondered if that would translate into passion in a bed. He shook the thought away as the door opened.

LaVere' walked in with a tray of food. He froze in the spot at the sight of the woman tied up as she was. He tilted his head at Joshua. "You seem to have a way with women."

Joshua smiled. "I think she likes me."

LaVere' put the tray of food on the table then glanced at the angry woman tied up on the bed. "I am not getting that feeling. Are you making any progress?"

"Yes," Joshua replied as he walked over to the table, picked up a slice of toast and bit into it. He pointed the toast in her direction as he spoke. "She speaks English."

"That should make communications easier."

Joshua looked at her. "I don't know. She just tried to hit my jewels."

"Ouch." LaVere' folded his arms and stared at the woman. "Your mother would not be happy if you are unable to give her grandchildren."

"True," Joshua replied as he picked up the tray and carried it over to the bed.

"Can you handle her or do you need me to stay?"

Joshua looked incredulously over his shoulder. "Is that an insult?"

"You're the one with the woman's hands and legs tied behind her back," LaVere' laughed. "Since she speaks English this may be a good time for you to explain your life's mission for women." He smirked, then walked out of the room.

Taking a seat, Joshua smiled. There may be something to LaVere's suggestion. "You may not believe this, but women generally love me. I think we just got off on the wrong foot." Still receiving daggers from the woman, he decided to switch tactics. He turned to the food. It was mid-morning, maybe she was hungry. "This looks good." He crossed his legs as he sat back and bit into a slice of mango. Closing his eyes, he moaned. "Mmm, this is really good." He picked up a napkin, held it under the fruit. "Here, taste." She turned her head away. "I bit it first so you would know it's not poisonous."

The woman watched him, then her eyes narrowed. She opened her mouth and he placed the fruit inside. She bit down on his fingers and would not let go.

"Damn it." He dropped the napkin on the bed, then squeezed her jaw applying pressure until she released his fingers. He shook his fingers as if the bite was nothing. "Okay." He shook his head. "That was my fault. I tried to force you to eat, when I should have asked if you were hungry." He sat forward. "Let's try again. Hello. My name is Joshua. Is it okay if I call you Triple A."

"That is not my name. My name is Akande Ariana Aubree," she angrily replied with an accent.

"Okay, okay, see, now we are getting somewhere." He looked at his fingers to make sure she had not drawn blood. "Since we are making progress, tell me this. Were you being held against your will?"

"As I am now?"

"There's a difference," he replied as he pointed his finger. "I rescued you and even had breakfast brought in as a peace offering, thinking you may be hungry. In payment for my thoughtfulness, and bravery, I might add, what did you do? You attacked me without cause or provocation. All I want to know is if you were being held against your will, do you want to go home?"

A flicker of surprise appeared in her eyes, then quickly disappeared.

Sitting back in the chair, Joshua crossed his legs at the ankles, staring at her and thought. *Masking your reactions takes years of practice. The stance she took before attacking him was not amateurish, it was professional. Where did she learn that,* he wondered.

She had beautiful eyes, a slight slant to them. Dark lashes, against smooth chestnut skin. Her natural hair was twisted in a large single braid that was wrapped around her head like a crown. To him she looked like a temptress, in a neat little package. A wildcat. He liked that. "Where are you from?" he asked.

The room was silent as he patiently waited for her to reply. At some point, she would realize he was not the enemy.

"Asmere."

"Finally." He threw his hands in the air. "Okay, next question. Do you want to return home?" He watched as the question played in her mind. He wondered why she had to think about the question. One would think she would be excited with the possibility of seeing her loved ones again.

"Yes."

"Okay." He stood, and placed the tray back on the table. He walked back to the bed and stood over her. "I'm going to untie you. Make a wrong move and I will take you out. Do you understand?"

"Yes," she replied.

With one flick of his wrist, she was released. She immediately jumped up from the bed and kicked his legs from under him. He fell to the floor. She sat on his back, grabbed the scarf, tied it around his neck and pulled with all her might. "Where is the girl?"

"Whoa. That was good," he laughed as he reached back grabbed her by the neck and flipped her over. "One good turn deserves another," he said as he sat on her back. "You got the drop on me." He shook his head as he pulled the scarf from around his neck then ripped it in half. "I was looking at your lips instead of your eyes." He huffed as he ripped the scarf again. "My bad. What you don't know is I have six sisters who have tried that maneuver on me. You could take lessons from them." Angry now, he stood, putting his foot in her back to keep her down. "First you tried to kick me." He tied her feet together. "Then you tried to hit me in my balls, of all places," he yelled as he turned her over and tied her hands. "Then you bit me." He tied a strip around her mouth placing a knot behind her head. He stood over her to take a look at his work. Satisfied, he picked her up and sat her on the edge of the bed. "I pride myself on being a patient man, however, you are slowly pushing me over the edge. The only thing keeping me from knocking you the hell out is I think you have the girl's best interests at heart." He huffed, then pulled the chair up and sat in front of her. "The girl is back with her family. What was your role in her capture?"

The woman angrily mumbled something.

He realized she couldn't speak. Frustrated, he reached behind her and pulled the scarf from her mouth. "I kill people for a living. Keep that in mind the next time you think about doing something to piss me off. Now answer me!" he yelled.

The woman flinched at the controlled anger he was displaying. With fire coming from her nose, she replied. "I had no role in her capture," she seethed. "I was only told to care for her. Where am I?"

"Not important." He crossed his legs at the ankle. His legs were so long they almost reached where she was sitting. "I'm not a mean person. I do however kill people when provoked. If, I'm so inclined I rescue a few. I'm good at both–damn good." From time to time I return people to their families. You hesitated when I asked before. Are you sure you want to go home?"

All Akande could do was stare at the tall dark man before her. Friend or enemy, he was an imposing figure. How she came to be here, in his presence, she did not know. The last thing she remembered was hearing steps at her door. Her confinement had heightened her senses. The moment the steps stopped at the first door, she immediately awakened. Not moving, she watched as a light swayed around the room. The click, he thought was silent, vibrated through her mind, as if it had been a bulldozer. She sprang up and grabbed the heaviest thing she could find, a book. After waiting for a minute, she heard no movement. She took a step towards the open doorway and peeked around in the room. Her next memory was of a few minutes ago when she opened her eyes.

Fear, more so uneasiness, spread through her. She did not recognize him or know where she was. Anger filled her. She was tired of people just taking her and locking her away. Did he just ask something?

"Are you?"

She heard him ask again. "Am I what?"

"I need you to stay focused. Are you sure you want to go home?"

"If I am, what are you, as the Americans say, my knight in shining armor?"

"I've been called that from time to time." He smiled.

His smile jarred her senses. She did not believe men who looked like him really existed. This man, she could look at for days and never blink away. He was dressed as if he was on vacation, not like a warrior, yet, there was something clearly in his eyes indicating he was dangerous. For some reason, unknown to her, she felt drawn to him. She shook the feeling away. "I want to leave here. I want to go home."

"Where is home?"

The sight of the fiery woman of five minutes ago, with her head now down, bothered him. He placed a finger under her chin, she quickly pushed it away. "That's more like it. I like my women fiery. This is the last time I'm going to ask. Where is home?"

He stood, giving her the feeling he was towering over her, as her eyes traveled up his body to reach his eyes. Another feeling invaded her senses, but this was not the time to figure it out. This may be her only opportunity to escape.

She exhaled. "My uncle is King Tarik of Asmere."

Chapter Five

Queen Nasheema was not a woman to be dismissed. When she said she wanted something done, the men in the palace, including both Kings, Ahmed and Aswan, ordered the task done. The task Joshua was attempting to block was two women sent to see to the comfort of his captive. Queen Nasheema wanted to care for the woman who'd cared for her child.

When he turned the women away, King Ahmed, himself, came to the guest house and ordered Joshua out. For twenty minutes he explained how it was imperative that the woman was dependent on him for everything during his interrogation. The King in turn explained, on my grounds, Queen Nasheema ruled, to a certain extent. She wanted the woman who cared for Zsa Zsa, bathed, dressed and fed. His interrogation would have to wait. Before leaving, Joshua insisted on seeing every guard and woman allowed near the guesthouse.

Sitting in the family room of the palace, King Aswan, and Prince LaVere', were discussing the night's events when Joshua appeared.

"Do you people not understand the art of interrogation? How am I supposed to make this woman believe I will kill her if she does not give me the information I need, when your father is demanding we treat her as if she is a heroine in a romance novel? There's a damn brigade of women with scented soaps and oils to bathe her?"

"Where did you come from?" A shocked King Aswan stood.

"Don't take it personally Aswan," Lavere' explained. "He has a way of popping up anywhere at any time. It's something we all have gotten used to."

"It comes in handy at times."

King Aswan pointed around. "There are several doors for you to enter."

"I learn more my way." Joshua grinned. "We have an issue."

"My mother?" LaVere' asked.

"No, the woman confirms she is the niece of King Tarik of Asmere."

"He is not the true King of Asmere," King Aswan stated. "It is believed he was behind the death of his brother, Tochi, who was the true King of Asmere. Some believe he was murdered. I pray that was not the case."

"Is Tarik behind the kidnapping?" LaVere' asked in an anger filled voice.

"That we don't know," Joshua replied. "We may find out more when I take the woman home."

"Joshua, we are not on friendly terms with King Tarik," Aswan explained. "When his people wish to defect, we welcome them with open arms. If he connects you to Emure he will kill you."

Joshua flashed a grin. "Many have tried, and I'm still here."

"Did you get anything else from the woman?" LaVere' asked.

"Not yet, however, as you know, I have a way with women."

LaVere' moaned, as Aswan smiled. "If I have not said it, thank you for bringing our Zsa Zsa home."

"It's what I do. Where is she?"

"She is upstairs with Mother," LaVere' stated. "I think she is a little afraid to venture too far from my parents."

"It's understandable, she has been through an ordeal," Joshua offered.

"Well, she is home and safe now," Aswan said. "There is no reason for her to be afraid."

"Are you certain of that?"

"Do you mean to insult me? Do you believe I am incapable of protecting my family?"

"No." Joshua sat forward. "What I'm saying is there are a few unanswered questions that need to be addressed before we can declare the grounds are safe. You have a baby boy, six weeks old. I would think you would not want this to happen again."

Aswan looked from LaVere' to Joshua. "Please, accept my apology. I do feel responsible for what happened."

"This was something planned out," Joshua stated.

"I have to agree." LaVere' patted his brother on the shoulder to show his support. He knew the burden placed on Aswan's shoulders when their father decided to step down from the throne. Unlike his brother Raheem, he did not envy the role Aswan was now forced to take. "There was nothing on the security tapes. That could only mean, whoever did this knew where the cameras were located. None of them showed any disruption in the viewing."

"How it was done isn't as important as the fact that it happened on my watch."

"I understand your position King Aswan." Joshua nodded. I can say this from experience. You do not want to leave a traitor in your midst. The safest step to take, is to find out who planned this, how and why? The answers to that will begin with the woman in the guest house and Zsa Zsa. I really need to speak with the Princess."

King Aswan called out, "Pharell." A servant appeared from behind the wall. "Ask Mother to bring Zsa Zsa downstairs."

"As you wish, Your Highness."

"How many servants do you have?" Joshua asked, noticing how the man appeared out of nowhere.

"In the house or on the grounds?" Aswan asked.

"Both," Joshua replied.

"Twenty live-in staff; approximately fifty on the grounds who come and go throughout the day."

"What type of access do they have?"

"You cannot think a member of our staff is involved in this?" Aswan questioned.

"Until we know exactly what happened and how," Joshua stated, "Everyone is under suspicion."

"Excuse me." All eyes turned to see Zsa Zsa, who looked like the young Princess she was.

"Zsa Zsa," LaVere' opened his arms to his sister, who ran right into them.

The two had a special bond. He was fifteen when his mother announced she was having a baby. After rebelling as the youngest child who was about to be replaced, LaVere' welcomed the little bundle of joy as if she was his. As a child, she spent more time with LaVere' than with her own mother. LaVere' looked up at his mother as tears glistened in her eyes. They shared a knowing smile. She knew and understood, Zsa Zsa was a part of him.

"I knew you would find me," she beamed as LaVere' sat her back on her feet.

"Exactly, how did you know that?" He touched the tip of her nose with his finger.

"I just knew."

"I don't think you have been properly introduced. Princess Zsa Zsa, this is Joshua."

She walked over to Joshua. Smiling, she motioned with her finger for him to bend down. She kissed him on the cheek, then wrapped her arms around him the same as she did the night before. "Thank you, Joshua for bringing me home."

Joshua picked her up and kissed her cheek. "Whenever there is a Princess in need, I will be there." He sat her back down on the floor. "Will you do me the honor of taking a stroll with me, my lady?"

"Outside?" Zsa Zsa looked to her mother then LaVere' then back to Joshua. Fear appeared in the young girl's eyes, as well as her mother's.

"No," Nasheema cried out as she stood up from the seat she had taken next to Aswan. To her it was too soon to have her daughter out of her sight.

He placed his hand on his mother's. "There is no time like the present. We will watch from the balcony," Aswan stated.

This fear gripping her was something Joshua would not allow to happen. He suspected Zsa Zsa was a ball of energy, just like his little sister Phire. He did not want her to lose that or be afraid to live. "What good is it to have a beautiful Princess on my arm if no one sees us? I have a reputation to uphold."

"You think I'm beautiful." Zsa Zsa blushed.

"Why, my lady," He smiled down at her. "You are the fairest in the land," Joshua replied as he put her hand in the crook of his arm and walked outside. He felt her fingers tense on his arm, so he took his other hand and gently rubbed his thumb across her hand as they walked out the door along the path leading to the maze of a garden.

The area was covered with lush green grass, a water fountain to the right, a gazebo directly ahead, and about a mile away, a lake. Several guest homes were on both sides of the property. "You have a very beautiful home, Princess Zsa Zsa."

"You may call me Zsa Zsa."

"No, I cannot." He smiled down at her. "You are a Princess, a member of the royal family. And even if you weren't, I would still call you Princess because you look like one."

She beamed up at him. "Man, you are smooth."

He roared back with laughter. "I know. I've been trying to tell people this." They walked a little further into the multicolored garden that lined the path on both sides. "I feel the fear in you. You are now home and as King Aswan stated, you are safe and secure here." The young girl was poised, and knew her role as a member of the royal family. As they passed house staff members along the way, she smiled and spoke to each of them by name. They in turn welcomed her home, yet he could feel her tremble.

"My mother would love this garden. Every time she tried to start one at home one of us would trample on it."

"You are not an only child?"

"No." Joshua grinned. "I grew up with five brothers and six sisters. Our father refers to us as his Gems and Gents."

"Why does he call you that?"

"He would tell you all of his girls are precious gemstones in his eyes and anyone who wanted to be a part of their lives had better treat them as such."

"And the males?"

"We have a reputation to uphold because of our names. We were all named after men in the Bible. As gentlemen of the Bible, we are expected to, above all else, believe in God and try to live by his words. Do you know about the book of Joshua?" He looked down at the girl as she acknowledged his question. "Joshua, Chapter 1, Verse 9 states, and I quote, 'Be strong and of good courage; be not afraid or dismay, for the Lord thy God is with thee wherever thou may go,' or something very close to that. My mother taught me how to use my faith to protect myself. You will learn to do the same."

Zsa Zsa bowed her head so he could not see the tears in her eyes. "I do not feel safe here. I know that is an insult to my brother, who is now King and has vowed to protect us all." She stopped walking, then looked up at him. "When I was little, my father had an escape tunnel built directly from my room. It made him feel secure that his little girl would have a way to escape if the palace grounds were taken, as it had been in our neighboring countries. Yet, someone came into my home and took me from here. How do I close my eyes and not expect that to happen again?" She shook her head, then turned and continued to walk. "I cannot dishonor my family by speaking of this to them. I have to be strong. It is expected and I know that is important to them. What I am about to say may not be kind, but I felt safe in your arms last night. I felt safe in LaVere's embrace, for neither of you were here when I was taken. The other members of my family were here." She stopped and pointed to a window on the east side of the palace overlooking the garden. Whoever took me either climbed that wall to my window or knew about the escape tunnel." She looked up at him. "Take a look at that wall."

Joshua looked at the wall. With the right tools, it could be scaled. He looked around the grounds. It was an open, garden style area, nowhere for a person to be concealed. He looked at the strategically placed camera. There was no way a person could have scaled the wall without being caught on camera.

He looked into her knowing eyes as they turned and continued to walk the path. "Only family knows about the tunnel. Tell me why I should not think someone in my family was involved in this."

They walked over to the gazebo. He sat and pulled her down next to him. He put his arms around her shoulders and gently placed her head on his chest. She giggled and he liked that. That's what a teenage girl should be doing. "Boys do not get to hold you like this, understand."

"Understood," She smiled.

He nodded. "Tell me everything that happened that morning."

Zsa Zsa exhaled as he rubbed her shoulder. She nodded and began telling him all she could remember.

When she finished, he held her head up, wiped away her tears and told her, "If anyone ever harms you in any way, know that I will find out and it will be the last thing they will do in life. Understood?"

"Understood."

"Believe me?"

She stared into his eyes, then nodded. "Yes."

"Good." He smiled. "When you come back to the states you should meet my little sister, Phire. You remind me of her." He sighed missing his family. "Let's go back inside before your brother sends the guards after us."

"I would love to meet her." She exhaled and looked at her family. "You do not fear any of them, do you?"

"I fear no man. They bleed the same as I. Why do you ask?"

"I believe you will have to confront one of them before this is over."

They reached the entrance to the patio, just as Queen Nasheema and King Ahmed walked down the stairs. "How is my Princess?" King Ahmed kissed the top of her head.

"Better, Daddy."

Queen Nasheema smiled at Joshua. "Your visitor has been bathed and received nourishment. I'm certain she will be more forthcoming now."

Why people thought nice was the way to get information, he would never know. "Thank you. I'll take my leave now." He bowed, then winked at Zsa Zsa, and left the room.

Chapter Six

Akande Aubree was stunning. He was certain there were other words befitting the woman standing at the window with the sunlight framing her face as if she were an angel from heaven. At the moment, nothing else came to mind. She must have sensed him standing there, for she suddenly turned around.

The temperature seemed to have jumped a good twenty degrees when she turned to see him standing there in a suit. He had changed from the leisure wear of the morning and now stood before her as if he was attending a business meeting. She did not know a lot about men's clothing, but this suit looked perfect on him. Other men in her country wore suits sometimes. None of them made her mouth water. She swiped at an imaginary loose hair as she became self-conscious about her appearance.

A serene smile appeared on her face. "I believe I owe you an apology. This morning I was concerned with the girl's safety." Her head tilted towards the window. "I see now, you simply brought her home to her family. Please accept my apology."

The outfit she was wearing, a silk sleeveless dress filled with vibrant orange, purple, and tan stopped at the ankle. The sandals on her dainty feet, her toes decorated with rings, made him smile. The colors enhanced her skin tone, making it shimmer. Her hair was freshly braided and wrapped around her head. Matching earrings dangled down to her shoulders. It looked as if the ensemble was made for a Queen.

His blatant perusal of her body caused her to frown. It did not make her feel dirty, like when Uncle Tarik would watch her. It just made her feel unsure, insecure.

"Ms. Aubree, I must say you are a sight to behold." Joshua flashed that megawatt smile, exposing those double dimples as if they were sexual weapons. The compliment made her smile again, and he liked it. Shaking the thought off, he strutted into the room. He had business to handle.

"It's time to talk." Joshua pulled a chair out from the table and motioned for her to take a seat. He held the chair out for her and the fresh scent of jasmine filled his nostrils as she sat. He was tempted to touch her skin, it looked so soft. Pushing the urge aside he walked around the table and sat across from her. "Start at the beginning."

"The beginning started so long ago."

Joshua sat back, stretched his long legs out, crossed them at the ankles, and smiled. "I have a little time."

Akande crossed her legs and sat back. "Two weeks ago I was on my way to purchase garments for my trip to meet my father. It was a trip I had been looking forward to just about all my life. You see my mother died when I was young. My aunt raised me. She promised once I was older she would grant me permission to meet with my father." Closing her eyes as if thinking back, she slightly nodded her head. "I never thought the day would come," she looked up smiling, "But it did." Her smile faded. "On our way, our vehicle was forced off the road. My driver and I fought with our attackers. Unfortunately, there were more then we could overtake. I was rendered unconscious and I am not certain of my driver's outcome." she sighed. "When I awakened, I was in the basement of a mansion. For days I had no idea where I was or what would become of me. On the third day, the man who brought my meals said my family had been notified. Once the ransom was received, I would be sent home. Days passed as I watched others removed, while more were brought in, yet I remained. Each day I would ask what was happening, why was I not released? Some guards would talk, others would just glare." She rubbed her arms as if thinking back. "One guard told me, my family had not sent the ransom. I would remain until they complied. I knew, before he told me, it was the case. For my Uncle had always stated the country was not financially sound. You see, our family had to use personal funds to keep the country stable until things settled in the region. Three days ago, I was placed in the room in which you found me. I was told I would earn my keep until my family complied. The girl was brought to my room. They supplied food and clothing. I would cook and watch over her during the day. At night she would sleep in the panic room. That is how I came to be with Princess Zsa Zsa. She was different from the others, for she was older and a female. That is dangerous around our captives. On her second night there, I heard a sound outside my door. I thought it was one of the guards coming in after the girl. I remember getting out of bed to walk into the outer room to see who was there. The next thing I remember was waking up here, to you."

The story was plausible, and she delivered it well. Stopping at certain points, dropping her head low as if remembering, however, some of the story did not ring true to him. He did not know her reasons for lying, that would come later. There were other matters more important.

"Do you know who your captors were?"

"No."

"How did you communicate? Did they speak your language, English or another?"

"English," she frowned wondering why he asked.

"Any idea how long you traveled before you reached the location?"

Getting a little testy, she narrowed her eyes. "I have no idea. As I stated before, I was unconscious. Similar to how I ended up here."

Unfazed by the spike in her voice, Joshua continued, "How many captors did you see?"

"There were different ones each day. I have no way of knowing."

"Catch any names when they spoke?"

"No."

"Descriptions. Tall, short, heavy anything at all that could lead us to who kidnapped Princess Zsa Zsa or why?"

"No."

"Were you raped?"

"No, of course not."

"Not touched, even once?"

"No," she replied more adamantly.

"Nothing. You were there for weeks, captured by men of questionable character. Your family made no effort to find you or pay your ransom. You were not raped or beaten. In fact, from what I saw, you were living rather well for a captive. You were not in a cell, but in a room behind locked doors. Other than that, there was nothing. I find that amazing. Here's why." He cut her off when she was about to say something.

"The man, whose home you were in, he's about money. His name is Naftali Conteh. He does nothing out of the goodness of his heart, nor do any of his men. If your family did not pay the ransom, he would have used your body to get his money one way or another. Or, he would have simply killed you. That leads me to believe one of two things. You are involved in the kidnapping of Princess Zsa Zsa or your family placed you there and paid him to keep you untouched. If it's the latter, I have to wonder why? But that's not what I think. I think in some way you are a part of this kidnapping. You may be Naftali's mistress, whom he put in my path to find. If that's the case I have to again wonder why? Did he know we would come if he took Princess Zsa Zsa? Everyone in this region knows of the friendship between Emure and the United States. Was this a way for Conteh to pull us into the region?" He slammed his fist on the table. "Answer me!"

She jerked up. "I know nothing of what you speak. I was taken, same as Princess Zsa Zsa. I may not be royalty, but my family loves me just as much as hers and would do whatever was in their power to free me." She leaned across the table, with anger in her eyes. "I am no man's mistress."

Damn if those gold flecks in her eyes weren't shooting daggers at him. Inside he was smiling. "Why were you there?" He stood and towered over her, causing her to move back and look up. "He did not feed and clothe you to receive nothing in return." He shook his head. "No. I don't know the answer, yet. Make no mistake, I *will* get it out of you."

Joshua walked out of the room. He needed more Intel before he made another move. Using his secure cell phone, he dialed Ned.

"I am at your service. What do you need, my brother?"

"Ned, you're Jewish, you cannot be my brother."

"I'm your brother in spirit, my man."

"You sound chipper," Joshua put emphasis on the last word.

"I am, my man. Life is good."

"I'm about to change that outlook."

"Oh hell, what have you done?" his tone dropped an octave or two.

"It's not what I've done but what I'm going to do."

"I'm listening."

"Akande indicates she was taken a few weeks ago. Check the satellite feed over the Conteh compound. See if you can determine exactly when she was taken and visuals of her on the compound. You work on that, I'm going to take a short trip to get a few answers."

"Absolute, we were lucky last night. We have permission to be in Emure only."

"I need to know what's at stake before we return Akande to Asmere."

"No," he spoke emphatically. "We have sanctions in place. The leaders of Asmere will not allow you in their country."

"From Emure, it's as simple as walking across the street at some points. Lay low Ned, my brother. You know how I work."

"Yes, I do. That's why I'm concerned."

"Send any Intel to the chopper." Joshua disconnected the call before Ned could continue his disapproval.

Next, he went in search of LaVere'. As he descended the stairs, he stopped on the landing. Looking through the window, he noticed a number of black sedans and SUVs pulling into the circular driveway of the palace. When he reached the lower level of the guesthouse, Joshua took a seat at the dining room table, pulled out his handheld device and began to dig further into the life and times of Akande Aubree. A female servant, one he had seen the night before, asked if he needed anything. The suggestive way she asked, caused him to smile, however, he knew he had work to do and pleasure would have to wait. He declined the offer. Opening the file Ned sent the night before, he began to learn all he could about the woman. Akande Ariana Aubree, twenty-six, unmarried, no children. Mother and father, nothing was listed. That was odd, there was information in all fields. Where the parents names would be listed, or categorized as deceased or unknown, there was nothing. He made a mental note to ask Ned about it. He continued to read.

He came to a file with a password security attached. He tried several, but could not open the file. There were only a few people who had a higher security level than Joshua, the President, the Secretary of National Security, the Secretary of Homeland Security and the Senator of Foreign Affairs, to name a few. Hell, Joshua's clearance was higher than most Senators, yet, he could not open the file. He made a mental note to ask Ned about that as well.

"Mother, I will take care of it," LaVere' said into the phone as he walked in the guesthouse. Joshua looked up when he took a seat at the table. LaVere' disconnected the call and looked at Joshua. "It seems two staff members had a slight altercation this afternoon. We have a family-like atmosphere amongst our staff. Imagine my mother's surprise when the two women began calling each other names. As it turns out, they both spent a little time with you." He looked at Joshua, who sat there with an unconcerned expression.

"They weren't complaining, were they?" he responded.

"No, the argument was to determine who would have you first tonight." Joshua sat up as if contemplating the question. "My mother is very upset about this. Keeping the peace with the staff is her responsibility. You are to have no further contact with them."

"Just the palace staff, the other women in the countryside are not off limits?" Joshua asked.

All LaVere' could do was shake his head. He knew of Joshua's reputation with women. However, this was his first time experiencing it firsthand. "No, they are not off limits," LaVere' replied. "How in the hell do you find the energy or time?"

"Women happen to be my favorite pastime. They help build my stamina." He grinned at LaVere'.

"Will you please take it easy on the house staff? While my mother is grateful to you for returning Zsa Zsa to us, she will not have her household in turmoil."

"Okay, I'm busy tonight anyway." Joshua shrugged his shoulders. "I'm doing some recon later. Want to join me?"

"Count me in," LaVere' replied. "My father and Aswan are here. The family will be fine."

"Where is Raheem?" Joshua asked.

"He left for California. Since Zsa Zsa was secure he wanted to return to handle some unfinished business." LaVere' shrugged his shoulders. "He feels unneeded here." The look on LaVere's face indicated he did not approve of whatever Raheem was doing. "He is doing what he feels he needs to do."

"Cool, you can hang. But, I don't want to hear anything from you when I kill somebody," Joshua said as he stood. "Or, if we run into any women. No lectures."

"Hey, this is a mission. No women allowed."

"No women?" Joshua smirked as he stood. "You have lost your mind. I'm going to secure Akande and will meet you at the chopper in ten."

Joshua set guards at the door of Akande's room, changed clothes and was walking towards the chopper dressed in one of his signature Armani suits, this one gray with a crisp white shirt, gray and white striped tie, with his long trench coat swinging from the cool breeze of the night. The closer he came to the chopper the slower his steps were. He was used to running, jumping into his seat and taking off. He stopped ten feet from the chopper, lowered then shook his head. He sighed and looked up. "No one," he paused, "No one pilots my chopper but me."

"I'm an excellent pilot, Joshua," LaVere' explained.

"You have planes?"

"I do."

"You can pilot them. This one is off limits."

LaVere' threw his hands up as he moved to the passenger seat. "As you wish."

Joshua flipped his coat up and out as he took his place in the chopper, put his sunshades on, then took off to the West.

LaVere' gave him a sideways glance. "It's a style thing."

"Damn right," Joshua responded.

LaVere' laughed. "I'm getting the swing of things."

Joshua's lips slowly curved into a smile. He wasn't sure what to expect from Prince LaVere'. From what his brother Samuel told him, LaVere' could hold his own. They would soon find out if that was true.

An hour later, Joshua landed the chopper in a remote area of Nigeria not far from where he was the night before. The stealth helicopter was loaded with any and every piece of technology imaginable and some not. The quietness of the chopper allowed him to land it just about anywhere undetected. It was equipped with night vision technology therefore, lights were not needed. Once the chopper was secured, a shield was placed around it, rendering it practically invisible. It wasn't invisible, it simply took on the persona of its surroundings, allowing it to blend in, as if it was a part of the scenery.

Inside there were weapons of all kinds, guns, knives, tasers, and darts filled with tranquilizers. There was a state of the art computer system with a direct connection to Ned. Further in the back were suits, shoes, shirts, and ties. All the things necessary for an operative like Joshua.

Joshua looked at LaVere'. "Do you know how to shoot?"

LaVere' understood Joshua did not know him or his capabilities. He simply reached in, took a glock from the collection, loaded it, and placed it in the back of his pants. "Are we ready?"

"Let's roll." They climbed into the vehicle Ned had waiting for them.

Less than an hour later, Joshua, and LaVere' stood on a hill one hundred miles away, surveying the mansion where Zsa Zsa had been held. The jeep they drove had made the journey up the ninety degree angle road with little effort. According to Ned, it was the safest viewing point, without being detected. The home in question had the most sophisticated surveillance equipment available.

"One thing is for certain." Joshua reached into his blazer to pull out a pencil type device. "They are well financed." He stripped out of his coat, and placed it on the ground. Lying on his stomach, he used both hands to maneuver the slim device. A few seconds later he spoke. "This is the complex."

"How are we going to get in?" LaVere' asked.

"We are going to drive up and knock on the door. First we need to determine how many people are on the grounds."

"What do we have Joshua?"

"Looks like a small crew, less than twenty. However, I don't see Conteh."

"You can actually see everyone on the grounds?"

"Come down here," Joshua motioned to LaVere'.

LaVere' laid on the ground next to Joshua. His loose hair fell across his shoulder. "Close your eyes and move your hair out of your face."

Joshua gave the object to LaVere'. "Look through the top."

LaVere' brought the device to his eye. He flinched and dropped it on the ground. "My God man."

Joshua picked it up, twisted the end, then gave it back to him. "Try it now. Tell me what you see."

LaVere' slowly lifted the device to his eyes. The men on the roof did not appear to be right on top of him as they did before. This time they seemed to be sitting in front of him.

"Four men on the roof. One in each corner, armed with semi-automatic weapons."

"Look through the front window to your right. What do you see?"

Lavere' moved slightly to his right. "A woman sitting in a chair talking to a man."

"Now." Joshua reached over and pushed the head of the device. "Just point at the building and tell me how many heat images you see."

LaVere' did as he was instructed. "Twelve."

"Judge the weight and size of each. Are any of them less dense than the lady sitting in the room?"

LaVere' shook his head. "No."

Joshua hit LaVere' on the shoulder. "Unless there is a really big woman in there, we are dealing with eleven men and one woman."

"I pulled up blueprints of the mansion," LaVere' stated. He pulled out his cell phone and held it out. "This is a blueprint of the mansion below." He pointed to the screen. "This area was reconstructed a few years ago. There was a shaft leading to one of the diamond mines beneath the original building."

Joshua pointed to the screen, "This is the area I was in last night. This is where we are going to enter. Let's take out the men on the roof. Then we will find Conteh to see what he has to tell us."

"How are you going to take the men on the roof out?" LaVere' asked.

"Watch and learn," Joshua smiled as he walked over to the jeep. From the back, he opened a case and pulled out two long tubes, giving one to LaVere'. The two walked back over to the ledge, and lay on their bellies.

Joshua pointed. "I'll take twelve, two and four. You take six and eight." LaVere" watched then followed Joshua's movements. "Range," Joshua pushed a button on the tube.

LaVere' did the same.

"Set."

LaVere' did the same.

"Aim," Joshua said as he put the tube to his lips. LaVere' did the same.

"Fire." Joshua blew through the tube. LaVere' did the same.

They watched as two men on the roof grabbed their necks, then fell to the ground.

"Reload." Joshua and LaVere', reset the range on the device.

"Set," LaVere' stated.

"Aim," Joshua said. "Fire." They blew through the tube again.

LaVere' laughed as two more men dropped. "I've got to get me one of these."

Joshua aimed again and took out the last man on the roof, then grinned. "You like this, don't you?"

He stood and placed the tube back in its case. Joshua picked up his coat, hit LaVere' on the shoulder. "Ready for some action?" he asked and jumped into the jeep.

LaVere' climbed in the back, hitting the rooftop. "Let's roll."

Joshua pulled the jeep up in front of the closed, double-gated driveway. Using his handheld device, he pushed a few buttons and the gate opened. He shoved the device in his coat pocket, then drove up to the door, and jumped out of the jeep. Coming out were two large men with weapons drawn. Joshua grabbed the weapon from one, releasing the bullet casing, which dropped to the ground. He swung the empty gun hitting the man twice with the butt rendering him unconscious. LaVere', jumped and drop kicked the other man, knocking him backwards into the door.

The sound of a gun being cocked came from the doorway. LaVere' ran and jumped, kicking the door inward, then landed on his feet. The man behind the door fell backwards, but did not stay down. He hopped right back up and met with the force of LaVere's booted foot in his kidney, knocking the wind out of him. Several fast punches with his fist and the man fell to the ground. LaVere' turned to find Joshua staring at him. He picked up the gun. "Let's go."

Joshua grinned then followed him inside. "You got a little kick in you. Not bad for a Prince. You can hang with me anytime."

"Come any closer and the lady dies," A voice
commanded as they entered a room as richly
decorated as the family room of the palace. LaVere'
hung back. Joshua stepped into the doorway, the gun
he had taken, leaning causally across his shoulder and
his coat swinging out from behind him. A man stood
behind a woman sitting in a chair, with his arm
around her neck and a gun pointed to her head.
Another man with a gun pointed at Joshua, stood next
to a man who was seated with his legs crossed,
smoking a cigar, as if he did not have a care in the
world.

Joshua recognized the man seated as Naftali
Conteh. He stepped inside the room. "Mr. Conteh, I
presume."

"And you are?" the man asked with a controlled
voice.

"My name isn't important," Joshua replied as he
took a seat in the chair next to the door. It did not
escape him that there were only four people in the
room. There was another man somewhere in the
house. "How you answer the next question is."

"Why is that?" Conteh asked.

"It determines if you live or die."

The man released a low chuckle, took a puff of his
cigar then released the smoke. "You apparently do not
know who I am."

"Of course I do," Joshua shrugged. "I don't
randomly break into places without a purpose. For
example, last night, you had Princess Zsa Zsa. I
wanted her, so I took her."

The man placed the cigar in the ashtray on the
table. "You dare to enter my property, steal from me
and return today." He revealed a wicked smile. "You
are either very stupid or you believe you are
invincible."

"Neither. I returned today for information on the other woman I took."

"Hmm," the man nodded. "Akande...she is beautiful, is she not?"

"Why was she here?"

Naftali smiled. "The information you seek will cost you a million."

Joshua noticed a movement in the back of the room. Apparently LaVere' had taken care of the other man they could not see and was now positioned behind the man holding the gun to the woman's head. "I have a better deal."

"I'm listening."

"You give us the information we seek and I'll let you live."

Naftali's eyes narrowed. "Do not try my patience. You are still alive simply because I am a business man. I have something of value to you. There is a price attached. We only need to negotiate, then you will leave and I will kill my guards who allowed you to get in. There is no need for you or I to die today."

"Have it your way," Joshua flipped a button from his coat and jumped behind the chair. The man next to Naftali raised his gun and fired, but it was a fraction too late. The button, which landed in front of the woman, exploded taking out the woman and the man. LaVere' jumped, hitting the gunman from behind, causing his bullets to hit the ceiling. When the smoke cleared Joshua was on Naftali with a knife at his throat.

LaVere' collected the guns from both men and the one the woman had hidden behind her back.

"Mr. Conteh, no one has to die today. Tell us about the woman and we will be gone."

Naftali's nose flared with anger. "The woman was placed in my care."

"Why and by whom?"

"I don't know why!" the man shouted in anger.

Joshua tightened his hold around the man's neck and pushed the blade in, breaking the skin. A drop of blood trickled down his neck. "I hate to have to explain an international incident when I don't have to. "Who and why?"

"King Tarik of Asmere," Conteh caved. "He indicated his wife did not want the woman around because she feared he was attracted to her."

"Isn't the woman his niece?"

"By marriage only," he snarled. "Here, if we want a woman, we take her."

"Did you?" Joshua pushed the point of the knife in a little deeper. The answer was important to him.

"No! No!" the man yelled from the pain. "The agreement was she was not to be touched. None of my men touched her."

Joshua eased up from the man and pulled out a handkerchief from his pocket. "Wipe the blood off." He whispered something to LaVere'. He nodded. Joshua pulled a chair up in front of Naftali, sat in it then leaned forward. "Tell me a story, Mr. Conteh and you will receive your million."

Naftali narrowed his eyes. "You have the upper hand here, for the moment. Yet you offer to pay me, why?"

"As you stated, you are a business man. You were hired to take something that belongs to us, we took her back. It's economics, you fulfilled a demand. We simply want to know who you were supplying?"

The man looked skeptical. "And you will pay me my money for the information? How do you know I am telling you the truth?"

Joshua explained, "I've entered your mansion three times, without much effort. I will do it again."

The man raised an inquisitive eyebrow. "I was here the day before I took the girl, back doing recon, then again last night." Naftali looked surprised. "I know every angle to your house. So if you lie to me, I will come back."

Naftali looked at him as if he was crazy, but then he shrugged his shoulder. "What the hell. You're paying me."

Joshua sat back and listened as Naftali told him of Queen Sermyera's visit when she indicated an opportunity to make millions had come her way. "All we had to do was kidnap her niece Akande and Princess Zsa Zsa for a sum of a million American dollars. We were instructed to allow the Princess to be rescued and place Akande in the path for an American to save her as well."

"Why?" Joshua asked.

"I cannot say. But I will tell you, I did hear the mention of an official in Washington." He shrugged his shoulder. "If you ask my opinion I will tell you I believe it is all a set up for Akande to be taken to America, to find this man."

"For what purpose?"

"I am not privy to that part of the plan." he sighed. "Did you notice there was no retaliation for the girls being taken? You know how I operate. If I had not received payment, there would be dead bodies. There are none."

Joshua and LaVeré glanced at each other.

LaVere' stepped forward. "You were paid? When?"

"The money was wired into my account this morning. Therefore, I assumed the Queen was satisfied with my performance." he smirked, "It is my belief that Princess Zsa Zsa was a ploy to get an American here to act as an escort to take Akande to

America. Why, I do not know. But, as you Americans would say, there are bigger fish to hook."

"Bigger fish to fry," Joshua corrected as he sat there staring at the man. After a few moments, he nodded his head satisfied, then stood. "I appreciate the information." He gave Conteh a card with a number on it."

"What is this?"

"A get out of jail free card, when you need it." He turned to walk out. "Oh, stay away from the Ashro family. LaVere', pay the man."

LaVere' arranged to pay the man as agreed. As they returned to the palace, a few things were bugging Joshua.

"Why did we pay him?" LaVere' asked.

"Conteh is a man who works for the highest bidder, but he also works from the gut. We could have killed him and everyone who was inside that house. We did not. He is going to remember that."

"What are you going to do about Akande?" LaVere' asked.

The answer wasn't simple for Joshua. There was something about the woman that intrigued him. However, Conteh confirmed his suspicions, he did not trust her. If she was targeting an official in Washington, that made her an enemy of the United States, which made her his enemy. "I'll return her to her country. If she makes a play to be taken to the Washington, I'll play it out until the plot is revealed, then take her down."

"The U.S. Calvary to the rescue." LaVere' smiled.

"It's that arrogance the Queen of Asmere was betting on to initiate her plans," Joshua cautioned.

"True," LaVere' replied. "Unfortunately for them, they have never encountered the likes of you. May God have mercy upon them."

Joshua turned to his friend and grinned. "They are about to get a taste of the Absolute experience."

Chapter Seven

Monday morning, Royce walked into his office located in the Russell Senate Building in Washington, D.C. He placed his briefcase on the desk and pulled out the secure document that was delivered to him in the wee hours of the morning. Normally, he would brief the Secretary of Defense on any situations he believed would cause an issue for the United States. It would be difficult to do today for he had no idea what was in the report. That was telling, for he was a highly intelligent man. Reading, comprehending then interpreting was something he had done daily in the past. It was those briefings that had granted him the position he held now, while other third term Senators were still on regulatory committees.

This was his third term in the U.S. Senate, representing the State of Virginia. Royce had been appointed to the Committee on Foreign Affairs during his first term, and became Chairman on African Affairs in his second term. He was now Chairman of Foreign Relations.

Until a few years ago, he was thought to be the lead runner for the Democratic nominee for President. A family scandal that ended his marriage also altered his future. When the details of the scandal unraveled, the citizens of Virginia opened their arms and re-elected him to the Senate. Working closely with Senator Gavin Roberts and Governor J.D. Harrison, Virginia was thriving as one of the best run States in the country. Ranking number two as the best place to raise a family, start a business and boasting an AAA credit rating in addition to being one of the most sought after states for foreign enterprise. The last accomplishment, in no small part, was due to Senator Davenport's relations with foreign governments.

Under normal circumstances, after reading the latest reports, he would make recommendations to the Secretary. He read the document several times, unfortunately his mind continuously wandered. He was considered the top in his field in foreign negotiations and people depended on him. It was inconceivable that a woman could invade his thoughts to the point of distraction.

Looking out of his window, thoughts of the woman were foremost in his mind as they had been since the meeting on Saturday. The most staggering concern was that what the woman thought of him might matter for some ungodly reason.

Since his divorce, five years ago, he had not allowed any woman close enough for him to care one way or another. Oh, he'd enjoyed being in the company of women on multiple occasions, but after the third or fourth date, he was done. They just did not hold his interest. After a few years on the dating scene, he gave up trying to have a relationship with any of them, and settled for the occasional sexual romp here and there. Even with that he was very selective. A man in his position had to be cautious. The type of information he was privy to could have international ramifications if seen by the wrong eyes. He knew the media coverage made it seem as if he was on a date every night with a different woman, but the truth was he preferred quiet nights at home. It was his ex-wife who craved the limelight of the D.C. society. He couldn't care less about it.

"Good morning Senator," Kathy Paxton, his secretary of fifteen years, spoke as she entered his office with his agenda for the day. "How was your weekend?"

"Good morning, Kathy," he replied as he took his seat at his desk. "The weekend was too short."

She smiled. "It always is." The slim stylishly dressed woman of fifty-six, took a seat and began reciting his agenda and any information he would need to make the day smoother. If that was possible, most days the agenda was shot to hell by ten in the morning.

Kathy looked up when she mentioned dinner with Governor Harrison and his family. Normally, that subject would generate a lively conversation on the Governor's possible run for President of the United States. This morning–nothing. "Is everything all right, Senator?"

Royce looked up. "I'm sorry Kathy, did you say something?"

She closed her calendar book placing her hands on top of it in her lap. "After good morning, I said I was running off to marry Will Smith–*The Wild Wild West*, Will Smith, not the *Ali*, Will Smith."

"Let me know when you get back."

Kathy tilted her head. "Where is your mind this morning?"

Sitting back in his chair, he picked up a pen and began tapping the desk with it. "You wouldn't believe me if I told you."

Recognizing the nervous action, Kathy sat back in her seat. "Try me."

He stopped tapping the pen and looked up at her. Thinking, she was about the only person in his life he completely trusted other than his parents and Grayson. If he could talk to anyone about this absurdity, it would be her. He stood, removed his suit jacket and placed it on the back of his chair, then retook his seat. "I had a run in with a woman."

Kathy's heart leaped. It had been years since they'd had a real conversation about a woman. Not since the conversation they had concerning his divorcing Penny and that was five years ago. She stood, placing her calendar on his desk trying her best to keep her cool and not get too excited, "What kind of run in?" she asked as she removed the jacket from the back of the chair and put it on the hanger located right behind him. He had retrieved the pen and was tapping the desk again when she returned to her seat. Kathy couldn't help but smile, it had been a long time coming, but maybe he was finally letting his guard down.

"I wouldn't say it was exactly a run in, it was more like a confrontation that was entirely one-sided."

Picking up the calendar, she crossed her legs. "Why don't you just tell me what happened?" It was a statement more than a question, for a question would have given him a choice and she was too interested to give him an option. He revealed the events from the meeting as she watched him intently. At times it was what a person was not saying that spoke volumes. When he finished she picked up the calendar. "Was she attractive?"

He closed his eyes. "God, yes. Even in anger she looked like an angel."

"My, my–an angel," she teased while smiling at him.

Catching the amusement in her voice, Royce opened his eyes and sat up. Clearing his throat he nodded towards her calendar. "What do we have scheduled today?"

"No angels, that's for sure." Kathy laughed as she opened her calendar and began reading off the agenda for the day again. After they finished, she stood and walked towards her office. "Would you like the regular breakfast?"

"Sure," he replied slowly. She waited, for she knew something more was coming. "Kathy."

"Yes, Senator."

"Would you vet Shelly Knight for me?"

Smiling inwardly she replied. "Of course, Senator. Would you like it to be professional or personal?"

"Professional," he decided. "Make that personal." A second ticked on the clock, "No wait...professional."

She stood at the doorway and looked at him. "Professional it is." She turned to take a step and before he could say anything she said, "I'll do an in-depth."

"Thank you, Kathy. And make sure you do this, don't give it to anyone else to handle."

"I'll take care of it personally." She closed the door behind her and smiled. "It's about time." She sat at her desk and decided this task took precedence over everything else on the agenda. If there is a woman out there that has captured his interest, she wanted to know all she could about her. The last thing he needed was another Penelope Parker Davenport in his life.

An hour later, Royce had finally cleared his mind enough to concentrate on the intelligence report he received the night before. The report indicated Princess Zsa Zsa was safely returned to the palace. He was certain his friend King Ahmed and his wife were relieved. The region was going through a social transformation. The country was now led by the newly crowned King Aswan, the eldest son of his friend King Ahmed. For health reasons, Ahmed felt it was best for the country to be lead into the social change by someone younger and open to change. He remembered praising his friend for making the unprecedented move to step down. It was a clear indication that he was ready for his country to progress. Some neighbors in the region rebelled against Emure, because of Ahmed's decision to liberate his country and there had been talk of war. The region had become unstable and the United States was keeping a close eye on the developments.

Reaching under his desk, he pushed a button. Nothing could be seen by the naked eye, however, a few seconds later the small indicator near the button went from red to green, indicating the room was now secure. Any electronic devices attempting to pick up conversations would only receive silence. From his desk he pulled out a secure phone, then dialed a number. The call was answered on the second ring.

"Hello, Senator."

"Good morning, Ned. Update me on the situation with the woman rescued with Princess Zsa Zsa."

"She is being returned to her home."

"The royal family provided her with an escort?"

"Not exactly," Ned slowly replied.

"What do you mean, not exactly? They would not have sent a woman into the unstable territory without protection. How is she being transported?" The hesitation in his reply caused a frown in Royce's brow. "Tell me Absolute is *not* in Asmere."

"Absolute is not in Asmere. He's in Akrue, therefore, technically outside of Asmere."

"Do I seem amused Ned?" Royce roared.

"No Senator, you don't," Ned stammered. "However, it's important that we look at the larger picture here."

Royce waited for the handler of the most dangerous operatives the United States had at its disposal. On one hand he appreciated the fact that Ned was defending the actions of his operatives. On the other hand, he should never defend them to him. "I'm waiting."

"On what?"

"The larger picture, Ned. Hold that thought," Royce interrupted before Ned could speak. "Absolute is in a region that is unstable with no orders from this office. A larger picture would be he blows up something while he is there, which with his history, has an eighty percent possibility of occurring." Royce's voice began to gradually rise. "A larger consequence of him going rogue, is a war in the region if something goes wrong with whatever he is up to and we have to go in to get him."

"Senator...Senator," Ned, attempted to speak.

"Now would be a good time for you to tell me what in the hell he is doing in Asmere, near Asmere, or around Asmere. Then explain to me why I was not notified." There was no reply. "Ned."

"Intel from the woman rescued with Princess Zsa Zsa Ashro had implications of a plot against a United States citizen. After, questioning the man who held the women, who I am happy to report is still alive, more details were revealed. We believe it was in the best interests of the United States to follow up. Absolute is en route to Asmere to return the woman to her family. They were on a hot trail. There simply wasn't time to check in, Senator."

"Unacceptable. When it comes to matters of National Security you make time. Period. Connect me to Absolute."

"He went dark when he entered Asmere."

"So he *is* in Asmere," Royce stood and hit his desk with his fist. "There are things connected with Asmere that are confidential on the highest level. One wrong move on his part will set off a chain of events we will not be able to alter. Get him back."

"That could be problematic, but I will do my best."

"Ned, does the King of Asmere know an American is coming?"

"Not to my knowledge. An undercover delivery was planned. However, there is some concern for the woman's safety. There may be an overlap between the time he delivers the woman and the time he leaves the country. If all goes well, he will be back in the United States in twenty-four hours."

"Ned, I don't want any excuses. You contact me the moment you have an update on this situation."

"Yes sir," Ned spoke quickly. "Senator, before you go. There is a sealed file in the folder on Asmere. Any chance on us gaining access?"

"Need to know basis. At this time, you don't need to know."

Royce hung up the phone, took a deep breath and then dialed the Secretary of Defense's office. He explained the events of the last few days and the status.

"Are they aware of the sanctions against Asmere and the countries hostility towards us?"

"Yes, Mr. Secretary they are aware. However, a woman's life is in jeopardy. What they do not know, sir, is there are more sanctions on the way and a possible coup about to happen in that region. Perhaps opening the file to..."

"Negative, Senator. Under no circumstances is that information to be released. The rightful leader of that region's life could be jeopardized."

"Understood, Mr. Secretary."

"Get that operative out of that region before he negates all we have worked to accomplish for the last twenty years."

Royce sat back, concern clearly appearing on his face. He stood and walked over to the bookshelf located on the right side of his office. He pulled a book partially out, then pushed it back in. The bookshelves slid five feet to the right. There was another shelf, consisting of three shelves with several disc cases, organized by date. There were three file drawers under the shelves. Royce pulled out the top drawer, fingering through the files until he reached the one he was searching for. He took out the picture of his friend, at the time Prince Tochi of Asmere, and his wife, Maya. Then he took out another picture of a woman and smiled. The woman was and to this day remained one of the most beautiful he had ever seen. Lowering his head, he put the pictures back, closed the drawer, and returned the bookcase to its covert location, effectively securing his thoughts of the past.

Chapter Eight

As sure as there were stars in the sky, Shelly Knight knew she was about to be grilled. Her behavior was uncalled for. The weather was crisp. One could smell the first signs of snow in the air as they rode to the airport. It was Monday morning. Rochelle Delaney, her foster sister was on her way back to Atlanta where she taught chemistry at Morehouse and Spelman College. She was catching the six a.m. flight to arrive in time for her ten o'clock lecture.

Shelly had hoped the cool air from the cracked window in her 1999 Ford Explorer would keep the conversation, she knew was coming, from getting out of hand. She knew Rocy almost better than she knew herself. The events of Saturday night had yet to be discussed. Eventually she was going to have to fess up. She would have to explain why she reacted the way she had. Rocy chuckled, causing Shelly to give her a sideways look.

"Care to share?" she asked her friend who was now laughing so hard Shelly couldn't help but to join in. "What?"

Rochelle sat up and wiped the tears from her eyes. "Whew. The last time I saw you that pissed was when Larry Davis put the caterpillar down your blouse, and you were running around in circles flipping your shirt up and down trying to get it out."

Shelly smiled, remembering and nodded. "You started chasing me, trying to find out what was wrong."

"And you kept running around the school yard, screaming. Then I started screaming with you." The two women laughed together.

"Finally, you pulled my shirt over my head, and swatted the damn thing away. Until that day, I never thought you even knew some of the words you said to that boy. Hell, I didn't know some of them. I'll never forget the look on his face when Mrs. Blount pulled you off him after you beat his butt."

Rocy laughed as she looked out the window. "Damn right I whipped his butt. Nobody messes with my best friend and gets away with it."

"Whew, that was funny." Shelly laughed.

"Until we got suspended from school." Rocy shook her head.

"Yeah, but you got a butt whipping." Shelly frowned at the memory.

"It was worth it."

"It wasn't that big of a deal and definitely not worth you getting into trouble."

"Yes, it was." Rocy looked at her. "I saw how hurt you were then. It was the same look you had when we walked in that restaurant to find your husband all hugged up with his mistress." She touched Shelly's arm. "I saw the same look in your eyes the other night when you spoke to Senator Davenport." She waited a moment. "Now, I know you have never met the man before. So...you want to tell me what that was all about?"

Shelly glanced at her and turned her eyes back to the road as she put her signal on to enter Interstate 64

East. She exhaled, while contemplating how she would explain her actions. She took a quick glance at her friend. "Don't judge me."

Rocy, raised an eyebrow. "Have I ever?"

"You may after you hear this." It was four in the morning and thankfully, traffic going towards downtown Richmond and towards the airport wasn't heavy, for she knew how her friend Rocy, as she called her, was going to react. "Don't laugh."

"I will not laugh at you. Come on, you know me better than that."

Shelly took another quick glance at her friend to judge her sincerity. "He's my fantasy." She kept her eyes on the road, fearing the look she might receive.

"Fantasy?"

Taking a deep breath, she sighed. "Whew. When I want to...you know, get off, the Senator is...was my visual."

Rocy sat there, staring at her friend with a blank look on her face. She turned and looked out of her side window, composed herself then turned back to Shelly. "Let me get this straight. When you get your rocks off, with whatever toy you have at your disposal, the person you visualize is the Senator, not Denzel, Idris, Babyface, or Hill Harper? Your fantasy lover is the Senator?"

"You promised you wouldn't laugh."

"I'm not laughing." Rocy smirked. "I'm just surprised." She chuckled, then looked over and saw Shelly's deflated look. "Okay, I'm sorry. Hey, he's a damn good looking guy. I can, I can..." she was nodding her head. "I can see that." She shrugged her shoulders. "If it was me, I would go all out. Hell, if I'm going to fantasize, give me Boris Kodjoe or that brother from *Jumping the Broom*."

"Laz Alonso."

"Yes, both of them...at the same time. Now, *that's* a fantasy." She laughed. "Yep." She thought about it a little more. "That...is definitely a true fantasy."

"Too light, I like intelligent, strong, dark men."

"Okay, I can see the attraction." She paused. "So, when your fantasy lover didn't respond to a situation, the way you wanted him to, you became disappointed in him--the real him, not the fantasy him, to a point where you damn near cursed the man out?"

Shelly thought for a moment. "That sounds about right."

Rocy did all she could not to laugh out loud. Inside she was cracking up. "Honey, do you think you may have lost your grip on reality?"

"No." Shelly was adamant. "He should do the right thing and make a way for those children to attend that camp." She was pounding the steering wheel. "I don't care if he has to come out of his own packet to pay for them. Right is right," she huffed.

"Okay, okay, calm down. This is me, Rocy, you're talking to."

"I am calm. I sat back and watched Marc do things I knew were wrong and never opened my mouth. I'm not making that mistake again."

Rochelle reached across the seat taking her friend's hand. "Shelly, you can't compare Senator Davenport to Marc Knight. You don't even know the Senator, no matter how many fantasies you have about him. It's just that, a fantasy. That prick, Marc, was your husband, who cheated on you. They are as different as day and night." She released Shelly's hand then sat back in her seat. "Besides, we all have that fantasy man that we put on an impossible pedestal. We make them so perfect in our minds, that no real man would ever be able to meet our expectations. You've put the Senator in a no-win situation." She watched as Shelly processed her words. This woman was one of the most sensible, grounded people she knew. Yes, the ass of an ex-husband changed her ability to trust people, however, Royce Davenport was a decent man and one of the good guys working in Washington, D.C. Rocy couldn't allow Shelly to continue to think this way about him.

Shelly looked up, sheepishly, then began laughing herself. "I've lost touch with reality, huh?"

"A tad bit," Rocy smiled back. "Okay, a lot, but it's okay. At least you picked a fine man to lose your mind over." She hesitated. "Why fantasize about the man when you can have him." She sat forward. "Remember how Momma Brown used to say you can catch more bees with honey than vinegar?"

"Yeah, but who wants to catch bees?"

"It's a metaphor. The bee you want to catch is Senator Davenport."

"Girl, please, no." Shelly shook her head. "Now that I'm back, let's stick to reality."

"Why not, Shelly?" Rochelle was really getting excited about the thought. "You are the one always telling these kids to dream big. Well, a fantasy is just like a dream. Why not go for it?"

"You can't be serious. Have you seen his ex-wife?"

"Yes, she's not all that. Look Shelly, you are an intelligent, beautiful, full grown woman. You saw something in the Senator you liked, why dream about it. I say go for it. Get your grown and sexy on." Rocy watched as her friend considered her words.

Shelly shook her head. "No. After the other night, the man is not going to want to see me again...ever. I'm sure his sights would be on someone a lot younger than me."

Rocy gave her a sideways glare. "I don't know what you are talking about. I look damn good and so do you." She huffed, "Besides, I think you have a perfect opening. You could always call to invite him to dinner as a way of apologizing." Allowing the thought to take root, Rochelle looked up at Shelly and asked, "Why settle for the fantasy when you can have the man?"

Later that day, after her class had ended, Shelly took a moment to consider Rocy's advice. Thoughts of the conversation came back to play in living color in her mind. She was thirty-five years old, had been married for five years to a certifiable ass, and divorced for eight years. There had been dates in between, but they either wanted someone to play the role of their mother, or wanted to have a harem of women chasing behind them. Shelly did not have time for either. What she wanted was a man she could have decent conversations with, who would not mind going out and dancing every so often, and someone who knew how to satisfy her sexual urges every now and then. As if reading her mind, her cell phone rang. She looked at the caller ID. It was Rocy.

"Hey, I made it to class, and wish like hell, I had stayed in Virginia."

Shelly, smiled. "Hey, yourself. What happened in class?"

"One of my students mixed some chemicals and damn near burned down the building," she laughed. "Now, I have the Dean on my ass about possible charges against the student for creating a bomb. I swear, I understand national security better than most, but we tend to take things too far. And here's the kicker. The kid is trying to perfect a device to deactivate bombs. Do you know we have agencies trying to do that same thing, yet we are talking about suspending and charging this student? There is something wrong with this world."

"Is everyone okay? Was anyone hurt?"

"No, we responded quickly, just a smoky building. We had to cancel classes for the rest of the day. We will be back in business tomorrow. Are you home yet?"

"I'm pulling into the driveway now."

"Good, I have a phone number for you."

"A phone number." She hesitated. "For who?"

"Royce Davenport."

Shelly laughed. "You had time to find a number to Senator Davenport with all you just told me?" She turned the ignition off, and stepped out of the car.

"See how far I will go for you. I had to promise his brother a date for his private number."

"Grayson? Oh, that's a hardship."

Rochelle laughed. "I know that's right, with his fine self. So, are you in the house yet?"

"Wait a minute, I'm turning off the alarm." She put her purse on the table in her kitchen and silenced the alarm. "There. Now, what do you expect me to do with the number?"

"Call him."

"I can't just call him out of the blue."

"Shelly, man up. You owe the man an apology. Write down this number." She gave her the number. "Did you write it down, Shelly?"

Shelly rolled her eyes upward. "I put it in my cell phone."

"Read it back to me."

"What? You don't believe me?"

"No. Read it back."

Shelly read the number back. "Satisfied."

"Yes. He is not in the office at the moment. So I suggest you make the call now and leave a message with his secretary. Her name is Kathy Paxton. She's a sweetheart."

"How do you know this?"

"I just called. I started to leave the message for you, but I think you should do this. According to Grayson, the man is not seeing anyone. I'm sure he will appreciate a dinner not connected to the Washington who's who."

Shelly sat down at her kitchen table and sighed. "I don't know, Rocy. It's been years since I've called a man about a date."

"This isn't about a date. This is about an apology, which you do owe the man. If you happen to get a date out of it, that's icing on the cake. Call him, now. Then call me back and tell me what happened." Rocy hung up the telephone before Shelly could respond.

Shelly looked at her cell, with the phone number glaring at her. She closed her eyes and pushed the button.

"Senator Davenport's office, Kathy Paxton speaking."

"Hello." Shelly was surprised the call was picked up on the first ring. But then she remembered, this is his private line. "Yes, Mrs. Paxton. Umm, my name is Shelly Knight I would like to leave a message for Senator Davenport."

Kathy smiled. "Ms. Knight, Senator Davenport is available, if you hold I will connect you."

"Umm, no," Shelly said surprised at the woman's response. "I don't want to disturb him."

"Not a problem, Ms. Knight. Hold please."

"No, no, no..." She shook the telephone when she realized the woman was no longer there. *Just hang up. Just hang up*, she kept saying as she walked circles around the table, putting the phone back up to her ear, then holding it away from her.

"Royce Davenport."

She heard his voice on the other end of the phone and froze. He had a really smooth voice.

"Hello?"

"Yes." She took a deep breath and rattled off her apology. "Senator Davenport, I'm sorry for interrupting your day but I need to apologize to you. I was wrong, very wrong to speak to you in the manner I did. Please accept my apology and again I sincerely apologize. Yes, that's it. I'm sorry," she spilled out.

He recognized the voice from the word 'hello'. Containing his smile was difficult. "Thank you."

He sounded strained. She lowered her head and exhaled. "That wasn't very smooth at all was it?"

"I think it was a good start."

She smiled, than exhaled. "That's because you are a kind person, Senator. This is Shelly Knight, the woman who attacked you unmercifully on Saturday night in Richmond. I do apologize for interrupting your day. However, I really could not go another minute without apologizing for my actions." There was silence on the other end. Did she say too much? Was he still there? "Hello."

"I'm still here. You have me at a bit of a disadvantage. I have a cancellation on tomorrow. Is it possible for us to meet around six at a location convenient for you?"

Shelly opened her mouth then shut it. "Yes," she slowly replied, shaking her head no.

"Would you give the location to my secretary?"

"Umm, all right."

"I look forward to the meeting."

"Okay," she said puzzled. "Thank you."

"You're welcome. I'm going to transfer you back to my secretary."

She stared at the telephone, wondering what in the hell just happened.

"Hello, Ms. Knight?"

"Yes, I'm here."

"Senator Davenport indicated you were to give me an address for a meeting?"

"Yes, yes, umm." She looked around the house then gave the woman her address. After disconnecting the call, Shelly fell into the chair at the kitchen table and sighed. "I have a date with Royce Davenport." A warm smile surfaced. "I have a date with Royce Davenport."

He was going to have to have a few words with Kathy, Royce thought. *Then kiss her.* She knew he was at the White House in a meeting with the Chief of Staff. Putting the call through was inappropriate. After he reprimanded her, he would send her a bouquet of her favorite flowers. There was a smile deep down, even with the information the Chief of Staff was giving him about the declining state of affairs in Asmere.

Chapter Nine

Joshua landed his chopper ten miles on the outskirts of the capitol city of Asmere under the cover of night. LaVere' flew the chopper back to the palace for safe keeping until Joshua was ready to return to the United States. With the technology on the chopper, there was no way he would leave it anywhere in Asmere.

Joshua and Akande walked the ten miles, sticking to the back roads leading to the palace. The country was a direct contrast to Emure. This country was poor. The lands were ravished. The homes they passed were no more than one room shacks with roofs falling in. As they walked closer to the capitol, the homes were in better shape, but still not great. The area was a little more populated, which caused Joshua to proceed cautiously. He checked constantly to ensure they had not been detected. One would think, with his mind occupied on keeping them alive, the sway of the woman's hips in front of him would not affect him. Wrong. It did, damn near to distraction. He couldn't figure out why. Women did not affect him the way this one was. Something in him needed to protect her and that was problematic. For now, she was an enemy. He needed to keep reminding himself of that as he continued to watch her. His head involuntarily moved from side to side with the sway of her hips as he followed her. She turned to look over her shoulder at him. His head stopped until she turned back. He then resumed scanning of the countryside and his head movement.

It dawned on him, he had come to admire the way she was handling the situation. Not once did Akande complain about the journey. Most women would have. What concerned him was, he noticed the closer they got to the palace, the more tense she became. It was an odd reaction for someone returning home. Right now, he would not question her, he would let things play out.

For the life of her Akande could not understand why the man behind her sent heat surges through her body. Every so often she would glance over her shoulder at him. It appeared he was looking elsewhere, but she knew different. She could feel his eyes every time he looked at her. There was an attraction between them. She had never experienced this with a man before, but she knew for certain it was something she could not afford. She had to fight it, at all costs.

"It is hot. Why do you wear a suit to walk miles?"

"You don't like my suit?" She heard the amusement in his voice.

"It is not a question of like. It is not practical."

"Practical," he snarled. "Who in the hell wants practical? Practical is boring. I want bam, in your face excitement. Besides my suits let people know I'm ready to handle business. You shouldn't diss the suit. This suit will provide your cute little behind with protection if there is trouble. Why are you looking at my suit anyway? I know," he grinned, "A brother looks good, don't I?"

She abruptly stopped and turned to him. "That has nothing to do with it. This is a serious situation, yet you stand here with jokes and your careless way. We could be surrounded and killed at any moment."

He stared down at her. "Do your know you accent becomes more pronounced when you are angry? It's kind of sexy."

She glared at him thinking, so was he. "Argh," she huffed, turned and resumed walking as she mumbled, "Arrogant man. Of all the men in America, they sent you." She stopped and turned back to him. "Are you the best they have to offer?"

"Damn right I am," he scowled down at her. "I got your little ass out the dungeon alive." He held her glare and then walked off."

The palace was less than a mile away when they stopped for the last time. Joshua pulled Akande down by her arm. "Are you going to be safe walking from here to the entrance of the palace?"

"This is my home. Of course I will be safe."

"Why do you look so worried?"

She shot him a glance. "It is nothing. I am anxious to be home."

"Un huh," he held her gaze until she looked away. "It's not too late. We can leave here, if you want." He saw a flash of uncertainty in her eyes as she looked up at the palace then turned back to him. "No," she shook her head. "I must return home."

"Okay." He reached into his suit pocket. "Take this." He placed a small thin band around her wrist. "If you have any need to contact me just rub the band. I will come."

Confusion filled her eyes. "Why?"

"I read people pretty well. You're frightened. I don't know of what or who, but you are. When you are ready, you'll tell me."

"I will probably never see you again after today."

"Sounds like you're going to miss me." He raised a teasing brow.

"I will not. I do not like you."

He saw a hint of a smile tug at her lips. "I believe the woman protests a bit too much. Seconds ticked away as they held each other's stare. He bent over and gently kissed her lips. They were as soft as he imagined. *She is the enemy.* The thought caused him to pull away. "It was the fight. You felt the electricity too, right. I know, you want me, don't you?"

It took her a second to register his words. Her lips were still tingling from his kiss. She jumped up. "Of course not. I am no man's whore."

He pulled her back down. "Okay, okay, I'm just teasing. I was trying to lighten the mood for you."

She glared at him for a moment then settled back down. "Thank you for bringing me home."

"You're welcome." Something was telling him not to let her go. But it was his sworn duty to protect his country against all enemies. At the moment, she was the enemy. "You have to go now before someone walks up on us." He pointed to her arm. "Use it if you need to."

She nodded, then walked around the outside of the brick wall surrounding the grounds of the palace. She looked back, but he was gone, just that quick. She looked around, no sight of him. She wondered if she would ever see him again. Sadness fell over her spirit. It had only been a day since he appeared in her room. For some reason she felt safe with him. She had an idea of what awaited her inside the palace. Nothing felt safe about that. Turning back, she began walking towards the palace. Rather than walking to the front entrance, she squeezed into the opening leading to the back of the palace. Half way in, shouts began piercing the air.

Joshua watched as two armed men ran towards her. Then another two joined them. With weapons drawn, they ordered her to the ground. With her hands behind her back, he watched as they picked her up by her arms and carried her into the back of the palace.

Unknown to the guards, Joshua entered the palace the moment the security detected Akande on the grounds. By the time the men ran out, he was at a back entrance to the palace.

Checking his hand held device, he monitored the movements of the men who intercepted Akande. Through the shadows of the hallways, he listened as a call was placed informing someone of Akande's presence. On her knees, with her hands behind her back, a guard snapped a picture of her with his cell phone. He sent the picture as one of the other men was questioning her.

"How did you get here? Did someone come with you?" When Akande did not reply, the guard raised the butt of his gun. Another guard stopped him.

"The Queen will not be pleased if she is scarred. Instead of striking her in the face, the guard shoved the butt of the gun into her side. Akande grunted, but did not cry out. The man on the phone spoke and a few seconds later, Akande was picked up by the arms again.

Joshua wanted to kill the man for striking Akande, but he knew it would lead to other issues. Instead he turned to explore his surroundings, but he knew the guard would die before he left the palace.

Akande wasn't taken to her room as she expected. The hallway they were in led to the common area, not the residence area of the palace. A man who she determined to be royalty from the way he was dressed, with guards around him, hurried from one of the rooms to the exit leading to the front entrance of the palace. When their eyes met, he quickly turned his head and walked hurriedly out the door. The man looked surprised to see her, but she did not recognize him and had no idea why her being there would be an issue. However from the way he quickly turned, it appeared it was.

"Sit," one of the guards ordered. "Queen Sermyera will speak with you soon."

For the last four hours, she had been preparing herself for the encounter that was about to take place. She knew her aunt would act disappointed. She was certain the Queen still wanted the mission completed. It was imperative that she not allow her temper to get the best of her until she was able to get information on the new plan.

How her life had changed in the last few weeks. The day she left the palace her thoughts were on the mission her aunt had prepared her for, avenging her mother's death and the restoration of the country's honor. The mission could be accomplished with one task. Kill the man who had dishonored her mother by impregnating her and then spearheaded sanctions against Asmere by the United States. One man alone was responsible for the devastation of her family's honor. His actions alone, had caused Asmere's economic demise when sanctions put in place by the United States prohibited any commerce between the two countries. Their countrymen had to sit back and watch as neighboring Emure prospered from economic growth, enriching their lands with factories and trade agreements.

From a very young age, she had been taught how to manipulate, and coerce others. At times, she was forced to test her skills on her friends, whom she soon lost after they discovered her duplicity. Her aunt made sure her few friends knew what she had done. Soon she learned it was the way her aunt wanted things. She wanted her to be alone with no friends or anyone around who cared about her, leaving her only means of support, being Sermyera, the Queen of Asmere. Once Akande learned what was expected of her, she began to shield her thoughts, from her aunt and others. It was her only means of dealing with the mental cruelty she sustained as a child. She began to understand she had one purpose as far as her aunt was concerned and once she was older and prepared, she would fulfill that purpose.

She was trained to use her interpersonal and communication skills that had been perfected by the same people who trained military personnel in the United States. Her specialty had been designed with this one mission in mind. To portray any personality needed to get close to the man she was to kill. For that, her greatest strength meant she had to think on her feet and adjust to whatever situation arose. This was more than just a mission to Akande. This was her opportunity to restore her family's honor.

When she was first kidnapped, it had not come to her that it was her aunt who was behind it. After days in captivity, she pieced together all that had taken place, leading her to only one conclusion. Her aunt was behind the kidnapping. The question was why? The plan was in place for her to go to Washington, get a position as an intern at the White House and use the position to get close to the man, by any means necessary. She could have easily requested that the man who rescued her take her to the United States, however, she needed to know what had changed before she moved forward with the plan.

Her thoughts turned to the man, Joshua. There was something about him that made her instincts of self-preservation kick in. He was intelligent and dangerous. Not many men looked the way he did. The affect he had on her was intense and scorching. The only thing she could think to do was fight him. Even now, when she should be concerned with her life, her thoughts went to his kiss. She reached up and touched her lips. It was sweet, gentle...lingering. She dropped her hands. Therein lie the problem for her. Her thinking, judgment, all were cloudy around him. When they were talking at the table, she thought about telling him all, but she quickly clear that from her mind. Her fear of failing at her task overrode her curiosity about the man. The one thing she knew, he was not the one for this task. She would have to find a way to impress that upon her aunt.

"The Queen will see you now," a guard commanded.

Akande stood, shielded her soul and walked into the room.

Sermyera entered the room with the authority of a ruler. She was draped in a two–piece, purple, dress, trimmed at the bodice and edged in gold, with a matching purple headpiece. Many countries had done away with the traditional throne room, Asmere had not. King Tarik and Queen Sermyera reigned. If there were any doubts, the two deep red, gold trimmed, throne chairs were a not too subtle reminder. They sat high above the others on a stage with steps leading to them.

The guards, who entered the room on each side of her, carried weapons under their suits. They did not look as good as Joshua. The men standing behind her carried weapons as well. However, none of them intimidated her more than the woman now standing before her, for she knew none of the men would act without her say for fear of the consequences. Queen Sermyera's consequences were never minimal or swift, for she lived to see people suffer. It was for this reason, Akande never wanted to disappoint her aunt.

Sermyera's eyes roamed over her niece. The sight of her niece displeased her, for the garment the woman was wearing made her look regal and that was the last thing she ever wanted Akande to feel.

"You dare to stand before me in such rags!" she all but roared.

Akande thought the dress was beautiful but could see it displeased Sermyera. She kept her head low, never looking the Queen in her eyes for she would believe that to be insolent. Akande had felt her wrath before and did not wish to experience it again. "It is what I was given to wear from the Queen of Emure."

"You believe her garments to be of better quality than what we have here in your homeland?"

"No, my Queen. I had nothing else to wear."

Akande referring to her as her 'Queen' always pleased Sermyera. "Very well, I will endure it through this conversation." She looked at the men with Akande. "You may leave us now. Tell no one she is here."

The men bowed. "Your Highness," they said as they left.

Once the men were gone Sermyera turned to one of her guards. "See to it that we are not disturbed. The two guards walked out of opposite side doors. Once closed, Sermyera turned back to Akande. "You have been gone for weeks, Akande. Did you complete your mission?"

"No, your highness."

"So, the American is not dead and the sanctions have not been lifted from Asmere?" Sermyera lifted a questioning brow.

"No, your highness. There was a delay."

"A delay? You have been gone for weeks. Yet you return without accomplishing your goal. What possible excuse could you have for failing your country?"

Akande lowered her head. She hated the word failure. It was too close to the words used all her life to describe her mother, dishonor, disappointment, and traitor. Her aunt, Queen Sermyera, never allowed a day to go by without a reminder. There was no question her life would have been different if Sermyera was not her only means to food and shelter. There was little else afforded her from her aunt, certainly no signs of love or caring. She wasn't allowed to have friends. The few she made were soon disheartened by the history of her heritage, usually shared with them by her aunt. Now, to have the same words used to describe her damaged her pride.

Akande held her head high. "I was kidnapped." She narrowed her eyes. "I believe you are aware of this."

"Why would I be aware?" Sermyera inquired. The girl was smart. Sermyera knew she would eventually figure it out. Now, she truly had to tread lightly, for she still needed the girl to kill the American.

Sermyera yelled, "If you had been kidnapped as you say, why was there no ransom demand! Did you not tell your kidnappers you were my niece?"

"I was not kidnapped in this area. We were hours away when this occurred. When I did not return, did you not wonder at my whereabouts? Did you not once send someone to search for me? Putting that aside, did you not think something was amiss when my driver did not return?" Her eyes were now level with Sermyera's and she knew the moment the words left her mouth, she had allowed her temper to get the best of her. Seconds later, the confirmation came; she was correct.

Sermyera slapped her across the face. The contact was so forceful, Akande stumbled backwards. "You dare to question me? Tobyn!" she called out. The guard who accompanied Sermyera to the throne room reappeared. "Take her to the dungeon." She commanded as she turned back to Akande. "For your insolence, you will receive twenty lashes. If you survive, you will be banished from our lands."

Tobyn, grabbed Akande by the arm. "My Queen I will take the lashes, but do not banish me from my home."

"What good are you to me, Akande? I gave you one mission to restore your tarnished life, yet you failed." She rallied on the girl. "I cannot continue to carry the burden and shame of your mother's actions, by having you in the palace. You do not deserve my generosity."

"Have the plans changed? You no longer want the American dead? Is this why you had me kidnapped and imprisoned?"

Sermyera nodded to Tobyn. He released Akande's arm, then stepped back. "You are smart. I have always said this." Sermyera walked over and sat on her throne. "An opportunity to earn funds came to me. We had to delay the plans. Now that we are better financed, we can resume."

"The man who was here earlier, did he provide the funding?"

Sermyera frowned, but quickly recovered. "He is not important. However, I fear your dedication to the mission has been compromised. Since you returned here, you no longer have access to the American.

"I have the means to get to the American."

Sermyera looked up at her niece. "How?"

"It was an American who rescued Princess Zsa Zsa of Emure."

The smile within almost surfaced as Sermyera glared at the girl. The plan had worked. By assisting an ally with the kidnapping, they had received one hundred million dollars and a direct connection to Royce Davenport. As their ally had indicated, the friend of Prince LaVere' had stepped in to help recover the Princess. Whenever military personnel were involved with actions in foreign lands, the Senator of Foreign Affairs took the lead. Davenport was the lead Senator. Knowing how the Americans loved to open their borders to all, they would ask if she wished to receive asylum in the United States or return to her country. His office would process her request for asylum. She had trained her niece well. There was no doubt in her mind that Akande would be in a room with Davenport soon. With her powers of persuasion, Sermyera knew it was only a matter of time before she would kill Davenport. Of course if Akande failed, no problem, there was a backup plan in place.

"Where is this American now?"

There was no way Akande would tell her about the band the man had given her. That would cause a wrath she was not ready for. Another thought crossed her mind, which she was not pleased with. Sermyera could have the American killed. "He brought me here. I'm certain I could find him."

"You will tell this American, you wish to be taken to Washington to search for your father."

"My Queen, I will use this American to get to Washington. But I do not think we should involve this American with the plan."

Sermyera narrowed her eyes. "Why is that?"

"He is an intelligent man and not one to be easily fooled."

"He is a man, an American at that. They only think of carnal satisfaction. Have you so quickly forgotten your mother's disgrace to her country, her family?" she screeched. "One look in the mirror should remind you of your mother's treachery. It is your purpose, your duty to make the American pay for the dishonor he brought on your mother and still holds over our country, your country. It is the only way for you to receive forgiveness for your mother's sins. The sanctions that have held your homeland in turmoil are on the shoulders of the American. Do you not wish to restore your country to its rightful state?

Akande held her head lower in shame. "Yes, your highness it is my wish to restore my family's name to honor. The sanctions against my country will be lifted and we will again rule in this region. I pledge my life to this mission."

Sermyera was pleased with the passion of her niece's words. It was imperative that the fear of failure was deeply imbedded within her for the mission to be completed. Once Akande reached the United States, she would kill the only two people in the world who could take the throne away from her and Tarik, Royce Davenport and her niece standing before her. "I believe you my child. For I believe you love your country and its people. If you fail at this mission you have been raised to complete, you would not only fail your people, you would fail your chance at restoring your mother's honor." Sermyera narrowed her eyes. "Tobyn will give you a reminder of the consequence of failure."

Akande knew if she failed, she would take her own life before returning to Asmere in disgrace.

Joshua moved about the palace effortlessly. This place did not have much in the way of security features, unlike the mansion where Zsa Zsa was found. No, this place was secured by men. While the lands and homes surrounding the palace were deteriorating, this place was not. The luxury of this palace paled in comparison to Emure's palace. However, it was more luxurious then the lands leading to it would imply. It was clear any funds coming into this country were used for the comfort of the residents of this palace. A leader should live the life of his people. This King was living far beyond his means. The rooms were lavishly filled with paintings, statues, and furniture fit for a King. On their way to the palace, it was clear the sanctions from the United States were having a significant impact on the country. It angered him to think of the poor conditions of the homes he'd passed coming there as compared to the lavish furnishings of the palace.

Someone is living well, he thought as he silently entered a bedroom. Standing behind the drapes made of soft silk, trimmed in gold, and framing the balcony doors he had just entered, he listened to the conversation taking place.

"My King, the girl Akande has returned. She is downstairs with Queen Sermyera," a woman's voice spoke.

The man sounded startled as he spoke. "When did she arrive?"

"According to Tobyn about an hour ago."

He heard the man move. "Did she see our visitor?"

"I believe he had left before she was brought to appear before the Queen." The man seemed to relax at the woman's words. "The Queen is questioning her now. What will you do if the girl learns the truth?"

The man sneered, "The girl is not an issue. Once her role is complete she will die."

"I don't want her here. You lust after her. It was only due to the Queen's plan that you did not have your way with her. Banish her from our lands."

"You do not order me. Your duty is to pleasure me," his voice eased. "Bow before me. I wish to be pleasured, now."

For a moment, Joshua thought he would have to intercede. It sounded as if the King had physically injured the woman from the sound of her gasp. That, he could not allow. However, from the sounds of things, the King was now being pleasured, for he could hear the man's moans. It may not be the most professional picture, Joshua thought as he pulled his handheld device out and snapped pictures of the King and the woman. He looked at the picture. *Technique wasn't bad*, he thought as he sent the picture to Ned, with one word-*identify*.

There was a knock on the door. "My King, Queen Sermyera is en route," a man's voice came through.

Joshua watched as the woman attempted to get up, but the King held her head in place. "Finish," he commanded. The woman was trapped and had no choice but to comply. Once the deed was done, the King fell back on the bed and the woman fled out a side door. The King closed his robe just as the doors opened.

Joshua shifted his position to get a better view of the woman walking through the door. She was regal, as she walked through the sitting area of the bedroom. He snapped her picture.

"Tarik, the transfer has been completed." He could hear the joy in her voice. "We now have the funds needed for our mission." She ran into his arms and they embraced.

The King held her once the kiss ended. "Sanctions are still in place my sweet. We must kill the American who threatens our throne."

"The delay of Akande's mission in America was necessary. The opportunity to add significant funds to our accounts was fundamental to our mission. If we are frugal we can survive off the funds we just received."

"I am King. I should not have to be frugal."

She took the Kings arm and wrapped it around her shoulders. "Soon, very soon, Akande and the American will be dead. The lands of Asmere and the surrounding countryside will be under our control. Then we can again live without fear."

"Where is the girl?"

"I have ordered Tobyn to take her to the basement."

"Why."

"A reminder of her purpose was necessary."

"The girl is too strong willed. You should have allowed me to tame her."

"She will be on her journey soon." Sermyera stepped away. "As our friend promised, an American saved Princess Zsa Zsa and Akande. This American, he has connections in Washington. His presence will reduce the time Akande will need to establish a relationship with the Senator."

"How is it possible if Akande is here?"

"She will be back on her journey to America very soon."

"For twenty years now, I have been denied the life of the King of Asmere. I do not like our fate being in the hands of a girl."

"All we need her to do is get an audience with the American. The rest will be taken out of her hands."

The King smiled down at her. "You have a contingency plan?"

The two laughed.

Joshua had heard enough. Pulling out his handheld, he had to find another escape route. There was no way he could leave the way he had entered for the couple were now seated on the balcony. He pulled up a schematic for the palace, then slipped from behind the drapes and out of the room. Now he knew a Senator's life was in danger. He had to find out who. Akande was going to have to lead him to the target. Before they reached the states, he had to find out what happened twenty years ago.

Chapter Ten

At precisely six p.m. there was a knock on her door. Shelly nervously looked around at the dining room one last time. The table was set, the china was sparkling, wine was cooling, everything seemed to be in place. As she walked through the hallway into the living room she stopped by the mirror just to check her appearance. She smoothed her hair down just to make sure it was neat, then she rubbed her hands down her size twelve frame to calm her nerves. When she got to the door, she took a deep breath and opened the door with a smile. It quickly turned into a frown, then confusion.

"Ms. Shelly Knight," a man dressed in a black suit, white shirt and tie, flipped an ID and badge at her. "Secret Service Agent McNally." He turned and pointed behind him. "Agents Johnson and Scott." He stepped inside past her, with the other two agents in his wake. "We need to search the premises. It shouldn't take long ma'am." The two agents briskly walked through the living room. One went in the direction of the kitchen and family room, the other went upstairs. Agent McNally stood next to her, discreetly scanning the living room.

"What is going on? Why are you doing this?"

"National security, ma'am." He continued to look around. "Is anyone else in the house ma'am?"

"No," Shelly replied a little frustrated. "Why do you have to search my home?"

Agent McNally turned to her. "As I said ma'am, national security."

The man from the kitchen walked back into the living room. "All clear," he said then disappeared as if he was never there. All Shelly could do was stare at the man's back as he walked out the door.

A minute later, the other agent appeared from the back staircase. "All clear." He also disappeared out the door. Agent McNally nodded his head to someone outside, then turned to her. "Have a good evening, ma'am."

When Agent McNally walked past her, Shelly looked up and there was Royce Davenport standing on her front porch, as if he appeared out of nowhere. The entire process took all of two minutes, but it left her already frazzled nerves shaken. "What in the hell just happened?" she asked looking out the door at the men now departing in a black SUV, which had been parked in front of a black sedan.

"Security detail," Royce replied as he also watched the SUV pull off.

"Well, what are they doing?" she asked seeing the two men still outside her home.

"I'm afraid they will remain until I leave."

She stood in the doorway staring at him with a quizzical look.

"May I come in?"

"Of course," she shook her head. "I'm sorry." She closed the door behind him as he walked in. "This all took me by surprise." They stood there for a minute staring at each other. Then her manners kicked in.

"Please," she said with a motion of her hand, "Do come in."

He held up a bottle of wine in a carrying case. "Peace offering."

Taking the gift she smiled. "Thank you. I should be giving you a peace offering." She walked to the left towards the family room. "Please make yourself comfortable while I put this on ice." He watched as she continued into the kitchen, which had an open connection to the family room. Smooth jazz was playing in the background. *Najee,* he thought. Taking a look around, gave him a sense of home. From the moment he walked in the door, that's what it felt like, home.

The furniture looked comfortable, with an overstuffed matching sofa and chair set. Not like some homes he walked into that felt like a museum. No, this felt good. There was a table at the corner of the sofa and a coffee table with an arrangement of callas and tulips in a glass vase. On her walls there were pictures of her and her foster sister, and some of an older couple. "Are these your parents?"

Shelly looked where he was standing, and thought the room looked small with him in it. "Yes," she replied as she walked over extending a glass of wine to him. "My foster parents."

"Thank you," he said as he accepted the glass. "Do you keep in touch with them?"

"We did. They have both passed away now."

"My condolences."

"It's been awhile. But, we do miss them. Please, have a seat. Dinner will be ready in about fifteen minutes. I just put the bread in the oven."

He raised an eyebrow, "You made bread?" He asked as he sat on the sofa.

"Homemade rolls." She nodded as she sat in the chair.

"Yeast rolls?" He smiled.

"Laid them out this morning," she explained. "They had all day to rise."

"Do you do this every time you have to apologize to someone?"

She lowered her head and smiled. "Believe it or not, it's a rare occurrence. I'm usually a pretty nice person."

"There's something about me that brings out the opposite reaction?"

"No," she anxiously replied. "No, I did not mean to insinuate that at all." She looked up to see him smiling, and exhaled with a grin. She cleared her throat. "Please," she placed her hand over her heart. "Allow me to apologize properly." She placed her glass on the table, then unconsciously ran her tongue over her bottom lip and sat forward with her hands clasped together in her lap. "I sincerely apologize for my actions and the words spoken. I have never behaved that way in public. My only excuse was that I was upset and disappointed with the outcome of the meeting. However, that gave me no right to speak to you in that manner." She looked up at him. "Please forgive me."

It took a moment for Royce to compose himself. From the moment he followed her curvy body into the family room, he had been trying to control his reaction to her. When she gave him the glass of wine, their fingers touched and heat, the likes of which he had never known, surged through him. Now, she sat there nervously licking her lips and all he could think about was how her tongue might taste. *What on earth was wrong with him? He was a forty-five year old man who knew damn well how to control his body.*

She was trying, really trying not to jump the man's bones. After all he was a United States Senator. There was a certain amount of decorum, she had to maintain in his presence. But, damn if he didn't look good and smelled even better. Lord, the way he looked at her was as if he had stripped her of every stitch of clothing. If he didn't stop soon, she was sure her body would burn away the fabric just from his stare. "Senator?"

He looked up from her lips. "Royce." He repeated it when she looked confused. "My name is Royce." They sat there gazing at each other as if there were nothing else important in the world.

The alarm from the oven buzzed. "I'm burning!" Shelly blurted out as she abruptly stood. "Not me," she fluttered pointing in the direction of the kitchen. "The rolls! I need to take the rolls out!" She almost ran into the kitchen.

Royce sat back a moment, closed his eyes. *Whoa. Okay get yourself under control.* He exhaled, and stood. "Do you mind if I remove my jacket, it's a little hot in here?"

Shelly had the pan of rolls in her mitten clad hand as she looked over to see him remove his jacket. "Sure," she replied, "You can remove anything you like." She snapped her fingers, catching herself. "I mean, you know, make yourself comfortable." Still standing there with the hot pan in her hand, she watched as he walked into the kitchen.

"It smells good in here. May I help you with that?" He nodded towards the pan of rolls in her hand as she stared up at him.

"No." Clearly shaken by his nearness, she quickly sat the pan on the island. "Why don't you have a seat in the dining room while I butter you...these down?"

"Are you sure you don't need help with that?" he asked as he walked back into the family room to retrieve their wine glasses.

"Yes, umm, I'm sure." She removed the mitten and began to spread butter on top of the rolls. "The dining room is right through there." She pointed to the opposite side of the kitchen as he walked by her.

"You have a very inviting home, Shelly. May I call you Shelly?" He asked as he looked back over his shoulder at her.

"Yes, please do," she replied trying not to look up so she could at least finish the simple task of putting butter on the damn rolls without thinking about how intense his eyes were.

"Good, because I like the way it sounds on my lips."

She froze and stared at him in the doorway, staring back at her. "Senator..."

"Royce."

"Royce," she corrected as she sighed. "I'm not good at picking up signs and notions and things like that. I'm kind of the 'go straight at it' type of girl. So, forgive me if I'm being a little blunt, but are you flirting with me?"

"Yes," he replied then walked into the dining room. "You cooked a smorgasbord."

It took a moment for her to recover from his blunt reply. She took the rolls from the pan and placed them on a platter. Shelly walked cautiously into the dining room. He was seated at the head of the table placing the linen napkin in his lap as if the question was never asked or answered.

Shelly placed the rolls in the center of the table. "I wasn't sure what you liked to eat, so I cooked a little of this and that," she said as she sat at the opposite end of the table and placed her napkin in her lap. "You don't know me. Why are you flirting with me?"

"You don't know me either, and I think we should change that."

She hesitated and stared at him as he took a sip of his wine. "What exactly do you think is going on here, Royce?"

He smiled at hearing his name on her lips. "An apology."

She nodded and smiled at his reply. "And how far do you think that apology is going?"

"As far as you like, however, it doesn't matter." He shrugged his shoulder. "We're going to be doing this again, aren't we?" He held her eyes and they both smiled. He tilted his glass towards her, motioning for her to do the same. "Apology accepted. Here's to new beginnings."

She liked the man. More than that, her taste in a fantasy man was reaffirmed.

An hour later, they were back in the family room on their second bottle of wine. Royce was at one end of the sofa, with his tie pulled loose, his shoes on the floor and his feet propped up on the table. Shelly was at the other end of the sofa, sitting with her shoes off and her feet under her, laughing at a story Royce had just told her. "Are your constituents always so animated?"

"You would not believe half of the requests we receive. I try to do what I can to make life a little easier for all of my constituents. The one thing I cannot do is make their neighbors mow the lawn after ten in the morning."

She laughed again. "I think there should be a law against mowing the lawn at six in the morning. Are you sure you can't make that happen?"

He really liked the sound of her laughter. There was something magical about it. Lord he wished he could bottle it up and take it back to Washington with him. He held her gaze and sobered. "Tell me about the children in the program."

They had sat in the dining room eating dinner and talked about everything under the sun, his career, her career. Their marriages, what happened, why they didn't work out and about his two children, one in college and one in high school. With all of that, they did not discuss the details of his job or the situation that brought them to this point.

Shelly took a sip of wine, and exhaled. "You know we were having a perfectly good time until now."

"We're still going to have a good time. I promise." he grinned. "However, I need to know about the children."

Shelly threw her head back and exhaled. "The children are priceless." She held her head back up smiling. "They don't have much. Most of them are in single parent homes with limited income and love. They've lost faith in the system and don't believe they have any future other than what they see every day in their neighborhoods." She shook her head. "I used everything in my arsenal to get participation in the Abstinence Pays project. Do you know that over half of my senior class homeroom is pregnant? The other half has contracted a STD at least once. That should not be happening to children. We have babies having babies, and they don't know how to teach their children right from wrong, or good from bad, because they haven't had time to learn these things themselves. I'm telling you, if Congress wants answers as to why our education system is so poor compared to other countries, it's because teachers have to spend so much time on raising the children and in some instances the parents, too. Then we have to teach to this ridiculous 'standards of learning' crap that doesn't give a true assessment of jack shit. And most, of the questions on the damn test are geared to one class of people." She sat up, "I'm telling you, if I had the money I wouldn't open up a school in another county, I would open my own school right here at home and say the hell with what law makers think I should be teaching, and teach these children what I know they need to survive in this world." She took a breath, looked up at him and raised an eyebrow at his exasperated look. "Well...you asked."

He laughed. "I did. And I see you are not one to hold back, are you?"

"Not when it comes to children."

"Why didn't you have any children?"

She sighed. "My ex didn't want any. The one time I thought I was pregnant he told me to abort it." She shrugged. "Thank God I wasn't. I would have aborted him before I did my child." Royce laughed a deep rich laugh that made her heart flutter. Everything about this man made her insides quiver.

"You will be happy to know, the other children in your program will be attending the camp."

Shelly beamed, "You did that?"

"I did."

The look in her eyes filled him with pride. Being with her for the last few hours was like fresh air whipping through the clothes on a clothesline in the backyard of his grandmother's house. When he was young he would hold his hands up under the sheets as the wind whipped through them. The breeze was warm, fresh and invigorating. That's what she was to him. Royce watched as the play of emotions showed on her face. "If you ask me to...I will."

"You will what?"

"Kiss you."

The heat had simmered and now it was speeding back through her veins as he held her gaze. "If I ask...and you adhere...I might want more."

"There's no might in it, Shelly. I do want more."

He sat up and put his glass on the table. Took hers and did the same, then he pulled her on top of him as he laid back. "I'm going to do what I've wanted to do all night."

The contact, her body on his, started her inner lips pumping, as if they were saying, *feed me, c'more feed me.* And why shouldn't her body want this. They were two grown, consenting adults who happened to be very attracted to each other. She stretched out against his chest, wrapping her arms around his neck. "What are you going to do?" she whispered against his lips.

"Kiss you until I can't breathe." His lips descended on hers like a moth to a flame. Nothing, absolutely nothing, compared to the feel of her lips, other than the feel of her body in his arms.

Yes, her lips were as luscious as he imagined with the sweet taste of wine on them. A moan escaped as he slanted his mouth over hers again, parting her lips, tasting the sweetness of her tongue as his slowly glided over hers. He broke the kiss and looked at her. When she opened her eyes he liked the sassy, *why in the hell did you stop* look she gave him. He smiled. "It's going to be a long night." Royce dove right back in taking her mouth with a greed he did not know he possessed. What he did know, was she was the sweetest tasting woman he had ever kissed.

The fantasy of Royce Davenport had nothing on the reality. Her body was pulsating in areas the fantasy never reached and they still had clothes on. She moaned as his tongue explored every inch of her mouth. The passion in his kiss, his hold on her body, had her nipples straining against her bra. His hands roamed down her back, curving over her behind and pulling her feminine mound in direct contact with his thick penis. Lord, it felt as thick as his thighs. The A-line dress didn't allow her to spread her legs, as she wanted. She reached down and both their hands pulled the sides of the dress up to her waist. Now, the only thing between them was his zipper. She exhaled at the thickness she could feel through his pants.

He moaned at the heat in his hands from the globes of her behind. That just fueled his fire more. He wanted to squeeze those globes while he was submerged deep inside of her. Damn, this was going too fast, but there wasn't anything he could do, or wanted to do, to stop the feelings of indescribable desire that were building inside of him. He felt as if he was sixteen again and this was his first time, only, this time, there was no wondering. He knew exactly what to do. He broke the kiss again and stood her up on her feet.

A shaken Shelly looked up at him. "You have Got to stop doing that."

She was adorable, standing there pouting up at him. He pushed the dress off her shoulders and watched as it fell and gathered at her waist. She wiggled to get the dress over her hips then stepped out of it. Taking a seat on the coffee table, in her bra and panties, she crossed her legs and looked up at him. "Your turn."

She watched as he pulled his shirt from his pants and released the two top buttons. Royce pulled the shirt with the tie still in the collar and his tee shirt over his head. Her breath hitched. She wasn't sure what she expected. There was no ripple of a six pack. There was smooth brown skin with a flat firm stomach, a wide chest and shoulders you could just snuggle in and sleep for days. He unbuckled his belt, unzipped his pants and allowed them to drop. Her mouth went dry at the sight of him bulging through the boxer briefs. She licked her lips nervously with a frown. "Hmm, um," she began, never taking her eyes from his bulge. "It's been a minute for me. I mean, you know, since I've..." she cleared her throat, "Had sex."

He reached out, took her hand and pulled her body flush with his. "We're not having sex." He removed her bra and gazed down at her. "I'm going to make love to your body." With that, he picked her up and laid her on the sofa, then took her breasts in his hands and held them. Enjoying the way they filled his hands. He kissed one, then the other as she squirmed beneath him. "This one," he said just before he covered it with his mouth, sucking, twirling his tongue around and over the nipple until it hardened to his satisfaction. He turned to the other. "Now, it's your turn."

Shelly laughed. She didn't remember sex being fun with her husband. The thought fell away as sensations ricocheted through her. It was true one breast was more sensitive than the other and she marveled at the feel of her nipples growing hard and taut at his touch. Her body came to life as her legs wrapped around his, rubbing up and down almost to the same rhythm of his mouth on her breast. His bulge, which was pressing right on her nub, caused her to move against him, anticipating his thickness inside of her. He must have sensed her restlessness, for his mouth moved from her breasts to kiss her navel. She felt him lift her behind to slide her lace panties down. As he pulled them over her thighs and down her legs, he stood, removed his briefs and covered himself with a condom he retrieved from his wallet, which he flung over his shoulder. She watched as he moved between her legs. Royce stretched his body on top of hers. He entwined their fingers and looked into her eyes.

"I want to see you when I enter you this first time."

"You're confident there will be a second?"

He revealed a sexy grin and slowly entered her. They held each other's eyes until she had to close hers from the sheer pleasure of his thickness. He pulled out and waited for her to open her eyes. Slowly he entered her again, this time going deeper. He stopped. "Oh, yeah...we are definitely doing this again." He kissed her and continued to move in her with slow deliberate strokes. His body matched his tongue strokes with every demanding thrust, hitting every corner of her. The slow strokes began to increase, when her lips kissed the side of his neck, his concentration centered on pulling her to the edge, then he would pull out, just to push back in with an intensity that made her scream out in pleasure, holding him tighter, so he could go deeper still.

She did not want this feeling to stop. His body now moved feverishly, in her and she could feel the control of her body and mind leaving her and she did not care. All that mattered was the glorious feeling that was building. A few moments later, a cascade of lights filled her eyes. Shelly's body hitched up higher to meet his as the explosion burst through.

He didn't stop, in fact he slowed, returning to smooth, unhurried strokes, pulling her back to the brink, then slowing up again until she screamed out his name. Royce pushed up on his hands, arched his body and vigorously thrust inside her time and time again until he growled out her name.

Blood pumping wildly through their bodies, he pulled her on top of him and wrapped her in his arms.

Shelly lay there on his strong chest, hearing his body still reacting to their lovemaking. He gently rubbed her back from the base of her spine up to her neck.

Royce lay there with one hand behind his head and the other stroking her. He could not break the contact. Not yet. The way her body pulsated around him, making him feel as warm and safe as a baby in a mother's womb. He lay there smiling, relishing the moment as she stroked his chest.

"Damn," she said. They both began to laugh. "I mean really, damn." Shelly laughed.

"My sentiments exactly, Ms. Knight," Royce praised. "You can lay me out anytime."

"Is that what I have to do to get a repeat?"

His cell phone rang. He closed his eyes and sighed. He was not ready for this moment to end. However, he knew if his phone was ringing there was a situation. Shelly started to sit up, but he held her down. "Not just yet." She laid back down as he reached to the floor for his pants.

"Yes," he said as he answered the call. She felt his body tense as he listened. His hand continued to stroke her back as if it was not a part of the rest of him. The strokes were even and tender, while the rest of him was tense. "Absolute." He listened more. "Have Lieutenant General McGary meet me in the situation room at eleven hundred hours with an exit strategy." He disconnected the call and dropped the phone on top of his pants. He pulled her up to straddle him. She folded her arms across his chest, placed her chin on them. Shelly looked up at him with lustful eyes.

"This is not going to sound good. I have to go."

"No, it doesn't sound good. Will you at least leave my brains, which you screwed out, at the front door so

I can think clearly the next time I open it for you and your security detail."

He laughed so hard, his body shook hers. Royce pulled her up by her arms and kissed her lips. "I'm keeping you."

She kissed his chest. "Yeah, well for now, I'm taking one part of you." She sat up and eased her body down on his thick, throbbing shaft. He closed his eyes and sighed at the feel of being embedded inside of her warmth. She pressed against his chest, lifted her body and eased back down on him. "Do you think you can handle one more round before you go?"

He opened one eye at her teasing smile, grabbed her hips and proceeded to fill her with every ounce of energy he had left.

Chapter Eleven

Joshua looked around wondering why Akande was in a cell, chained to a bed. Under any other circumstance, this would fulfill a fantasy of his. He could have his way, do all the things he could to make this woman feel like a woman should feel—wanted. However, seeing her this way, knowing someone else did this to her, pissed him the hell off. "If this is the way your family welcomes a relative home, I would hate to meet your enemies."

Akande almost, almost smiled at the sight of him. She thought he was long gone. She promised herself, no matter what, she was not going to use the band until she was far away from her aunt's hold. She jumped up to go to the cell door, but the chain prevented her and she fell. "You have to get out of here."

Taking a step back, he observed the cell, the bars, and the lock. "Trying to get rid of me so soon? I just got here." He smiled, displaying those deep dimples. "I'm looking for a way to show you exactly how much this scene is turning me on."

Akande stood, worried he would be found. "Please leave. She will kill you if you come in here."

"Many women have tried, but you hold that thought, sweetheart." Joshua walked off to the right following the outline of the cell. "Aw, this one will work," he mumbled as he pulled his lock pick from his pocket, inserted it into the lock, made a few twists, and pushed the door open. Standing in the doorway, he scanned the area for any security features, but was certain there weren't any. He walked over to her and frowned. "What happened to your clothes?" She was now dressed in a pair of dull brown pants with a tie at the waist and a yucky yellow shirt. You look like Mr. Potato Head with mustard on top. Dry, dull mustard at that."

"Who?"

"Mr. Potato Head. My brother Mathew had one. Funniest looking thing I've ever seen."

"You are comparing me to a potato?"

"It was a toy."

"A toy made out of potatoes?"

"You know, you took the funny out of this about two questions ago."

She shook off his comments. "I don't have time for this, you must leave, now. I will find you later." He ignored her protests and walked over to examine the chain around her ankle. She looked over her shoulder in the direction of the guardroom. "Go away, you arrogant man!" she quietly cried out as she pounded on his back.

At first he ignored her. The strikes on his back did not bother him. However, the laser he was about to use could burn her if she didn't stop moving. He reached behind him and yanked her down to the bed. "Sit still," he demanded, then turned back to what he was doing. The laser burned through the metal and she was free. "Where are you shoes?"

"I have none."

"Where are the shoes you wore here?"

"They were taken."

"What kind of place is this you call home?" he stood and shook his head. Joshua started walking towards the cell opening. "Did they at least feed you?" He stopped when he realized she was not behind him. "Are you coming?"

"No. She will kill you if they catch you. Don't you understand?"

"Would I be safer if you show me the way out?"

"How did you get in here?"

He smiled mischievously. "I followed you."

The statement made her pause. Did he hear her conversation with the Queen? "You followed me to see the Queen?"

"No." He pulled out his handheld device and smirked. "I tracked you. As nice as this place is," he looked around, "The ambiance of it all, I can't stand here arguing with you all day. I have to go home."

Akande hesitated. The last thing she wanted was for him to lose his life at her aunt's hands. She had to get him out of there. "Okay, I will go with you. Will you take me to your country?"

Disappointment settled in him. A part of him had hoped the request would not come. *Here we are*, he thought as he contemplated his reply. "If that's what you want."

"Yes, it is. Will you promise to go about your business once we reach your country?"

He thought about that one. Since she is his business, he had no problem agreeing. He didn't like making promises he couldn't keep. "Yes, I can promise you that too. Now, can we leave?"

"Yes. This way."

She ran past him and all he could do was shake his head. "We've got to do something about that outfit."

Akande slowed as they reached the guardroom, but Joshua kept walking. "Wait." She pulled on his arm.

"Wait for what?"

"Shush."

"Don't be shushing me woman. Come on."

When he walked by the door and nothing happened, Akande peeked in. The guards seemed to be asleep. "What happened to them?"

"They received a taste of some really good drugs." He grinned as she stared at him. "Let's go."

She was beginning to realize, this was not an ordinary man. The mansion she and Princess Zsa Zsa were in wasn't an easy place to get into, yet he got in and took them out somehow. He had found his way into the palace and again he came to her rescue. He was like a warrior of olden times. Whenever a princess was in distress, he would ride in on his horse and save the day. Most of the time the princess would fall in love with the warrior and if she weren't careful, this man would become *her* warrior. That she could not afford.

"Wait here," he said as he pushed her into a corner near the guard station.

"Where are you going?" She looked down the hallway to see if anyone was coming. When she turned back, he was gone. Looking around, she could only wonder where he had disappeared. "How does he do that?" she shook the thought away.

The man was exasperating, arrogant, too darn good looking for his own good or hers. There were too many things she had to figure out now. Leaving with him meant she had no financing. What would she do once she reached America? She would have to find a way to contact Sermyera once she arrived. How would she get rid of him? This is where her problem began.

She didn't want to get rid of him. Her heart skipped a beat when she saw him outside her cell. Akande was happy to see him. Closing her eyes, thinking of his gentle kiss, the way her body felt when he touched her. All these things about him clouded her judgment. This she could not afford. She couldn't afford anything when it came to this man. She opened her eyes. He was standing in front of her.

"You were thinking about me, weren't you?"

Akande's beautiful smile appeared. "You are exasperating."

"You have no idea," he seductively replied, bending down. "Put these on."

She braced herself against his shoulder. "Where did you find them?"

He stood. "On that note, we really need to go. I had to take someone out to get your shoes." They left through the guard door.

Once they were outside the palace grounds, she turned and looked back wondering if she would ever see her home again.

Joshua also looked up at the palace. The escape was too easy. No, they did not have the security of other places he had entered, but they were still the royal family. His eyes roamed from window to window, until he saw what he expected. From the balcony of one room, a woman, he was certain was Queen Sermyera, watched from the window. She wanted Akande to escape.

Joshua waited until they were on the rural road they had taken hours earlier, to begin his questioning. "You want to give me some idea what's going on here?"

Akande was hurting, hungry and desperately wanted a bath. She was certain there was dry blood on her back from the lashes she had received. Thankful she'd only received five of the twenty Sermyera had ordered, for the result would have been much worse. Her thoughts were on how she would accomplish her mission when her savior asked his question. He deserved an answer, if for no other reason, than he had saved her twice even though she did not ask him to.

"I will tell you what I can without endangering your life once we are in a safe location."

"We are in a safe location woman. You need to recognize I have skills..."

Shots rang out before he finished the statement. They dropped to the ground. "What the...," he heard vehicles coming towards them. He grabbed her hand. "Stay low," he said and ran into the woods to shield them from the attackers.

"Someone is shooting at us!" Akande screamed.

"That would be correct." They pushed tree limbs out of the way as they ran deeper into the woods. Yet, they could still hear the vehicles. They stopped behind a tree trunk as Joshua took out a device. He assessed their location. They were still a good twenty miles from the Emure border. "We can't out run a vehicle or bullets." He had just pulled Akande down to the monitor when another shot rang out, hitting the tree trunk right above her. He grabbed her again and ran further into the densely wooded area. Stopping behind another large tree, he said as he looked around. "Okay, I want you to stay here."

Fear clung in Akande's tone. "Where are you going?"

Joshua took off his suit jacket, then pulled out a thin tube. "Take this. Stay behind this tree. Keep your eyes in that direction. He pointed to the area where the shots were fired from. "If anyone comes within fifty feet of this tree, put this end to your lips, point it at them then blow hard. Understand."

"They are shooting guns at us and you give me a straw?"

He almost laughed. "It's a very powerful straw." The look on her face was priceless. "You're going to be fine. Remember, I'm your knight in shining armor. I will not let anything happen to you."

"Where's your armor?"

"God is my armor." he proclaimed with a smile. "I'll be right back."

Joshua had to draw the attacker away from her. He picked up a rock and threw it in the direction where he wanted to draw fire. It worked. They opened fire, giving him a clear indication of where they were positioned. It sounded like three guns. He circled around to where the shots came from. The first man was perched behind a tree. Years ago, his trainer had forced him to take ballet classes. At the time, he wanted to kill the man. After several missions, and at times like this, he could kiss the man. He had learned to move around soundlessly. He walked up behind the man, grabbed him around the shoulder with one arm and snapped his neck with the other. His lightning fast reflexes allowed him to catch the man's weapon before it hit the ground. "Sleep tight," he said as he eased the man's body to the ground.

Using the scope from the man's weapon, he counted two other shooters. Another tidbit his trainer had taught him. If you really want to kill someone, don't waste bullets shooting the body, go straight for a headshot. That's what he did. One single headshot and another attacker dropped to the ground. "Two down, one to go."

The third man was a little crafty. After hearing man number two go down, he pulled back. Joshua wasn't able to find him right away. It took a minute, but he now had him in his sights. The man shot at Joshua. The bullet lodged into a tree next to him. "You have to aim better than that." Joshua said from behind the man. "Too late," he said as he pulled the trigger leaving two shots in the man's head. He searched the man's pockets and found the keys to the vehicle.

"Hello honey, I'm home." Akande turned on him ready to fire when he grabbed her arm. "Whoa, now is that any way to greet your knight?"

She jumped up and threw her arms around his neck, almost knocking him to the ground. "Joshua."

"It's okay." He held her a little longer then he should hold the enemy. Pulling away, he smiled. "Now that's how you are supposed to greet a man."

"Are you ever serious? You could have died out there."

"It's the nature of the beast." He picked up his jacket. "Let's go. And on the way, you want to explain to me why your aunt is trying to kill us?"

Akande stopped. "I don't think it was my aunt. She would have no reason to."

"Like she had no reason to have you locked in a cell." He raised an eyebrow.

Questions about her home life, she was not ready to answer. She began walking again. "That is different."

They walked to the clearing and jumped into the jeep. "Who else would be trying to kill us?" Joshua asked as he pulled off.

Akande looked off in the direction from which the men had been shooting. "I do not know."

They drove a few miles in silence. Joshua's mind was working overtime. Akande may be right. Her aunt watched as they left the grounds, yet did not sound an alarm. Why would she now have men shooting at them? It didn't add up. Another mile in and the answer appeared in front of him.

Vehicles, at least three, filled with men with guns were traveling at a high speed towards them. At first he thought they were LaVere's men crossing the border to assist them. When several raised their weapons, he knew better.

"Get down!" he yelled. He took a sharp turn taking them into another wooded area. They had to get off the open road. "When I stop, get out and haul ass to the North. You understand?"

Akande nodded. "I don't understand any of this, but okay."

He pulled as close to the trees as he could and stopped. "Run."

Akande opened the door and ran into the woods. Joshua turned the vehicle in the direction from which they had come. He propped the gun he had taken from the other men against the gas pedal and the seat, then released the hand brake. The jeep roared towards the oncoming vehicles. He ran into the woods.

"Akande! Akande!"

"Over here."

He found her, grabbed her hand and they took off running again. They stopped momentarily to gauge their location. According to his device, there was a clearing behind the trees on two sides. Gunfire came at them again. "That was too close," he said as they continued to run until they reached another area with trees surrounding them. Joshua stopped, pulled out a button from his jacket, pushed the center and threw it in the direction of the shots. He pulled her under him and ducked.

The explosion cascaded through the trees. He grabbed her hand and ran towards the opening he saw on the device. They burst through the line of trees only to suddenly stop. Joshua had to pull Akande back to keep her momentum from taking her over a cliff.

"Whoa!" she screamed. There was at least a twenty foot drop into the river. They started to run back in the direction from which they came when shots rang out again. Following the line of trees, they ran to the North. Shots rang out from that direction. They were being surrounded.

"Oh hell," Joshua yelled as he pulled Akande and ran full speed over the cliff.

Joshua had no idea which was more deafening, shots ringing out over his head, Akande's scream as they jumped in the river or the impact of the splash when they hit the water.

Chapter Twelve

They were immediately submerged, losing contact with each other. Joshua swam back up to the top and looked around for Akande. She didn't come up. "Aw, hell... Akande," he called out, looking around to see if she surfaced anywhere. He went back under at the point of impact. *Thank God for clear water*, he thought, spotting her a few feet away. She was struggling to stay afloat. He swam over, grabbed her around the waist and pulled her up with him. She sputtered; water was coming from her mouth.

He had to get out of the open water so the men could not see them. He looked around and saw an opening behind a waterfall and quickly swam in that direction. He pushed her body up onto the ledge. He pulled himself up.

Akande lay there coughing up water, trying to catch her breath.

"Why didn't you tell me you didn't know how to swim?" Joshua was bent over, hands on his knees.

It took her a moment before she had the strength to answer him. "You didn't ask before throwing me into the river." His laugh was rich, deep and contagious. Akande came to her knees and could not help but laugh with him.

"I didn't throw you into the river," he continued to laugh as he stood, walked over and helped her up. He pushed her hair from her face. She looked a mess, but she was a beautiful water creature. The water on their bodies did nothing to contain the flame that ignited between them. Neither moved as they stared, smiling into each other's eyes. The pull was strong, almost too strong for him to resist. *She is the enemy.* His mind reminded him. He stepped back, still holding her gaze.

Checking his pockets, he pulled out his handheld. "Let's check this place out."

Akande stood, frozen in place. The heat that was there a moment ago was now gone. The chill from her drenched clothes replaced it.

Joshua turned away and took a deep breath to regain his composure. This woman...no enemy, was disturbing his concentration. No woman had ever deterred him from work. He was determined not to allow this one to do it now.

"It has never been submerged in water." He held it up now certain he was back in control. When the green light blinked he smiled. "Okay." He sent a signal to Ned, closed his eyes and said a silent prayer. "All right." He stood to assess the area. "What do we have around here?" Looking around, he walked into the opening. It was a large area, about the size of a ten by ten room, with a flat surface. "With a little cleaning we should be able to hold here until help comes."

"Will help come?" she asked.

He turned to see her hugging her body. The chill from the wet clothes was affecting her. That wasn't all it was doing. The outline of her nipples were pressing against the wet shirt. He looked to the sky and thought, *Lord, why? Why did you send me this temptress?*

"Grrrrr," he growled. He knew he had to get her out of those wet clothes. And as sure as he knew his name was Joshua Theodore Lassiter, if that woman took her clothes off they were going to end up bumping booties. There was nothing he could see to keep it from happening. *She is the enemy*, his mind screamed. "Oh, shut the hell up."

"What did you say?"

"You need to get out of those wet clothes."

"I have nothing to put on. I cannot."

"Yes, you can." He exhaled. "Give me a minute."

He pulled out his handheld and sent a short message to Ned. *Attacked. Emure? Extraction.* He knew from that Ned would pinpoint his location using the device's GPS system. Looking at her checking out the small cave they were in, he prayed someone would get there soon. "Do you know the story of Adam and Eve?"

She narrowed her eyes.

He walked to the edge of the ledge they were on and pulled up several large fern leaves. "Adam ate the apple, they saw each other's nakedness, then covered themselves with fig leaves." He took the leaves and placed them next to each other on the ledge. He took another leaf, rolled it up like a funnel then collected water. "Let's see if you are still working." He pulled his laser from his jacket pocket and flipped it on. He looked at her and smiled. "It's working." He held it above the leaf pointing the top towards the water.

"What are you doing?" Akande asked as she walked over to him.

"Don't stand too close," he cautioned. "I'm heating the water to sterilize the leaves. We are going to use the leaves to cover ourselves, then hang our clothes above the ledge to dry."

"You are just an Indiana Jones, aren't you?" she asked, amazed.

"More like MacGyver."

"MacGyver? Who is he?"

"You know Indiana Jones, but you don't know MacGyver? Ouch," he yelped from the heat of the water. He turned off the laser.

Akande laughed. "Smarty pants."

The sound of her laughter was pleasant. "I got your smarty pants all right." Joshua smiled. He held one of the large leaves up, then slowly poured the heated water over the front, then did the same process for the back. He did the process several times until he had four large leaves for her and two for him. Using his knife and string from his jacket, he punched a hole in the stem of a leaf and then ran the string through to attach the leaves.

"Hold these." He handed her his handy work and pulled his shirt off.

Akande quickly turned her head, but not fast enough to avoid seeing the ripples upon his stomach. "What are you doing?"

"Taking these wet clothes off," he replied enjoying her face blushing from the thought.

"Wait." Akande commanded. "You can't do that here."

He looked around. "You see somewhere else I could do this?"

"I don't know," she said and turned her back. "Go over there in the corner." As the words left her mouth, she knew it was too late. She heard the pants unzip and fall to the ground.

"If you don't want your world to be shattered, you may want to hand me one of those." When she did not move, he reached out and took the leaf he made for himself and wrapped it around his hips on both sides.

"You can turn around now," he said as he picked up his shirt and pants. He climbed two boulders, above the waterfall, placed his clothes there and placed a rock on top to keep them from blowing away. He came back down to find her staring at him with her mouth open. He walked over, put a finger under her chin and closed her mouth. "I understand."

Akande had never seen anything so magnificent as this man's body. Joshua's shoulders were wide, his chest was smooth; no hair. His stomach was like a washboard and his thighs... Good Lord, the muscles were bulging with definition. When he climbed the boulder, her mouth dropped from the pure power that radiated from his back and thighs. If she were a weak type of woman, she would have fainted dead on the spot from the pure masculinity of him.

She still hadn't moved. He took the leaves from her. "Do you want me to help you take off those wet clothes?"

There was no way she could take her clothes off in front of this man after seeing his body. She wrapped the wet material around her and violently shook her head no as she continued to look him up and down.

"We are really going to have issues if you keep looking at me like that." He arched an eyebrow then licked his lips. "I'm going to turn my back. You undress, then wrap the leaves, tying them on both sides. Then tie this one around the top. You will be covered more than a woman on the beach wearing a two piece bikini. If the leaves covered me, as you can see they do, they will certainly cover all of you. Now, get out of those wet clothes." He turned his back and waited. Inwardly he was smiling at her shyness. Finally, he heard her removing her clothes. He held the leaves out so she could reach them. She took the bottom and a minute later she took the top. A few minutes passed. Nothing. "Can I turn around now?"

"I can't tie the string."

"Hold it up to your chest. I'll turn around to help. Okay?"

"Okay," her voice was unsure.

He turned around and froze. He understood why Adam ate the damn apple. If Eve had looked like this, he would have eaten it too. Her head was down and he was glad. For if she caught a glimpse of his reaction to her, he was sure she would jump off the damn ledge. Seeing women's bodies was a daily, sometimes, twice daily occurrence for him. Why this little woman, with the toned legs, and thick thighs caused him to have an immediate salute he did not know. Her skin seemed to glisten, even in the semi-darkness of the cave. Her hair was still a mess, yet it did not take way from how sexy she looked. If he could just get his heart to stop pumping so fast, he could move from the spot to which he seemed rooted. His hand held beeped with a message. He pulled it from his fig wrap and read it. *Twenty-four.* He closed his eyes. If he did not know better, he would swear God was conspiring against him. It was going to be twenty-four hours before someone would reach them. How in the hell was he going to keep his hands off her?

He laughed to ease the tension. "We should have done a one piece for you. The leaves are almost longer than your legs." He willed his legs to move. "I'll tie it for you," he tried to sound as nonchalant as he could. "If I had a camera, I could make money off this....." His voice trailed off as he walked behind her.

He had seen many things in his life, and recognized them for what they were, fresh whip marks. Five thick, red lines resided brightly across her back. He took the strings with shaking hands and tied them. While doing so, he saw several old marks, which meant this was not the first time.

When he spoke, his voice was dangerously low. "Who did this to you?" He touched one with his finger.

Akande flinched from the touch and turned quickly to face him. "It's nothing."

"It's nothing," he repeated as he held her eyes.

Anger was shining back at her. Pure unadulterated anger was what she saw in his eyes. "I didn't do anything," she said thinking he was angry with her for some reason. "I swear I didn't."

"Why were you beaten?"

Shrugging her shoulders, Akande said, "It's just my aunt's way of keeping us in line. That's all."

She was talking as if this were a natural occurrence. He turned away from her, to curtail his anger. He picked up her clothes, climbed the boulder then placed them next to his.

Akande walked away. Getting distance between them was what she needed. She knew her body was not attractive. She was short, top heavy and had a big butt. Nothing a man like him would be interested in seeing. That thought should please her. The last thing she needed was to get attached to this man. They had to part ways when they reached America anyway. So why did him turning away, sting so bad? She folded her feet under her and took a seat in the corner. Her chin, she held high; her body was what it was. She was proud of it, regardless of what he thought.

Joshua stayed at the boulder for a minute. He wanted to scream. How could you do something like that to another human being, much less someone you are supposed to care for? He stepped down and found her sitting proudly in a corner. Chin high, hands folded in her lap.

"It shouldn't take long for the clothes to dry." He looked at the devices he pulled from his jacket. He picked up a long device and made it expand. It looked like a spear. "We are going to be here for a minute. I'm going to catch dinner. Me...Tarzan; you... Jane." he joked. She didn't laugh. *Probably never heard of Tarzan.* The sight of her back was a little more than he could take. He had to walk away, get his anger under control. Later, he would try to question her. He picked up the metal object he gave her before. "Keep this with you. I'll be back shortly."

Akande watched as he walked away. Tears stung her eyes. Why, she did not know. All she knew was his reaction hurt her more than her aunt ever could.

Joshua sat with his back against the boulder at the base of the waterfall. He had surveyed the area. So far there was no sign that anyone had been in the area recently. That was good, he thought. They could hole up here until morning. Next to him, he had several fish he had caught, but he wasn't calm enough to find out why this was done to her.

For a moment, he thought he had this whole thing figured out. The King and Queen of Asmere wanted sanctions lifted and a Senator in the United States killed. They were using Akande to draw the man out. He didn't know who, why or how she was to do this. The question he had now was why would she do this for people who clearly treated her poorly. Making matters worse, someone was trying to kill her. The location of every shot played over in his mind. They weren't trying to kill him. They were aiming at Akande. Again, who and why questions assailed him. He needed answers. Picking up the fish, he climbed back to the cave.

When he returned, she had cleaned the cave out and had started a fire in the corner, so it could not be seen from outside the cave. A few of the fern leaves were placed around the fire, which had small rocks around it, keeping it contained. The scene would have been a little romantic, if men weren't trying to kill them and she didn't have the damn welts on her back. He shook the thought from his mind.

"We are going to have to improvise on the cooking utensils, my lady." He almost got a smile from that one.

"If you will give me your knife, I will clean the fish and have them ready shortly." The statement was made with no emotion, just a matter-of-fact tone.

True to her word, she took the knife and fish, walked to the edge of the ledge and began cutting the heads off. Less than ten minutes later, she had taken his spear, shoved four fish on it, then placed it on the two 'Y' shaped sticks on both sides of the fire.

Twenty minutes later, they sat around the fire. The sun had set making the cave more sensual than it already was. They had cooked and were now eating in silence. It was time for some answers.

"Are you in pain?" Akande looked up at him. "Your back, does it still hurt?"

"It dulls after awhile."

Her attitude about this irritated him. "It dulls." He shook his head as he leaned against the wall of the cave. "What could you have done to cause your aunt to do something of this nature to you?"

"You do not have to do anything to earn strikes from Queen Sermyera. You receive them because she is. It's that simple."

"Because she is? What in the hell is that supposed to mean?"

She huffed. "Leave this alone. It does not concern you."

She was right and he knew it. What happens to her is not his concern. The fact angered him, because he was concerned for her, but there was nothing he could do about that. However, her plot to kill a United States Senator was another thing all together. "Why do you have to go to America?"

Akande sat on the opposite wall, with her feet under her. She had long ago stopped eating her fish. "I wish to meet a man there."

This was rich, Joshua thought. "There are many men in America. Can you narrow it down?"

"Not at this time."

Her evasive answers were beginning to irk him. "You want to go to America?"

"I have said so, yes."

"Then you better make the time."

She stood, and began picking up the bones left over from the fish. When she did this, her thighs flashed before him. He stifled down a moan. Joshua closed his eyes, exhaled then waited for her to finish her busy work.

When she sat back down, he poked at the fire. "The man in America?" he asked again.

"It is dark. Is it not time for us to rest?"

While she was cooking the fish, Joshua had gathered more leaves to make two pallets for them to sleep on and had placed them near the fire. This is where she was now sitting.

"I'm a patient man. Truly I am. I have six sisters and five brothers. Waiting for the bathroom took patience. I swear you are wearing my patience thin." He moved to sit next to her. "You asked me to take you to my country. What are you going to do when you get there?"

"I'm going to Washington and you are going home."

"Un huh. What are you going to do once you get there? You have no money. You don't know anyone there. So how will you live?"

"I will find my father," she replied defiantly.

"Your father?"

"Yes, I told you. My father is an American. I will go to this Washington place and find my father."

"Washington is a big place. How do you plan to find him?"

"My father is an important man. I will find him."

"What's your father's name?"

She hesitated. "I do not wish to say."

That pissed him off. Yet he had another piece to the puzzle. Her father must be a Senator. It's not far-fetched. Many legislators visit countries, have a fling and leave offspring behind. Could this be what occurred twenty years ago? No, according to the records he read on her, she would have been four years old twenty years ago. Besides, the U.S. would not have put sanctions in place because of a Senator having an illegitimate child. Hell, if that were the case, sanctions would be in place against every country in the world. There was something else going on here. The sealed file in the folder on Asmere probably had the answer.

"What position does your father hold?"

"I do not wish to discuss this."

"You're going to discuss this and more. See, I don't believe you are going to find your father. No. I think you are going there to meet a man. Your aunt is desperate for money. Did she sell you to this American because she caught you with her husband or something?"

She raised her hand and hit him. "I am no man's whore!" The anger flared quickly at his words. "You have no right to say such things. You do not know me." She slid away from him, he was sitting too close.

Joshua rubbed his cheek where she'd slapped him. Well, he knew how to get a response out of her. "You are right. I don't know you, but I know a lie when I hear it." He bent over to her. "And sweetheart, you are lying." His nostrils flared and he didn't have time to play this game with her any longer. Joshua needed answers. "I don't know what your reasons are. What I do know is those marks on your back are from your aunt. A person who cares for you would never do that. Yet, she is sending you to America for her own purpose. What exactly are you supposed to do to get this Senator? You claim this man is your father and can lift sanctions from your country? Are you supposed to seduce him? Hell, you are beautiful."

"I am no man's whore." She raised her hand to slap him again.

He grabbed her wrist to stop her and he could feel that damn heat again. Every time he touched her the heat consumed him. *What in the hell is wrong with me.* The anger in her eyes turned quickly to something different, something primitive as he stared into them. The soft light from the fire, made her skin glow. The way her lips parted at his touch. All of it was drawing him to her.

With all he knew, he still wanted her in the worst kind of way. *She is the enemy.* His body wanted his mind to shut the hell up. It did not care that the woman was an enemy of the United States, or that she would probably try to kill him once her mission was complete.

Controlling his sexual urges was something he never worked at doing. His job had taught him to live life to its fullest, never denying himself of anything. This woman, an angelic beauty, consumed him with desire so strong it caused his body to ache. That he would not allow. He pulled her forward, and willed his mind to close down, as his lips descended on hers.

Full soft lips touched his in the most innocent way. His tongue glided across her bottom lip. "Hmmm," he groaned, enjoying the soft feel of them as they parted. His tongue eased into the small opening and moaned at the taste of her. He cupped her head, tilting it back to give him deeper access to the sweetness of her mouth. Touching every inch of her mouth, Joshua savored Akande. The feel of her inner cheeks, the roof, oh and that inexperienced tongue of hers. The deeper he dove, the more he wanted. The heat intensified, as did his arousal. He pulled her onto his lap and immediately felt the heat of her naked behind on his thighs. His hands roamed up the softness of her thighs as he relished the intoxicating kiss. Her body jerked the moment his thumb rubbed against her untouched nub. She moaned. Her uninhibited reaction made him as hard as steel. His finger moved to her opening then slipped inside causing her juice to flow onto his hand. She arched her body and his finger went deeper. Her breath hitched at the invasion. He placed another inside her then softly tickled her nub. Her body squirmed with the motion of his fingers. As they increased in rhythm, so did her body. She was tight, and wet, as she bucked wildly against his slick fingers. He almost lost control. He slid the kiss from her lips to her neck, right below her earlobe, and sucked as she screamed out her first orgasm.

He abruptly stopped and looked down at her. That was the worst thing he could have done. Her eyes were filled with passion, her lips, swollen from his kisses. Akande's nipples were hard, pointing at him, knowing he was the culprit who made them that way,

commanding his mouth to cover them. "Oh hell."
Joshua pulled the leaf from her breast, taking one into
his mouth in the same motion. He cupped, then
suckled the brown tip until it was as hard as he was,
then switched to the next giving it the same pleasure.
It was as if he was in a candy store, tasting one sweet
treat after the next. The buds were so damn tasty; he
could suck on them for an eternity, rolling them over
his tongue. Her moans and body squirming required
him to pay attention to all of her. His tongue traveled
down the valley between her breasts, down to her
navel loving the scent of her heat calling out to him.
He wasn't one to linger when it came to women. He
never left them wanting, but he never intentionally
slowed his pace. With her, he wanted to take his time,
savoring the feel of her as his hand slowly followed the
trail of his tongue. Lingering at her navel, with his
long fingers spreading around her small waist, her
scent swelled his manhood. He moved her from his
lap, easing her onto the leaf pallet.

Joshua sat back on his haunches, pulled the leaf
away and gazed down her body. Graceful, even in her
naked state he felt honored to be gazing upon her.
"You are beautiful," he said as he lowered his mouth
into her warmth then kissed her there. Her body
bucked from the touch of his lips. Reaching under her,
he placed her legs over his shoulders. He smiled, then
lifted her to his mouth and began sucking as if he was
trying to get all the meat from between a wishbone.
My God, she is so sweet. Holding her in his hands, his
tongue glided slowly between her inner lips. The
nectar of her was so addicting, he stayed, partaking
with his lips sucking and his tongue dipping as if he
was at a dinner table. Her body convulsed, sending
more juice to quench some of his thirst. It wasn't
enough. He was hard as steel.

He needed to see her. Lowering her back to the ground, he swiped his hand down his face and sat back on his haunches. He marveled at her skin, glowing from the passion as her body jerked from his touch. Nothing filled him with more pride than to see her reach another orgasm. Now he had to be inside her.

Pleasure so powerful, she could not, did not want to move. Her body was pulsating all over from his kisses, his touch, his tongue. She felt the moment; his body was not touching hers. Her eyes slowly opened to see him sitting back looking down at her. He was a magnificent man. Everything about him screamed, secure, masculine, all male and dangerous. She wished she saw a little love in him, for she knew at that moment, with all the fighting, anger and distrust, there was one simple fact. She could fall in love with the man known as Joshua Lassiter. Tears came to her eyes as the realization began to settle in. She was falling for a man she was using and would have to leave. Maybe it was because he was the only person to have shown her kindness, she didn't know. Whatever it was, she didn't want it to stop. All thoughts left her mind when she reached out and touched his chest which glistened from the glow of the fire. The heat of him caused her to pull her hand back. She watched as he tore his leaf away. She drew in a sharp breath at the fully uncovered sight of him.

There was a stark difference between thinking and seeing. His strength showed through his clothes, but never had she imagined a mesmerizing body like his. The muscles rippled in his thighs. This was not the body of a weight lifter, who at times looked unnatural and awkward. No, this man's entire body was smooth, with the natural ridges of an athlete who trained regularly. More enticing than all of that was his male member extended out from his body, long, thick, and ready. Her mouth was watering at the sight, causing her to unconsciously lick her lips. She watched as he lowered his body to hers. His eyes focused on her so intently; she could not look away. Then she felt him, his thickness, the heat of him, at her opening. God help her, she knew she shouldn't, but without caring, she spread her legs, wrapping them around his waist, willing him to come inside, to fill her with all his glory.

The moment he touched the junction of her thighs, he knew this was going to be like no other. He lowered his body, covering hers, and then rubbed her forehead with his thumb as he looked into her eyes. He saw desire, anticipation, questions and fear.

"No more fighting." He brushed his lips against hers, as he slowly began to enter her. The sensation was so sweet, he had to stop the gentle caress of his fingers. He dipped his tongue inside her mouth, as he pushed himself further into her. His tongue and body cherished every taste as he continued to slowly enter her. He could feel the moist heat of her muscles adjusting to him, pulling him in faster than he wanted to go. *Slow down,* his mind warned again, but her body wasn't allowing him to. It was all consuming, inflaming him, inviting him...to go deeper. He pulled out and entered her again, this time going a little deeper. His kiss, mirroring his body movements, froze, as did his body. He knew it was there, the blockage verifying her virginity.

Closing his eyes and placing his forehead on hers, he knew he was in too deep to stop. The innocent kiss, the uncertainty, the fear and the tightness and if that wasn't enough, his mind was warning him. With his heart beating to the same rapid tempo of his penis, he wrapped one arm around her body and held her as he pushed through. Willing his body to stop, his tongue dove deeper, as he devoured her mouth until he felt the tension in her body begin to dissipate and the whimper of pain turned to moans of pleasure.

His body took over at that point and did what it knew to do. With her nails digging into his back, he rose up above her, moving his body that was now fully embedded in her, in and out, savoring every inch of her slick muscles surrounding him. The sheer strength of him, evident with each stroke, pounding with a purpose, bringing her to the brink, then pulling back only to bring her there again, and again, until he felt her body explode around him, and then, only then did he allow, the profound torment of unabashed pleasure to rage out of him.

"Joshua!" Akande passionately screamed out.

He tried to close his eyes and heart to the emotions she was pulling out of him. He couldn't allow this woman, not this woman, to invade the one place he had always held back from any other. The battle raging within, to release all to her, was killing him inside. Doing what he always did when faced with enemy forces, he prayed, asking God to guide his actions. He released all, but did not call out her name, as every fiber in him wanted to do. He gathered her in his arms, holding her tightly, for he knew the significance of what had taken place. What he did not know, was if her innocence was a trap for him or her target in Washington. That was the reason he could not, would not surrender all to her as she had done with him.

The fire burned down, as he held her. His arm rubbed her back, but stopped when it connected with the first welt. He closed his eyes to the possible pain he may have caused her. "Are you all right?"

She nodded her head against his chest. "She will kill me now."

Joshua held her tight. He was so torn. Should he simply console her or encourage her to talk? Country, or this woman, who had slipped under his skin? The answer, as difficult as it was, came quickly. "Why will she kill you?"

"I have disgraced my family the same way my mother did."

"Tell me about your mother."

Akande spoke quietly as if she were reciting a verse of the bible at a wake. "My mother was the daughter of the head servant of King Tochi. A soldier from America was here on a peace keeping mission and became friends with our King. While at court working, my mother met the American and it was said that she fell in love with him. Against her father's wishes, she gave herself to this man. When she found she was with child, the man abandoned her leaving her to deal with the disgrace of her actions. While her father was forgiving, he never forgot. From what I was told, when I was three, this man returned to visit with King Tochi. At my grandfather's request, the King addressed the issue of my parentage with his friend. The American became outraged at the insult. That night the King's palace was attacked. The royal family was killed leaving Tarik as our new King. My grandfather was banished from his lands by King Tarik. He was so angry he killed my mother and was about to kill me when my aunt stepped in to stop him. Soon after, sanctions were placed on our country. Life as it once was, existed no more. Our lands which were once aplenty and rich with produce are now poor, all because of my mother's actions."

He could feel the tears on his chest and knew she believed the story as it was told to her. In Joshua's mind, it was filled with holes. "What do you hope to gain once you find your father?"

"My only wish is to have him remove the sanctions and restore Asmere to its original status in the region."

"And if you fail in doing this?"

"Then I will die."

"You are not the bearer of your mother's sins, if there was indeed a sin."

"Of course there was," she sat up and looked down on him. "My mother was not the wife of the American, yet she gave herself to him. That is a sin."

Joshua sat up on his elbow. He pushed her hair from her face. "Do you believe that what we just did was a sin?"

Confusion played across her face. "No." A small smile appeared as she gazed into his eyes. "This has been the only moment in my life where I did not think about my mother's disgrace. To be honest, I think I understand it better now. She could no more resist the American, than I could resist you."

Joshua kissed her gently on the lips. "And just as I cannot resist you." The kiss that followed was not gentle. It was greedy, devouring, downright sinful, just as he intended it to be.

He made love to her again and watched as she fell asleep in his arms. The burden of guilt that had been placed on her was criminal. The beatings she had taken, were accepted by her as her punishment for her mother's sins. This task to have the sanctions lifted and kill the Senator, whoever he might be, is a foolish mission. There had to be another reason her aunt wanted the Senator found. This woman in his arms wasn't the enemy, at least not yet. She is a victim. *It is his duty to protect innocent victims*. At this moment Akande is just that and he vowed he would do all he could to prevent her from killing this Senator and becoming an enemy of the United States.

***

"Dress quickly, we're about to draw fire." Monique dropped the clothes she found on a boulder outside the cave at Joshua's feet. They had been trying to communicate with him for the last hour. The delay caused them to be detected by locals. Now, there was chatter indicating they were going to have company soon. To find her superior wrapped in the arms of some woman, rather than handling business pissed her off. His reputation as a womanizer was well established and she did not have an issue with that. She really didn't, hell she liked a good lay once or twice a day herself. However, what they did for a living was dangerous. If she found them and was able to walk up on him this way, so could the enemy. According to him, their job was to protect the United States of America against all enemies, foreign and domestic. You had to be alive to do that. She could have easily taken his life.

Joshua opened his eyes to see Monique Day, his trainee, standing above him. She did not look happy, but she rarely did. "Lower your voice." He looked at the sleeping form of Akande in his arms and smiled. Sleeping with a woman was one thing. Waking up with her was another. He liked waking up with this one. He covered her with one of the fig leaves, before rising.

"Really," Monique Day looked at him as if he had lost his mind. "I spent eight weeks in Quantico, three months training with you. I finally get a few days of R&R only to be cut short with a message, extraction needed. I come to your aide to find you here, doing this. I ought to cut your dick off, that's what I should do."

Joshua covered his jewels with his hands as if protecting them. "Hey, watch your mouth. I'm standing here naked." He began dressing, pants first. He had seen first-hand how well Monique handled a knife.

"You would have been a dead naked man if I was your enemy."

"Shh." Joshua glanced down at Akande as he pulled Monique to the other side of the cave.

"Don't shush me. You've lost your mind. And what's with the damn leaves?"

"Long story, Spicy. What's the situation?"

"There's a chopper above hovering. Bogey's about ten miles out; should be on us any minute. If we want to get out with limited casualties, the time to leave is now. You may want to wake up Eve over there." She nodded toward the woman lying on the leaves.

"Akande," Joshua walked over, bent down and kissed her temple. "We have to go, sweetheart." He picked up her clothes and gave them to her. "Dress quickly."

"Sweetheart?" Monique raised an eyebrow.

Akande turned over to his warmth, then slowly opened her eyes. A smile touched her lips when she looked at him. "Hello."

"Hi." he smiled. "We have to go. Let me help you up."

She took his hand and started to rise, when she saw a woman in what looked like a cat suit, looking at her with angry eyes. She jumped behind Joshua.

"Oh, please," Monique turned her back. "We don't have time for this." Her handheld came alive with chatter. She turned back. "Time to go is now." Monique climbed from under the waterfall to see the chopper above. The ladder was still suspended in the air, waiting for them to climb aboard.

"Go," Joshua yelled as he helped Akande dress. "Are you okay?"

His concern for her was so touching, tears surfaced before she could stop them. "Yes, I'm fine." In truth her back was throbbing and her thighs were sore.

He took her hand. "Follow her up the ladder."

"Who is she?"

"A friend."

Akande did not know if she liked the way the woman looked at her or the word friend. She climbed out to see the ladder. She looked back at Joshua.

"You can always stay your ass here." Monique grinned down at the woman.

"Stand down rookie," Joshua commanded, anger clear in his voice.

Monique gave him a look that would have some men running. "Yes, sir." She turned, grabbed the end of the ladder and began the climb up to the chopper.

Joshua held Akande by the waist and helped her, holding the ladder steady as she climbed. He took one last look around the cave. This place would be etched in his memory. He then followed the women. The moment his foot hit the ladder, the pilot pulled away from the fall. Shots rang out as they flew through the air, Joshua still climbing the ladder. He looked to see where the attackers were located. They were at the Emure border. *Why were they taking gunfire from Emure?*

Chapter Thirteen

"The situation in Asmere is escalating. There are reports of gunfire near the East border. The operative in the area is under attack by unknown forces."

Royce had examined the information on his way to the Pentagon. "Unknown? It's not Asmere forces attacking him?"

"We can't confirm or deny," Lieutenant General McGary stated. "I warned you this situation would get out of control, Senator. This region is unstable. Any disturbances in this area could affect future plans."

The Lieutenant General had no idea how close to the truth he was. The future plans he was referring to had little consequence compared to the actual plans to secure the region. "I did not request your commentary, General. Only the facts as they pertain to this situation. Why do we believe it is not Asmere forces attacking the operative?"

Angered by the Senator's remarks, the Lieutenant General's reply was terse. "The operative's message says it all."

Royce noted the tone of the Lieutenant General's reply, but really did not give a damn. He out ranked him as a Senator and as an ex-military General. "Why would Emure open fire on an operative who just rescued their Princess?"

"That is the million dollar question, sir."

"You have twenty-four hours to find me the million dollar answer, Lieutenant General. In the meantime, I want a conference with King Aswan. Make it happen." Royce stood. "General." Royce nodded, indicating that McGary was to remain.

Lieutenant General McGary looked bothered by the request for him to remain. The other men in the room took the cue. Once they were alone. Royce turned to the General. "Attention, soldier." The Lieutenant General immediately adjusted his posture and stood at attention. Royce stood in front of the man, legs braced apart, arms folded across his chest as if he was ready to do battle. "Are you forgetting your rank?"

"No, sir."

"No, sir what?"

"No sir, General."

"When you are in my presence, your opinion is to be kept to yourself unless I ask for it. Is that understood, Lieutenant General?"

"Yes sir, General."

"The next time you use a dishonorable tone with me, I will bust your ass down so fast you will wish your mother had never screwed your father. You are dismissed, soldier."

Lieutenant General McGary saluted, crisply turned then walked out of the room. Royce sat back in his chair drained. Under normal circumstances, he would have let McGary's disrespect slide. Royce was very aware of who he was in this world, but had no need to shove it down other people's throats. To Royce, McGary was nothing more than an irritating fly who wanted to be more than he was before his men. Royce understood that maintaining the respect of the men who serve under you was important, that was the only reason he did not reprimand McGary in front of his men. He was sure working on less than two hours of sleep added to his not so accommodating mood today.

Thoughts of the night before with the insatiable Shelly Knight brought an immediate smile to his face. He laid his head back, closed his eyes and he could taste her on his lips. The thought caused a rise against his zipper. God, he wanted her again. He sat up, looked at his watch. He called his office.

"Yes Senator," Kathy answered.

"How are things at the office?"

"Hectic, but manageable," Kathy replied. "How are things at the Pentagon?"

"Manageable, but they're about to hit the hectic mark. Anything there I need to handle?"

"It depends on what you are planning on doing instead. If you are planning on having another date with Ms. Knight, I can manage here."

A broad smile touched Royce's face. "I plan to do just that, if she will have me."

Kathy laughed. "I am so tickled by your reaction to this woman. Go, I'll handle the office. If anything serious comes up, I know where to reach you."

"Thank you, Kathy."

"Hold on. Ms. Knight's line is ringing now."

"Stop reading my mind."

"Why? I'm so good at it." She switched calls. "Ms. Knight, Senator Davenport is calling. Please hold." She put Shelly on hold. "I had to make you sound important."

"Go home to your husband, woman."

"Have a good evening, Senator."

Royce heard a click on the phone. "Hello, Shelly."

Shelly stood in her kitchen, waiting for the water to boil for her tea. Royce had been on her mind all day. Her mind was tired, but her body was humming just from the man's voice. "Hello, Senator."

"What happened to Royce?"

"You will get that when I see you again."

"Will tonight be too soon?"

"That depends. Are you bringing your weapon with you?"

"What weapon?"

"That body of yours. I'm humming for more."

His laughter rang out. "I needed that, Shelly. You have no idea how much."

"Having a rough day?"

He rubbed the back of his neck. "A very hard and long one."

"Sounds like the description I gave you today." He laughed. "Have you been there since you left last night?"

He sobered. "I'm afraid so."

"Wow. Are things that serious? Anything you can talk about? I'm a good listener."

He hesitated. The issues he dealt with were not something you could take home to the wife to discuss. That was one aspect of his job his ex-wife did not understand. "It's classified information."

"Oh, no, you keep that to yourself. I can't have you telling me stuff that will have unsavory characters coming after me. You keep all of that to yourself. I'll use other means to relieve you of all the pent up stress from keeping secrets."

If Royce had been anywhere near her, he would have kissed her. That was the very reason he never shared anything classified with his ex-wife. It was to protect his family. His ex had taken it as him being closed off from her and the children. Because he wouldn't discuss things that were on his mind with her, she began to shut down on him. Eventually she found someone who would tell her all and had an affair. That ended his marriage and his political career. He refused to tell the public why his marriage was dissolving. Of course the media came up with their own spin on things and that was just that.

"It doesn't bother you that I can't and will never be able to discuss my work with you?"

"No," Shelly replied. "There are going to be times when I will not discuss my day with you. When you can and you need to, you will. I'll be here to listen."

He stood and smiled. "Ms. Knight, you just earned another notch on my belt."

"You don't plan to beat me with it, do you? I'm not into the bondage, beating thing. You know with the whips and things."

Royce laughed. "No," he continued to laugh. "I might try a few toys here and there, but not whips or chains."

"Toys? I've got some toys for you. They're called East and West and they are straining for you with all this grown and sexy talk."

It took him a minute. "East and West." He laughed. "God, I'm going to bottle you up and keep you. I swear I am."

"I like having you around, too. So when are you coming over?"

"I think I'll be coming around eight, but I will be at your front door around seven, armed and dangerous."

"I got that. That was cute. I think I might be rubbing off on you."

He picked up his briefcase and turned towards the door. "You smack it up and rub it down."

They both said, "Oh no," and laughed.

"I'll be waiting for you, solider."

"I like the sound of that, Ms. Knight.

***

Joshua arrived at the hotel in Washington late in the evening. They made no stops between leaving Asmere and arriving in the United States other than switching from the chopper to a plane.

He walked through and surveyed every room in the hotel suite before allowing Akande to enter. Monique had a change of clothes for Akande and Joshua grabbed his things from the chopper. They'd washed up and changed on the plane. Joshua needed a thorough cleaning and he was certain Akande would appreciate the same.

Akande was still standing by the door when he turned around. "You are safe here." He took her hand and brought her into the sitting area of the suite.

"Is this your place?"

"No." He pulled her down into his lap. "This is where we are going to stay until we work out this situation."

She sat up. "There is no situation, Joshua. You fulfilled your promise. You brought me to America. Now, I must find my father."

"Back to that again." Joshua dramatically dropped his head on the back of the sofa. This brought laughter from Akande. He jerked up. "What, was that laughter I just heard?"

She playfully punched him in the abdomen. "Ouch."

"You'll hurt your hand doing that." He liked seeing her being this free. Her life had been so serious. He wanted to see her smile. "How about this, we'll jump in the shower, order some room service and live like

humans for tonight. Tomorrow, we find your father."
He kissed her lips. "Will you give me tonight?"

That was the first time he had kissed her since
leaving the cave. She liked it. She liked it too much.
They would have to part ways soon. God forgive her,
she wanted to feel him inside her again. For she knew
after tonight, there would be no more. "All right, you
have tonight."

Before she could change her mind, Joshua picked
her up and carried her to the shower squealing.

Joshua sat her on the floor in front of the shower
and began to remove his clothes.

"What are you doing?" A shocked Akande asked.

"Taking a shower."

Akande looked around and saw a tub in the corner.
"All right, I will bathe in the tub."

Joshua looked at the tub then back at her. "Okay,
the tub can be freaky, too. We'll bathe in the tub." He
pulled his shirt off.

She momentarily lost her train of thought seeing
his naked chest in the light. Shaking it off, she balled
her fist up at her side. "You cannot bathe with me. It is
not done."

The look on her face and the fist at her side made
him realize she was serious. He kicked off his shoes,
pulled her into his arms and proceeded to kiss her
senseless. By the time he was finished, they were
completely undressed and under the shower with her
back up against the wall. He turned the shower on
allowing the water to cascade down their bodies. His
hands moved over her smooth wet body as boldly as
hers roamed over his. The possessive kiss became
lazy. He now had her complete attention. He wanted
to take his time, go slow, say all the sweet words she'd
never heard and show her how a woman should feel in
a man's arms.

Akande never knew when they entered the shower because she was too busy trying to follow his kiss. It was powerful, forceful, possessive, and she loved it. She loved the feel of his hard body on hers, his muscle bound leg between her thighs making her heart pound and her stomach flutter. Now he was teasing her with feather like kisses down her neck, across her shoulder. She pulled his face back to hers, and sought his lips. She wanted his tongue merging with hers.

Joshua gave her what she wanted with a growl mixed with laughter. She grabbed his shoulders and began moving her body restlessly against his. She raised her thigh as if she were trying to climb him. He helped by wrapping his hands around her waist then picked her up until she was eye to eye with him. He leaned his body against hers and held her in place.

He touched the side of her breasts, loving the heavy weight of them in his hands. Her nipples had hardened at his touch. He gently rubbed his thumb across them anticipating their taste. He broke the kiss with one stroke and captured her nipple with the next. She inhaled and let out a deep moan. Her hands became wild, they were all over him as he sucked, licked and devoured her breast. He broke the contact and captured her lips again. Their kisses were ravenous and he liked it. He broke the kiss and looked down at her passionate face, waiting for her to open her eyes. When she did, he saw the passion, the desire, the need. He grinned, and then sucked the other nipple into his mouth. She moaned. He was beginning to like hearing that sound from her.

Akande was overwhelmed by his strength, his muscles, his entire body. She held his head to her breast, for the warmth of his mouth and the pull of his lips filled her with an indescribable sensation. The feel of his thigh was like steel between her legs. She was about to explode. "I'm burning, Joshua," she husked out. "I'm burning."

Her words drove him crazy. He ran his tongue down her stomach to her navel as his arms lifted her higher. He dipped, placing her legs over his shoulder, held in place with his hand on her stomach. His tongue lashed into her with a vengeance. She screamed at the sensation generated by him plunging in and out of her. She was so sweet, his knees almost buckled. He bent his knees and pushed back up as if he were lifting a hundred pound weight. Her thighs tightened around his neck, her hands holding his mouth to her, her body moving to the rhythm of his tongue until it shattered.

Pieces of light fluttered behind her closed eyelids as her body jerked.

Joshua, eased her legs down, held her under the shower and placed light kisses over her shoulders. Her body still trembled as he held her against him.

He smiled. "Now wasn't that fun?"

Akande couldn't move. She held him around his waist. All she had the strength to do was nod.

He carried her out the shower with a big terry cloth towel wrapped around her, laid her on the bed and proceeded to dry her off.

"You are so beautiful." His hands moved slowly over her body as he spoke. "I look at you and know there is a God in heaven. For only the creator would have such power to create you."

The sincerity in his eyes filled her with knowing. She knew she had fallen in love with Joshua. This man who could kill with his bare hands, yet touch her so gently. How did it happen? When? It was long before the cave. It must have happened when they were fighting and she sensed he was only toying with her. He could have easily beaten her. Yet, he allowed her to keep her pride intact. Joshua Lassiter was going to haunt her for the rest of her life.

She looked up at him, as he moved the towel over her legs. "Come into me, Joshua. I need to feel you inside me."

Her words caught him off guard. They were innocent, pleading, wanton. This woman was slowly draining all his will power to keep her at a distance. Joshua reached over to the nightstand and pulled a condom from his wallet. He dropped the towel to the floor and covered himself, never taking his eyes from hers. Kneeling on the bed, he spread her legs at the knee, covered her body with his and slowly entered her. At the cave, they didn't have protection.

He wanted to go slow, he really did, but her heat, as he slid in and out of her was so intense, so moist, so tight. He had to take it--all of it, for this, this woman belonged to him. He raised his body above her, wrapped his hands around her waist and plunged in deep, branding her with every inch of him, sealing them together with each powerful thrust. The sweat from his brow dropped to his nose, as he soared bringing her first to completion and then, only then, did he release what he had stored up.

They lay there, entwined, her hands roaming boldly over him. He, on his back, with one hand behind his head, leisurely twirling her hair in his fingers when she began talking.

"My aunt did not raise me. A family outside the village did. One day I was in the field working with the woman I thought was my mother when I saw a shiny black vehicle. It stopped in front of our hut and three men stepped out. The woman ran and stood in front of me. I was curious so I looked around to see and that's when I saw her. Sermyera. She was beautiful and so regal. One of the men pulled something from his coat jacket and shot. The woman in front of me fell to the ground. I was so shocked I just stood there. Sermyera looked down at me and said. 'You look just like your mother. I am your Aunt Sermyera, your Queen. You will come live with me.' I was eight years old." She stopped talking as she continued to trail a finger down his chest. "I don't remember the family I lived with anymore. I can't see their faces. My aunt said I was to forget them for I had a mission in life. The first time I was whipped it was because I said I wanted to go home to my mother. She grew angry and then told me the story of my mother, my real mother. Then I was whipped." She exhaled. "I had never felt such pain. Now, it has become a dullness. The story became my reality. The mission became my life. Convincing the man I know to be my father is the only chance I have to restore honor to my family. Not for my aunt, but for myself."

Joshua closed his eyes. He would not ask. If she is to tell him, it would be by her own choosing. It would be because she trusted him with the information. He knew they were coming to a crossroads where each would have to make a decision based on trust.

"My father was Lieutenant General Royce C. Davenport. He is now Senator Davenport of Virginia."

Chapter Fourteen

Royce arrived precisely at seven with a knock at the door. Shelly opened the door and stepped aside. "Agent McNally."

"Ma'am," he smiled as he and two other agents searched the premises.

It seemed to go faster this time. "Night, ma'am."

"Good night, Agent McNally."

Royce walked in, closed the door and pulled her into his arms. "I have thought about holding you in my arms all day." He kissed her deep, hard and ravenously.

"Is that right, Senator?"

"What happened to Royce?"

"Oh." She pushed him away. Reached behind her and unzipped her dress allowing it to fall to the floor. "Hello, Royce."

Royce stood there taking in every inch of her in nothing but a lilac lace bra and panties. They weren't bikinis or thongs. They were the high cut lace panties ending in a v-shape at her junction. He could see her natural skin through the lace. As tempting as it was, his eyes roamed up to hers. "Make me forget the last thirty-six hours, Shelly Knight."

Shelly wrapped her arms around his neck and kissed him as she eased his suit jacket from his shoulders. She then stepped back and turned towards the stairs. "Follow me," she said as she folded the jacket and placed it over the banister.

The sight of her from behind immobilized him. "Damn." There was nothing sexier than a woman who was confident in her skin. Shelly didn't have a child's body. She wasn't a size six, eight or ten. She had a woman's body, a good size twelve with all the curves just where he liked them. Her behind moved up the stairs with a rhythm that had him moving his head from side to side watching the lilac lace. The heels she was wearing, made her calves more defined, but it was those thighs, those smooth thighs that had his mouth watering.

She stopped and looked over her shoulder at him. "You coming? I'll be waiting for you in the bedroom." She continued up the stairs.

Royce pulled his tie loose and dropped it to the floor as he followed her up the stairs. "Oh, Ms. Knight, I do hope you have a sturdy bed." He growled as he removed the cuff links from his shirt and placed them in his pocket. Taking the steps in sync with her, he began to unbutton his shirt. By the time they reached the bedroom, all that remained were his pants, which he was unbuckling when she turned around.

"Oh, no," She walked back to him. "Allow me to do that." She held his eyes as she unbuttoned his pants, and slowly pulled the zipper down. She stopped midway and smiled. "I think you need a little attention down there." She started to kneel, but he stopped her and took her lips with a vengeance. The heat from her hands, now against his chest seared through him like a drop of boiling lava. He deepened the kiss, then pulled away. "You may continue now."

Shelly grinned and allowed her hands to trail down his waist to the top of his pants. She continued with the zipper and was pleasantly surprised to find him flowing free. She looked up at him to find him smiling down at her. "Why Senator Davenport where are your drawers?" she asked as his pants fell to the floor.

"They've been rather constricting for the last two days. I couldn't breathe."

"Well." She kissed him on the tip. "We certainly want you breathing." She licked her tongue up his shaft and reveled in his response to her touch. Reaching in his pants pocket, she pulled out a gold package, tore it open with her teeth then covered him. She stood, took his hand and led him to the bed. "We can play later." She lay on the bed, brought her legs up and spread them wide open. She touched herself through her panties. "I am so wet, Royce. I need you inside of me, like right now."

Royce reached up and pulled her legs down to the edge of the bed. He removed her panties, and threw them to the floor. He rubbed her thick smooth thighs, pulled them up and entered her with one fluid motion. He sank into her heat so deep, and completely he didn't want to move. Her muscles contracted so tight around him he had to do it again. He pulled out slowly, then thrust right back in.

Shelly moaned, "Again."

He placed his hands under her, and squeezed her buns as he pulled out again. She was angled higher now. Royce wanted to hit another spot. He thrust in again and heard her gasp. "Ahh." That was it. He hit it again, and again, and again until he felt her body rising to meet his. This woman, with no inhibitions, was drawing more than his seed, she was pulling at his heart. "Come get it, Shelly. Take what you want baby, just take what you want." She screamed letting him know, she was doing just that.

He wasn't finished. Her powerful muscles contracting around him fueled his passion even more. He held her legs up, closed them, then proceeded to plunge into her wetness, as her juices ran down her behind. "Ahh, Shelly," he moaned. She was so wet, so tight, so damn hot, he could feel himself still swelling inside of her. Her intake of breath, made him thrust harder, deeper, and deeper until he roared out his release. He didn't drop her legs. Instead, he wrapped them around him and covered her with his body.

Shelly started laughing first. Then Royce turned over bringing her body with him.

"That was so intense. Oh, God!" she exhaled. "You got any more where that came from?"

Royce unhooked her bra, lifted her on to the tip of him. "What do you think?"

Shelly braced herself on his chest. "I guess you do," she said as she eased down on him. She sat back, closed her eyes and licked her lips as she slowly moved against him. "There should be a law against this."

Royce had her breasts in his hands thumbing across her nipples. "I'm sure there is." He sat up taking one nipple into his mouth. He twirled his tongue over it to the rhythm of her body. His hands dropped to her waist guiding her movements that were now bucking wildly. He could feel her losing control and he wanted to go right over the edge with her. He sucked harder, nipping the bud with his teeth. She exploded and he followed right behind her. Her head fell to his shoulder, as his hands pulled her closer bringing their bodies together as one.

Hours later, they had showered, eaten, laughed and talked and were laying comfortably next to each other in bed, enjoying a quiet moment.

"Spend the weekend at my place."

Shelly sat up on her elbow. "You want me to come to Washington? You know I am not a member of the pearl society."

Royce laughed. "What do pearls have to do with you coming to my home?"

"It's in Washington, right?"

"Georgetown, but yes."

"That's even worse, the snob capital of the world. I don't have clothes to wear in an area like that."

"It is not that bad." Royce pulled her down into his arms. "They will love you in D.C."

Shelly laughed. "Yeah, I can see me now sitting at a dinner table with the wives of other Senators wearing one of my necklaces made by Nikkea and them sitting in their thirty-seven hundred dollar strand of Akoya Pearls. I don't quite see that working. You need a Washington insider on your arm."

Royce flipped her over and stared down into her eyes. "Spending time with you, during our uninterrupted moments," he smiled, "Has been an eye opening experience. I found out I was still alive inside." He became serious. "My life is filled with life and death and national security issues during the day and other than spending time with my family, I didn't look forward to the next day." He rubbed her brow with his thumb. "Since I met you, dealing with those issues has been a little easier to take. I've found someone I want to see when I come home. You bring laughter into my life and I want that. We talk about serious and crazy issues and I get the same exhilaration from every conversation. I don't know what to expect from you, and I like that."

"We've never been out in public, Royce. You have no idea how I would react to things."

"Then it's time we find out. I have no intentions on keeping you a secret. That's not my way. I want you in my life, public and private."

"But I don't have any pearls," she pouted. "All the political wives and girlfriends have pearls. I don't even know if I like pearls. You know what I mean."

"I'll buy you pearls."

"I don't want you to buy me pearls, Royce." She sat up and leaned against the headboard. "It's what the pearls symbolize." She exhaled. "I'm a school teacher, by choice. I lived the high society life and I did not like it, one bit." She ran a finger down his chest. "There is nothing I like more than the time we spend together. Believe me I am so enjoy spending time with you." She kissed him on the lips. "If you haven't picked up anything else about me, you should know I can't do fake. Look at me, no fake hair, nails, booty or anything." She laughed. "I am who I am and I like it. Washington is the backstabbing capitol of the world. We all know this. I call things like I see them. Your colleague's wives are not going to want to deal with me, which will end up affecting you and your politicking. I don't want to do that."

"You know what I don't want to do? I don't want to plan my personal life around what Washington insiders like or dislike. I don't have to sleep with them and don't want to." He pulled her down under him. "You, on the other hand, I desperately want in my bed. Be it here or in D.C. My work is at a critical point, I have to be in D.C. I should be there now, but I had to see you. You have me hooked like crack cocaine and I can't get enough of you. Come to D.C this weekend. Next weekend, we can stay here. Don't make me stand on the steps of the capitol calling your name. Shelly!"

he screamed out. She laughed. "Shelly!" he screamed again, then spoke almost in a whisper. "Come break me off a piece of your sweet, sweet love, Shelly." He kissed her neck.

"You are crazy," she giggled as he kissed the other side of her neck. "Really crazy." He crawled down and kissed her navel. She shook her head slowly back and forth against the pillow as he went lower still. "Oh, Senator," she moaned. "You got me." She felt his hand moving to the side of the bed. He looked up at her with a key in his hand. "You can let yourself in. I'm a little busy right now. He went back down on her and sealed the deal.

Chapter Fifteen

Monique walked into the hotel suite to find Joshua and Akande, sitting on the sofa, wrapped in each other's arms. This was not the man Monique had come to know. He was not one to play the loving boyfriend role like he was now. This bothered her, not out of jealousy. His actions were putting his life in danger. He might not be aware of it, but she saw in living color. To make matters worse, she did not believe the woman was being truthful to Joshua. Every fiber in her body screamed with this woman around. If Joshua hadn't taught her anything else, he taught her to follow her instincts. Her instincts were telling her Joshua needed her protection from the enemy. In her estimation of things, Akande was the enemy.

"You will be safe with her," Joshua smiled into Akande's eyes. "I trust her with my life. You're a part of that now."

"You will not forget I am here?"

"Never," Joshua replied before he kissed her. He lingered a moment then pulled away.

Monique was surprised at the parting. He stopped at the door where she stood. "Don't let anything happen to her."

"We're a little touchy, feely today, aren't we?" She gave him a sideways look.

"Don't."

"I won't if you don't. This is business, right?"

Joshua looked over her shoulder at Akande who was watching them. "Not anymore. It's personal now."

"That makes this easy for me. I will handle this as business. You are compromised."

He held her glare, not wanting to, but knowing she was right. The days with Akande had him turned inside out. He wanted her touch to be real. It's the thing Samuel, his brother had that he didn't, a woman who touched him deep. So deep, he wasn't thinking straight. There were too many unanswered questions. He ran his hand down his face. The dimples deepening as he thought. "Handle her as business."

Monique tilted her head, "Will do." She closed the door behind him and turned to Akande, senses on alert.

Akande seemed nice enough, but Monique learned long ago to trust her own instincts. Walking into the room, Monique moved the newspaper, and set it on the table as she sat in the chair. Being observant was a unique skill for her. For example, glancing at the article Akande was reading, just for a second or two, she read and would retain every word in the article pertaining to Senator Davenport. She had observed the shift in Akande's eyes when Joshua mentioned going to locate the Senator. The last observation bothered her more than any of the others. Joshua used the door to leave.

"Akande," she spoke standing behind the chair across from Monique. "I did not catch your name."

"I didn't give it."

Akande's eyes narrowed at the snappy reply. Uncertain of the reason, she waited a moment to see if the woman would say more. Was this someone who was involved with Joshua? She had never met the woman therefore was certain she had not wronged her in anyway. "There appears to be a bit of hostility in your reply. Have I caused you ill will at some point?"

There was an air of royalty in the way she spoke. And Monique could see where that may be a turn on for some. However, she was not one of them. Royalty or not, there was something off about the woman. "Not yet, but I am certain that you will. Take a seat, Akande. Let's talk."

"I'm not accustomed to speaking with someone so...how would you say?"

Monique spoke in her native tongue. "We may speak in any language you understand."

Akande looked up with shock radiating through her eyes, but never showing on her face. Quickly masking the reaction, she walked around the chair and took a seat.

"What shall we speak on?"

"Absolute."

She smirked. "So your hostility is about Joshua."

"No, my hostility concerns you coming into my country under false pretenses. Since we are speaking so forthwith, Absolute is a friend and valued colleague. I take exception to him being used."

"Joshua is a man quite capable of handling himself. This you can trust me on."

"No need to drop hints, Absolute sleeps with just about every woman who crosses his path. And yes, he makes each of them feel as if she is the only one in the world."

"Why do you insist on referring to him as that ridiculous name? Is it not clear to you he has shared his true identity with me?"

"Tisk, tisk. Your fangs are beginning to show. We would not want to tarnish that subdued persona, now, would we?"

"I do not like you very much."

"That gives you a one up. I don't like you at all." She uncrossed her legs and sat forward. "There's two things you need to know. First, I'm not buying your act. You have fooled an individual whom I admire and I am somewhat disappointed with that reality. The other thing you should know, and this is very important. I kill people for a living. I don't ask questions, I just take them out." The expression on her face changed as she glared at the woman. "I want to be sure there is no misunderstanding." Monique stood, walked over to where Akande sat. She placed her hands on the arm of the chair trapping the woman inside and glared into her eyes. "You've been warned." She held the woman's eyes for a moment then walked out of the room.

***

"Mommy," a small voice called out from her room. "Uncle Joshua is here."

Cynthia Lassiter walked into the room with her golden curls bouncing around her shoulders and a stomach that walked in the room before her feet did. "Joshua," she called out, a bright smile appearing on her face as she stretched her arms out.

"Good Lord, woman. What is that brother of mine doing to you?" Joshua's smile beamed as he embraced his sister-in-law. He looked down. "What? Do you have a beach ball in there?"

She hit him with the dishcloth. "When did you get back from Emure?"

"A few hours ago. Where's Sammy?"

"With JD." She knew this brother-in-law almost as well as she knew Samuel. She could tell when something wasn't right. "Can you stay for a minute?"

"No, I'm working. I wanted to see my niece." He bent down to retake his seat next to Samantha.

"Mommy, Uncle Joshua wants one of me. I told him, he don't have to. You and Daddy will share me."

"Doesn't have to sweetie," Cynthia corrected her two year old as she watched Joshua.

"Doesn't have to," Samantha repeated.

"Try this one," Joshua gave her a piece to the puzzle.

Samantha put it with the others and jumped into her uncle's arms when it worked. "Uncle Joshua made it work, Mommy."

Joshua kissed the child.

"Yes, he did." Joshua looked different. "Go wash your hands, sweetie. It's time for lunch."

"Okay," Samantha kissed her uncle on his cheek then skipped from the room.

"Use water," Cynthia turned to say. When she turned back, Joshua was gone. She stood there staring at the spot he'd previously occupied. Something was amiss.

***

Sally Lassiter loved three things with a passion, her husband, her twelve children and her garden. When her spirit wasn't right, that meant one of her children was in trouble. It wasn't Sapphire, her youngest. She was in school, eager for the Thanksgiving break. She had spoken with both sets of twins. Jade and Adam were fine, well except Adam, who almost blew up one of the buildings on the Morehouse campus. Opal and Timothy were at

Hampton University, both planned to be home for Thanksgiving. Luke was at practice. Since his NFL team did not have to play on Thanksgiving day, she was expecting him home. Mathew had just moved into his new apartment and was being frisky with some girl when she called. Her sweet Diamond was with her new husband, Zack, making babies she hoped. Pearl and Samuel were on a road trip with Governor Harrison. Pearl was his press secretary and Samuel was on his security detail. Ruby was at the shelter where she volunteered with the homeless. That left Joshua. She sat back on her heels, wiped at imaginary sweat on her brow, then bent back over her garden. This would probably be the last set of greens she would get before the winter really sat in. Joshua Theodore Lassiter, her gift from God. He was the restless one who was always trying to live up to his bigger than life brother Samuel. She prayed for him the most.

He was such a caring spirit and an accomplished man in his own right. But he always seemed to be searching for something. He would find it. Love. As soon as he stopped searching by bedding every woman who comes his way, he would find that one woman who would calm his spirit. That's what she prayed for, for all of her children. Samuel found Cynthia and Diamond found Zackary. Soon, Joshua would find someone. A smile crept into her heart.

"I have told you about sneaking up on me."

Joshua stood behind his mother in the backyard where he, his brothers, whom his father referred to as gents, and the wild bunch of sisters, his father called gems, because he thought they were all precious gemstones, would play. None of them, nor any woman he had met thus far, came within a mile of being as precious and rare as this one. His mother meant more to him than anything in this world. She would move heaven and earth for him and he would do the same for her.

Sally stood to see her son standing there with his arms folded across his chest, dressed in a navy blue suit, crisp white shirt, a striped navy, white and black tie. His trench coat swung open and free, looking like a modern day sheriff from the wild, wild west. Aww, this one. This handsome double dimpled devil stole her heart away the moment he came into the world. She loved her children, all of them. This one she worried about, because of his chosen profession. For the most part, Sally had no idea where in the world he was, but knew in her heart God would protect him. Yet, she worried.

"As I was with Moses, so I will be with thee. I will not fail thee, nor forsake thee. Book of Joshua, Chapter 1 verse 5. Hello there, mother of Joshua."

Sally laughed as she hugged him. "Be strong and of good courage, be not afraid, neither be thou dismayed for the Lord thy God is with thee whithersoever thou goest. Book of Joshua, Chapter 1, verse 9."

"So why are you fretting?"

"What makes you think I'm fretting?" She wiped her brow, then put her hands on her hips and looked up at him.

"You've beat the poor greens to death with the spade."

Sally looked at the garden and had to laugh. She turned back to him. "Come in the house smarty pants. I have a hot pan of peach cobbler in the oven."

He grinned and followed his mother into the house. "You are the second person to call me that. Where is everyone?" Joshua took off his coat and placed it across the back of the chair as he sat at the kitchen table.

His mother was at the oven, busy, pulling out a saucer and filling it with cobbler then dropping a big dip of vanilla ice cream on top. "Well, your father is upstairs asleep. He has to work tonight." She placed the saucer and a spoon in front of him then counted off. "Everyone else is at, work, work, work, practice field, apartment, school, school, school, school and school. She thought for a minute. "Yeah, that just about covers everyone." She smiled and sat at the table with a cup of coffee. She took a sip as her motherly eyes roamed over him, assessing, looking for the things only a mother's eye can find. "So, tell me about her."

Joshua sat back and laughed with a spoonful of cobbler in his mouth. "Cut right to the chase, Mom."

"You don't have time for me to be subtle about things. So spill it."

This was the reason he came home. He was tied up in knots. If anyone could clear his mind, it was his mother. "I met this woman. I can't tell you where." he sighed. "Mom, she is beautiful, and courageous. She touches something deep inside of me that I can't explain. She's had a sad life and I find myself wanting to change that, you know make it right for her." He told her about Akande without giving too much detail. Instantly, he stopped talking.

Sally waited. "But?"

He smirked. "I don't know if I trust her."

Speaking from her heart was the only way Sally knew how to be when it came to her children. She wanted all of them happy and the only way she knew to ensure that was to do all she could to make certain they ended up with the right person in their life.

"Trust is the cornerstone of any relationship, be it brothers, sisters, husbands, or wives. In your line of work trust is paramount. Every human beings life is built on trust. You have to trust the people around you to do their part to ensure a successful mission, for your life is on the line. You trust your brothers and sisters will always be there to support you and have your back in all things. A relationship is built on love, respect and above all else trust. Without trust, you cannot love. Without love there is no relationship. See in a relationship, you entrust your heart to another person. You have to trust they will protect it above all else. Once trust is broken it is not easily repaired. Ask your father. He was with a woman before me."

"No," Joshua had sat back in his chair, legs stretched out, crossed at the ankles, ready to receive any wisdom she had to offer. "Say it ain't so."

"Yes, my son. Your father was stupid at one time. But I love him anyway." she smiled. "This woman was beautiful, intelligent, wealthy, had just about everything going for her. She was fierce. She had your father too." Sally picked up her cup of coffee. "Mmm hmm, she sure did. Then she lied to him. It wasn't even a big lie." She took a drink as if thinking back, then sat the cup down. "When he discovered the lie, he was devastated. He tried to forgive her, for it was a petty issue she had lied about, but he never could. You see. When you put your trust in a person, you have to believe they will cherish and protect it. They will put your interests above their own. She did not."

"Whatever happened to her?"

"She married someone else. You've met her."

"Really?" Joshua sat up. "Who?"

"Her name is Sofia Thornton."

"No." Joshua laughed. "No. Daddy was with Cynthia's mother? That lady is a bitch on wheels."

"Don't curse in my house. Yes, he was too. Hell, that man is lucky I came along."

"Thank God he came to his senses."

Sally reached over and covered her son's hand with hers. He pulled hers to his lips and kissed it. "Trust in the Lord, Joshua. He will lead you in the right direction."

He had barely touched his cobbler, Sally noticed as she watched him walk out the door. This woman had him confused, but she wasn't concerned. Not once did her son ever mention the word love. She prayed that all of her children would recognize it when it appeared, and knew to turn away from what only looks like love.

***

Joshua started his jeep and was about to pull off when his side door opened.

"Hello, little brother."

Joshua did not fear many things. Only three: God, his father and his big brother, Samuel Lassiter. He may be CIA, but Samuel was ex-Navy Seal. He had experienced things Joshua could only dream of doing one day.

"I heard you need me."

"Cynthia?"

Samuel smiled. "Let's have a cup of coffee."

"Make that a cognac and you are on."

Samuel looked at his watch. "It's nine in the morning."

Joshua pulled off, as he looked sideways at his brother. "Yeah."

Ten minutes later, Joshua and Samuel walked into one of their favorite hangouts. The Renaissance, which was owned by a friend and not open to the public that time of morning. They had the place to themselves as Joshua told Samuel everything that happened from the moment he touched down in Emure.

"You have a hell of a situation on your hands and the week isn't over yet." They sat in similar positions, legs stretched out, crossed at the ankles, arms folded across their broad chests. "I know Senator Davenport. He's not the type of man to leave a child behind. I doubt that he is her father."

"Men do it all the time, Sammy."

"I agree. Not this man." He saw his brother begin to withdraw as he always did when he thought Samuel was questioning his judgement. "She may have been told this by this Sermyera woman and believe it to be true. But, I doubt the Senator is her father. There's something else." He sat up, which got Joshua's attention again. "We did a recon in that region about ten years ago. We were asked to try to locate a child. I remember because we failed. We had to close the file because we never found the child."

"There's a file in the Asmere folder that is sealed. I believe information in that file holds the answer to this situation."

"Ned can't get into it?"

"No, he's tried."

"That can only mean one thing." Joshua raised a brow. "It's sealed by the Secretary of Defense and it is related to a current security issue."

"I believe it's a current issue. I can't explain why, but the timing has me concerned." Joshua frowned. "Why the urgency now to take the Senator out? And there is something else. Princess Zsa Zsa said something to me and I didn't think about it until I was in the chopper watching Emure soldiers using us for target practice."

"What did she say?"

"She believes a member of her family was involved in her kidnapping."

"Did she say who?"

"No."

"I'll talk to LaVere' about it. He flew back yesterday. I think he's planning to bring Zsa Zsa here to stay with him for a while."

Joshua nodded. "I think that might be good for her. Is his security detail tight?

"I believe that's why he's here. He asked for Brian's contact information."

"His protection firm is good. Top notch. He could use a few tweaks, but not bad."

"Where's the chopper?" Samuel asked.

"Helipad on Leigh Street. Why?"

"We should go to D.C.; meet with the Senator. I'll call ahead to have the Governor arrange it."

"Will he? You know the man better than I do."

"JD will do anything to keep you from blowing up things in Virginia."

"I haven't blown up anything in awhile. Ned wouldn't let me." Joshua grunted.

Samuel laughed. "So tell me. Are you serious about this woman?"

"Akande," he smiled. "She can fight. She has a smart mouth. Easy to blush." He laughed thinking about the leaves. A frown appeared. "She's tough." He took a drink. "When we were at the waterfall, I was tying the leaf around her and she had five fresh whip marks across her back. Not once, the entire time we were together did she complain and I know she had to be in pain."

"Whip marks? Who in the hell would do that?" Samuel asked outraged.

"Her aunt." Joshua poured another drink and swallowed it down. "She's going to be the first one I kill."

Samuel studied his brother. He looked tired and angry. If he wasn't careful, he could cross the line. In a number of ways his little jokester of a brother was more dangerous than he would ever be. Joshua killed first and asked questions later.

"It wasn't the first time." Joshua poured another drink and held the glass in his hand. "There were older marks on her back. It looked like they were trying to beat her into submission or just for the hell of it. I don't know. I know no one deserves that type of punishment, especially a woman." Joshua swallowed another drink. "Did I tell you she was a virgin?"

Samuel smirked. "Was?"

"I like her, Sammy. I like her a lot."

"I couldn't help but notice you used the word like. There is a difference between like, lust and love. You are familiar with lust, so I'll stay away from that one." Joshua grinned. "This is the first time I've heard you use the word like since high school. Now love, love is easier to recognize for us because we have seen it all our lives. The moment I saw Cynthia at the Brooks mansion, it hit me right in my gut. I knew. Not a question in my mind." He looked up at his brother. "You have questions. I know because you are questioning your instincts. Don't. Go with what your gut tells you." Samuel stood, finished his drink and left money on the table. Joshua did the same. "Here's the only question you need to answer for yourself. Do you like her, more than you love your country? If what she plans to do comes to fruition, you will have to make that choice." As a sign of support Samuel squeezed Joshua's shoulder. "I'm always here."

Joshua drove to the helipad and parked.

"Can I fly the chopper?" Samuel asked.

"No."

"You let LaVere' fly it."

"Just to get it back home." The men climbed in as Joshua started the chopper and pulled off.

"You'll never steer my submarine," Samuel shrugged his shoulders. "So we're even."

Chapter Sixteen

Monique watched the satellite feed she received from Ned at least a hundred times. The clarity wasn't the greatest, but she knew something was there. Maybe there was something on the license plates of the cars, or a partial facial recognition; anything that could give her some indication who from Emure was working with Tarik. She had just hit the play button again when there was a knock at the door.

"Yeah," she replied knowing it could only be Akande. No one else was in the place but them. She had put sensors on all the doors and windows, so she knew no one had entered. What's more important is the little liar had not gone out.

"May I come in?"

What kind of bull crap did she want to try to lay out now? Monique thought. Monique placed her gun close to her hand, paused the computer then replied, "Sure."

The door opened and Akande walked in. "May I have a moment of your time?"

"What's up?"

"I'm worried about Joshua. It's been hours and he hasn't returned. Has he been in contact with you?"

"No," Monique replied. She had to give it to the woman, she really did look concerned.

"I know you do not understand, but I cannot stay here. I must find my father."

"What are you afraid of, Akande? I may not like you, but I will protect you and so will Absolute."

"It is not about me. It is about my country. I must do all I can to restore my country's honor. Secure its future."

"All of that sounds good. The way to do that is to trust the people who are trying to protect you. You have lied to Absolute and he knows it, yet he cares enough to still try to help with your mission. All he asks is that you trust him to do what's right by you. And you can't give him that." She pointed to the door. "Hell, the door's open. Walk out." She turned back to the computer monitor, pushed the power button on and continued working.

Monique turned when Akande didn't move. The woman was standing there, with tears streaming down her face. "Aww, hell, not the tears. Really, you want to pull out the water works?" Monique reached over to the desk, grabbed the box of tissues and handed one to Akande. "What?" Monique asked exasperated with the scene.

"I do not want to leave him." Akande wiped the tears away. "I know I must leave him behind and I believe it will hurt him." She began to settle down. "But this is my mission, my purpose, my duty to my country. I do not want him to suffer because I was weak and fell in love with him."

Monique stared at the woman. "You don't expect to live through this mission, do you?"

Akande squared her shoulders. "I will not. I always understood that. Once the sanctions are lifted, my purpose will end and I will die at the hand of the

American or my aunt will surely have me killed upon my return."

"Then why in the hell are you doing this? Out of some sense of honor, no less."

"Honor is everything."

"You speak of honor as if it's this badge you are proud to wear. Yet, you dishonor the man who cares for you with lies. See, I think your plan is find your father, who you believe is Senator Davenport and once you do you plan to kill him. Joshua has a sworn duty to protect all Senators for they represent the United States. You are putting him in a position where he will have to choose between you or his country. Which would you choose?"

Akande did not respond to the question. "Would you check on him? Please."

Monique gathered two important pieces of information in the five minute conversation. Honor was important to Akande and so was Joshua. She was still putting Joshua in a hell of a situation. However, she guessed the woman wasn't all bad. "I'll call, but I'm sure he's fine."

"Thank you." She turned to leave.

Monique watched as a proud woman's shoulders slouched. The sight wasn't pretty. "Hey, Akande, have you ever been to D.C.?"

"I have never been anywhere but Asmere. Unless you count when I was kidnapped."

"Well, I think some fresh air might do us some good." She stood. "You won't get kidnapped here." She picked up her gun and put it in the back of her pants. She grabbed her coat and gave another to Akande. "Let's get some fresh air." They walked towards the door. "You might get shot though."

Akande stopped and looked back at Monique. "I'm joking." Akande looked as if she did not believe her.

"Really, I am joking. You've got to loosen up a little, Akande."

Monique locked the door behind them. "D.C. is a great place for visitors. Sightseeing is one of its largest tourist draws. Hell, the White House is here. Everyone should see that at least once in their lifetime. Do you like basketball?"

"No."

"Okay, we're going to the Verizon Center. Check out the ball players."

"Where is your Senate Building?"

"In the opposite direction. Doesn't matter, you're not going anywhere near there today."

"Why not? It is my whole purpose for being here."

"You'll go when Joshua clears it and not before." Monique stopped in the lobby. "Hold up, that's not how you wear that jacket." She adjusted the collar. "You have to jazz it up a little." She stepped back and took a look at the woman. With the tears gone, and the attitude in check, she could see why Joshua would be attracted to the woman. "There, you almost look as good as me."

"You and Joshua and this clothes thing," Akande huffed. "The clothes are not important. What is inside is what counts."

"Really, hmm." Monique smirked. "Well, don't ever go to L.A. or Miami Beach." She opened the door and they walked out onto H Street. Akande did as most tourists do she looked up at the tall buildings. Monique surveyed the area.

They had been walking for a few minutes when Akande grabbed her arm. Turning she noticed that Akande's face had gone white as a sheet as she stared across the street. "What's with you now?"

"Who are they?"

Monique looked across the street to see men emerging from vehicles. "Prince Raheem of Emure." Her grip tightened. Monique quickly moved them from sight. She wasn't crazy about this woman, but it was her duty to protect her while Joshua was away. "You are shaking like a leaf. What gives?"

She looked up at Monique. "Are you sure?"

"I make it my business to know fine men," Monique looked up as security surrounded the man. They stood at a corner behind one of the columns of a bank giving them an unobstructed vantage point. "The man in front is Prince Raheem."

"I have seen this man before."

Monique looked down at her. "Which one?"

Akande watched the man closely. "Prince Raheem."

"That's possible. He is from your region."

"No, you do not understand," Akande cut her off. "When Joshua took me home, to the palace in Asmere, this man was there. He was leaving when I was brought in to see Queen Sermyera."

"Are you sure?"

"I looked him right in the eyes. That is the man who met with Queen Sermyera in Asmere."

Akande took a step out to get a better look. "Why is he here?"

Monique pulled Akande back behind her just as one of the security men looked up. "Did the man at the palace see you?" Monique asked never taking her eyes from the security guard who was still looking her way.

"Yes. Just as I saw him."

Monique held the guard's eye, until he turned away to speak to the man next to him. When that man looked up she pulled Akande around the corner. "Time to go."

She pulled out her handheld. Cell phones were not secure enough for this communication. *Need help. Track Me.* Surveying the area, she knew they could not go back to the hotel. They would follow them there. She put the device in her pocket and walked towards Chinatown. They had to get lost fast.

The busy tourist area allowed them to take a minute to assess things. Monique noticed two men dressed in suits with guns. The guns weren't visible they were under their suit jackets. Not unusual, this was D.C. after all. The area was loaded with agents of all kinds carrying weapons. As a precaution, she walked across the street, keeping Akande to her inside. Monique stopped at a storefront window pretending to be looking at the outfit. Through the glass, she saw the two men stop on the other side of the street to her left. In her peripheral vision, to her right she saw two more suspicious-looking men. They needed to lose the men and get back to the hotel. If she was alone she would kick ass, then find out who in the hell they were, however, Akande was with her and she did not want to put her in danger.

"You see them too?"

Monique looked through the glass at the woman. "The men?"

"Yes." Akande replied. "The men to our left followed us from the hotel. The others joined later."

"Do you recognize them?"

"No."

Monique hoped they would not open fire in a crowded area. They wouldn't be that stupid. Monique heard the swoosh sound a second before the glass shattered. She grabbed Akande and began running as some others did. She ran past the Verizon Center heading towards a building under construction. She couldn't take a chance that a civilian would be shot.

They ducked behind a truck near the construction site. Monique pulled out her glock and looked around. The area was less populated here. Maybe someone called the cops when the window shattered, but it was D.C., they might not. Monique pulled a button from the strap of her heel.

Akande must have thought her foot was bothering her. "You should remove your shoes and run bare foot. You will go much faster."

Monique looked over her shoulder at the woman. "Have you lost your mind? I'm not running barefoot on the streets of D.C." A shot hit the bumper of the construction truck. "Oh, hell. Too close." Monique pushed Akande back. She looked around. "We are going to run inside that building and straight out the back. On three. You ready."

Akande said, "One, two, three," and ran.

Monique tried to catch her but it was too late. All she could do was fire off two rounds to slow the men down. Then she ran into the building. A homeless man was sitting on the floor in the back. "Hide!" she yelled to him, then let off two more rounds on the men following them. She caught up with Akande, stopped her in the ally and hid behind a large green dumpster.

"You weren't supposed to run until I counted to three. Don't do that again. I count, you don't." Monique took a breath. She looked around. There wasn't anyone in the ally. Now all she had to do was hold the men off until Joshua got there. She had no idea where he was, but she knew he would show up.

***

Joshua was just about to land the chopper at Reagan National when Ned's voice came through the panel. "Absolute, I show you in D.C. and Spicy is under attack. I'm sending you Intel."

"Where is Akande?"

"With Spicy," he said. "They're holed up at a construction site not far from the Verizon Center."

"Shit. Sammy pull two semi's from the vault. We have a gun fight to get to in D.C."

Samuel came back to the front with guns in hand. He looked down over the city. "D.C. is a no fly zone. Where are you going to land?"

Joshua put the chopper in sleuth mode. "The Verizon Center is as good a place as any."

"That's not going to draw attention?"

"You have a better idea?"

"Take it to the fight. Land on the roof of the construction site."

"That has no flair about it, Sammy. You have to do things with style."

"Let's see how much style you will have when you have to explain landing this chopper with all its weaponry to Congress."

He looked over at his brother. "You always take all the fun out of everything."

***

Monique heard the accent filled voice and knew they were still a good distance away. She did not reply. That would give their position away. Her hand held beeped. She pulled it out and read the message. *Ten minutes.* "Hell, in ten minutes I could be dead." She put the device away.

"Can you fight?" Akande asked Monique. "We can try to take them."

"If they didn't have bullets, I would take you up on that." She shook her head. "I have to draw them away from you." She looked around. The brick wall covered their back, the large dumpsters kept them hidden from one direction. She looked up and it came to her.

She moved Akande, made sure she was covered then gave Akande the button she pulled from her shoe. "Hold this." She held the woman's eyes. "Do not. Listen to me. Do not throw this unless you have absolutely no other choice to save your life."

Akande looked at Monique and just shook her head. "Joshua gives me a straw you give me a button. Don't you people know about guns and knives?"

Monique glared at the woman. She grabbed the hand Akande was holding the button in. "This little button will go boom. You understand."

Her meaning must have become clear to Akande. The woman looked down at her hand. "This is a bomb. I do not want this."

"Hold this. Do not drop it. It will not explode until it hits something. The last thing I need to explain is a bomb going off in D.C."

"Keep me in your eyesight." Monique ran behind one of the large corner pillars holding up the building. She looked back to make sure she could see Akande. Staying low she ran further into the building behind another pillar. She heard a sound behind her. Turning quickly she raised her gun and froze. It was the homeless man, lying flat on the floor. "Get out of here," she mouthed to the man.

He shook his head, pointed to his eyes, then gesture with his hand. Four fingers, then pointed to his right, indicating four men. She nodded. He next closed his hand into a fist twice, then put up two fingers, indicating one at twelve o'clock. That meant a man was straight ahead in front of her. He stopped. Then put up a fist and four fingers. There was one at nine. He stopped. Put up two fingers. They were trying to surround her. He then closed his eyes, indicating he could not see the other men. She blew a kiss at the man, and looked over her shoulder to check on Akande. She was still where she'd left her. Good. When she took a shot, they would converge on her location. It might get a little sticky at that point. She saw a movement in front of her and took aim. One bullet, dead center and the man behind the construction wood fell out. Shots hit the pillar. She moved to the next anchor of the building. With the silencer on, the only sound that would have been heard by bystanders in the area was her one shot. To the untrained ear, a person would think it was just a vehicle backfiring. Nothing out of the ordinary. There would be no help from D.C.'s finest. She looked back. Akande was still in place, not as clear as she would like. But as long as the men were after her, Akande was in a good place. She turned to check on the homeless man just as a bullet went through her arm and hit the metal pillar. "Shit." She moved again and fell against a stack of wood. She sent off two rounds in the direction the shot came from. She dropped her weapon and quickly checked her arm. The bullet went through, but she was bleeding and it hurt like hell.

"We know you are hit," The accented voice called out. "All we want is the girl and we will let you live."

The voice was close. Monique heard a whistle and smiled. She picked up her gun, and counted to ten. "Sorry. You can't have her."

"Then you both will die."

Monique looked up and back to see the man point his gun at her.

"Get down!" Joshua yelled as he ran into the building. Monique hit the floor as sounds of a semi filled the air.

Joshua never hesitated as he sprayed the empty structure with bullets, taking the remaining men down instantly. He walked towards Monique and towered over her. When he saw the blood, he lost it.

He picked the man up off the floor. "You come into my country, after my woman and you shot my trainee. You have lost your damn mind." Joshua picked up the body and threw it against the brick wall. "Say something damn it."

"Joshua, he's dead." Monique released a nervous laugh. "He can't answer you." She stood and walked over to the homeless man.

Samuel ran into the building and looked around at all the dead bodies. "Did you kill all of them Joshua." Incredulously, he looked up at his brother. "How in the hell are we supposed to question them?"

"He doesn't ask questions," Monique explained then looked at the man. "Joshua, this Vet over here saved my life. You think we can ask him a few questions before you shoot him?"

Joshua was still pissed. "I'll ask them when I reach the fires of Hell. 'Cause if one more person starts shooting in my country I'm going to blow all their asses up!" he yelled and looked around.

When she heard his voice Akande peeked out from her hiding place. She had never seen this side of Joshua. It didn't frighten her. It made her proud, for he fought like a warrior.

"Where in the hell is she?" he yelled looking around.

"In the dumpster."

Joshua stared at Monique. "You put her in the damn dumpster?"

"Hey, she was surrounded by metal," Monique yelled back. "They didn't find her."

"Akande," Joshua called out. He saw something moving in the dumpster and ran over. He then pulled her out.

She put her arms around his waist and held him. She could feel his anger. This was one of those times she needed the jokester in him to come out. She held up the button. "A straw and a button. You Americans need real weapons."

He took the button from her then looked over at Monique. "You gave her the button?"

Monique was now talking to the veteran. "She is still alive isn't she?"

He looked down at Akande and slowly wrapped one arm around her, lowered his chin to her head and closed his eyes. He held his gun in the other hand.

"Can you two do that later?" Monique bent to one of the bodies. "Let's check some ID before the police arrive."

"It's D.C.," Samuel stated as he looked around. "We have time. Take the ID off of one and let's get out of here."

As the chopper took off, Monique looked down at D.C. MPD converged on the scene and she wondered why is Prince Raheem in D.C.?

Chapter Seventeen

Samuel and Joshua Lassiter were a sight to behold as they walked through the hallways of the Senate Office Building in Washington, D.C. Both were tall, formidable and handsome. Women and men took second glances as the two walked by.

"May I be of service to you?" one woman asked, smiling up at Joshua.

"No, thank you," Joshua replied and continued to walk.

Samuel looked sideways at his brother. "You feeling okay?"

"Yeah, why?"

"You didn't ask the sister for her number or flash the dimples or any of the normal things you do."

"Not interested. We have business to discuss with Davenport."

Samuel stopped. "You, not interested in a woman?"

"Sammy, the Senator."

"Wow, and serious too," Samuel said as he started walking again.

Joshua opened the door to the Senator's office. "I still got it."

Sammy laughed. "Now that's the brother I know and love."

"Good afternoon. May I help you?" A young blonde woman smiled up at Joshua.

He returned the smile. "We are here to see Senator Davenport."

"Wow, they are great," she said still smiling at Joshua. "Are they real?"

"Yes," Joshua replied.

"May I touch them," she stood, reaching out to touch his face.

"Sure," he bent over.

She touched his dimple with the tip of her finger. "Wow, they're deep, too."

Samuel cleared his throat. "The Senator."

"Yes. Of course." She picked up the phone. "Mrs. Paxton, there are two very attractive gentlemen here to see the Senator." She held the receiver. "Your names?"

"Lassiter, Samuel and Joshua."

She smiled. "Who's who?"

"I'm Samuel and he's Joshua."

She almost curtsied at Joshua. "Samuel Handsome and Joshua Hot."

The person on the other end of the phone must have said something because the woman straightened and got her act together. "Yes, ma'am, right away." She cleared her throat. "The Senator will see you now."

The two walked towards the double doors. "I can't imagine what life is like for you."

"Hey somebody has to live it." Joshua smiled.

"Good afternoon," Kathy said as she greeted the men. "My, my, my," she said then smiled. "Would you give me one moment?" She picked up the phone and pushed a button. "You're forgiven," she said and hung up telephone. "Right this way, gentlemen."

Royce stood as the Lassiter's walked into the room. "Samuel. It's good to see you."

"Same here," Samuel replied as he accepted the hand extended.

"You must be Joshua." They shook hands. "We seem to have a bit of a situation on our hands."

"One I believe we can end with a little guidance from you," Joshua replied.

"Have a seat, gentlemen. You want my help, after you landed a chopper on a building under construction and had a gunfight in the middle of Washington, D.C.? The appropriate time to have asked for my help would have been before all of that occurred."

"We were under fire from members of a foreign government." Joshua's tone elevated some.

"You had one of their citizens in your custody. Is that correct?"

"Yes."

Before Joshua could go on, Royce stopped him. "Why is a citizen of a foreign government here without proper documentation?"

"You know damn well why she is here." Samuel touched Joshua's arm to calm him down. Joshua took a deep breath. "As you are aware, there is a sealed file in the Asmere folder. I believe the information contained in that file will go a long way to shed light on a few unanswered questions."

"What has led you to believe that?"

"Oh, I don't know, being chased through the wilds of Africa with gunfire as the incentive to run, or, the fact that one of my agents took a bullet earlier today, may be an indication that something is amiss."

"Your choosing. Your instructions were to not enter Asmere. You went there against orders, possibly causing damage to current delicate situations above your grade level. Now you want to do a witch hunt into files that may affect national security."

Samuel touched Joshua's arm. "Senator, there are a few extenuating circumstances here." He nodded to Joshua.

Joshua sat forward and told the Senator what he knew of the situation, leaving out Akande's belief that he is her father. "I believe if we can get the two of you together, we can get to the bottom of this."

"You want me to be in a room with a woman whose sole purpose, according to you, is to kill me?"

"Senator, I know this sounds unreasonable. But it is our best chance to get answers."

Royce sat back. "Son, while I believe in your plight, you are asking a lot. This young woman has told you a tragic tale, one that many suffer in a foreign country. However, no one man can lift sanctions. That is something that would have to go before Congress." He sat forward. "However, there is a portion of your story that concerns me greatly. You believe a member of the royal family of Emure is connected to the kidnapping of their own Princess?"

"Yes, sir, I do."

Royce glared at Joshua. He was indeed an asset to the United States. His logical deduction of the situation was accurate. He only wished his manner of handling situations was less dramatic. "Give me twenty-four hours."

"Senator, time seems to be an issue here."

Royce stood and extended his hand. "Twenty-four hours."

Joshua stood and hesitantly shook the man's hand.

"Thank you, Senator." Samuel shook the man's hand.

Once the men were out of the office Royce paged Kathy. "Get the Secretary of Defense on the line."

***

Monique stood outside the hotel where Prince Raheem was seen. She couldn't let what Akande said go. She did not want to jump the gun and assume what she believed to be fact. It was far better to know the answers before you ask the questions. With that theory in mind, after the shootout at the D.C. corral, she was treated at the Quantico Medical Facility. Afterwards she went back to the hotel and did what she did best, she looked at the numbers.

Monique had a unique ability. Her analytical mind when it came to formulas was impressive and her ability to decipher codes was a skill that the CIA desperately needed. But, it was her ability to read or hear something once and repeat it verbatim that made her a candidate they couldn't afford not to secure. This situation in Asmere simply had her intrigued. She knew there was something more from the Akande end. It was her gut that told her there was more under the surface on the Princess Zsa Zsa end. Now there was another piece to the puzzle. Prince Raheem. The further she dug, the more disturbing the information became. It had to be handled delicately or a family would be destroyed. Diplomacy was needed in this situation. Joshua was not the person for this. She called the best diplomat she knew.

"Hi Aunt Tracy, is Uncle JD, around?"

"Yes, he's here playing with Jazzy. You need to speak to him?"

"Yes, thank you."

"Monique."

"What's up, Unc?" she laughed.

"You have five minutes."

She loved to pull the hood talk on her Uncle and he loved it too. She could hear his smile through the telephone. "Okay, sorry, I had to do that."

"Everything okay?" JD asked.

"Have a situation, I need your advice."

"Shoot."

"Ouch, please don't say that."

"Tell me you were not involved in the Absolute situation."

"Can't tell you that."

"Were you hurt?"

"Just a little, but look Uncle JD, before you start with the, 'this game is too dangerous for me,' listen to my situation and give me your take, then you can fuss. Okay. Oh, and you have to promise not to tell Aunt Tracy. She will tell Daddy and that will not be good."

"All right. What's the situation?"

"How well do you know Prince LaVere'?"

"Pretty well. Why?"

"Is he a true patriot to his country?"

"From what I know of him, yes."

She exhaled. "Well, I've come across something and will need to meet in private with him. Is that something you can arrange? Like now."

"I'll make a telephone call."

"Uncle JD, no one else can know about this meeting." She heard her Aunt Tracy in the background. "No one."

"I'll make it happen."

Here she stood, a few hours later watching, waiting, and wondering. If this goes awry, it could blow up in her face. But she knew she was right. Her cell phone chimed.

"Day."

"You good?" Joshua's voice came through the line.

"I'm good."

"What did the doc say?"

"The human body wasn't meant to take bullets."

"Sounds like him. You need anything?"

She smiled. "You love me. I know it."

"No, I don't. I just don't want you bleeding all over my suit if we have to do this shit again tomorrow."

It was good to have him back. "How is Akande?"

"She's good. She's tougher than she looks."

"I believe that."

"Thanks for keeping her safe. Any idea how they picked up on you?"

"An idea. I'm checking it out now."

"Be careful."

"You too, you're the one with the target now."

"Moved to another location."

"Good move." She hesitated. "Hey, she worries. That means she cares about you. Just thought you should know that."

He didn't respond for a minute. "Not sure if it's right."

"Well, it's not good, that's for damn sure. But you know how to handle business. Handle it. Check you in the a.m." The call was disconnected.

She watched as the black sedan pulled up and entered the parking garage. There was no turning back now. The back door opened and Monique slid inside. She bent over and kissed her Uncle JD on the cheek. "I knew you couldn't resist." she smiled. "Hey Brian, Sammy."

"Hey, Squirt," Brian Thompson, JD's body man, smiled through the rear view mirror.

"What the doc say about the arm?" Samuel asked.

"I'll live."

Then she turned to the man who had been invading her dreams for months now. "Prince LaVere', I'm pleased you could join us."

"I do not believe we have been formally introduced." He extended his hand. "LaVere' Ashro of Emure."

She hesitated for she knew before touching him, she was going to have a reaction. She placed her hand in his, and a warmth so delicious sped through. "Monique Day."

His hand closed around hers. "Ms. Day, it is a pleasure to meet you." He sat back and released her hand. "How may I be of service to you?"

***

Joshua sat at the window of the hotel room, where Akande was asleep. From the window he saw the activity below, but it did not register with him. People were going about their business, living their lives. One day he wanted to be like them. He wanted what Samuel and his sister Diamond now had: a loving family. He knew it was a long shot, but he believed he could have that life with Akande. Once this situation was over, she would have no reason to return to Asmere. The truth was, her aunt would kill her the moment she sat foot on Asmere soil. Her mission would be complete and her aunt would no longer have any use for her. The same question still gnawed at him, why Akande? Why was the Queen insistent that Akande carry out this mission? He did not have an answer to that question. Right now, he had to make a decision.

He pulled up his bible on his phone. As always he read The Book of Joshua, all verses in Chapter 1. His interpretation always came out the same. He believed

God knew Joshua's heart. He knew Joshua had a strong, righteous heart. God knew Joshua had the potential to lead, but just did not believe in himself. That's why he spoke to Joshua.

When he finished reading, he closed down the bible on his phone. He reached under his shirt for the cross his mother had given him years ago. He closed his eyes and prayed that he was making the right decision. This was one time he had to push past the fear of losing. He had to put everything on the line and let God lead him.

He pushed a button on his phone.

"It's about time you touched base. When did you get back?"

Joshua smiled at the image of his housekeeper Lucy. "Late last night." He smiled when he heard his dog Commando bark and run up to the monitor. "Hey boy. I miss you, too."

"You don't look good. What's wrong?"

Lucy had a way of picking up on his moods. She was ex-CIA with I.T. skills any company would kill for. She ran his command center from his home. It's his system and he had limited access, however, no one including him, entered Lucy's cave without permission.

"I need you to put something in motion for me." He explained what he wanted done and why.

"Are you sure you want to do this?"

"Yes, I'm sure."

"Then why do I sense some hesitation?" Lucy asked. "This is not something you do out of duty. These aren't the days of long ago when you were forced to take responsibility for your actions. There are other choices."

"I'm not being forced to do anything. This is the right thing to do."

"And, your career? Are you giving it up?"

"No, just adjusting."

Lucy stared at him through the monitor for a long while, and casually shrugged her shoulders. "I'll handle it."

Chapter Eighteen

The call Joshua was waiting for came through. A meeting had been setup with Senator Davenport and the Secretary of Defense at the Pentagon. He looked over at Akande who was sleeping next to him. Each day she pulled at another part of him. This morning it was especially hard leaving her.

He reached over and pulled her sleeping body into his arms. "Sleepy head, I need you to wake up." He took her bottom lip between his and sucked on it until she came awake.

"That is not the proper way to wake someone in the morning." She smiled up at him.

This was what he wanted to remember, her smile, her eyes sparkling. The way her body felt next to his. He prayed this would not be the last time.

An hour later he was at the Pentagon meeting with the Secretary of Defense and Senator Davenport.

"I received a call from Governor Harrison requesting I share what information I could," Senator Davenport started. "The problem was, until now I was under orders to withhold this information. Once you receive it you will understand why."

"You stumbled into a delicate operation when you went to Emure," The Secretary stated. "King Aswan and his brothers will be here today to address the issue of the attack by Emure's troops."

"As for the issue at hand, the United States knows King Tochi had a child. We believe that child, who is the rightful leader of Asmere, is alive and under Tarik's control. Once the rightful leader is put in place we will again, open commerce with Asmere."

"This all occurred over twenty years ago. The child would now be of legal age. If this person is under Tarik's control why wouldn't he present them?"

"That is the very question that gives us the belief that one day Asmere can be an ally rather than an enemy. Tarik may have the true leader, but has not been successful in corrupting them. He's giving the country and their people hope."

"Why now? It's been twenty years. Why the urgency now to have the sanctions lifted?"

Royce looked at the Secretary of Defense. A slight nod was given. Royce sat forward, then turned back to Joshua. "It's not about the sanctions. We believe Tarik has used what funds the country was able to secure to build an army. It is not a formidable army according to our stats, however, against a small country, such as Emure, this army could be successful. Some believe since King Ahmed stepped down, Emure is in a weakened state. While King Aswan is holding his own, he has empowered the people more, giving them more freedom towards establishing a democracy. As with any democracy, there will be factions, who do not necessarily agree with their leadership. To keep this under control, you will need a strong leader, who would bring down the abusers of this freedom with a clear, decisive message, dissuading others from following suit. King Aswan has not done this. He believes in diplomacy rather than force."

"Why would Tarik chance attacking a country we have a relationship with? He has to know we would aide Emure in this war? What is in Emure for him to consider such an attack? Oil?"

"No." Royce pushed a button on the table. The monitor showed pictures of military personnel and workers excavating the area. "When Emure began its quest to eliminate the class system of its country, they allowed citizens to expand into the countryside. One such expansion took place on the far Northwest region of the country. Many stayed away from this area for years because of its proximity to Asmere and Tarik's reign. Emure's military forces were preparing the region for possible settlement, when they came across this." He pushed another button and the monitor filled with pictures of diamonds.

Joshua sat forward.

"Uncut diamonds. Some of the clearest we have ever seen." Royce stated. "The find lines the border of Emure for miles. The area is about to become one of the richest in the region."

"Tarik wants a part of that," Joshua stated.

"Yes," Royce acknowledged. "Whoever controls Asmere, will share in the wealth."

"Tarik doesn't share. He wants it all."

"Affirmative."

"This Senator, who they want taken out, has some type of proof that Tarik is not the true leader of Asmere. They want this proof destroyed so they may have control over this vast fortune that has been discovered near their borders." Joshua shook his head. "All of this is based on greed."

"You stumbled on a highly volatile situation. If Tarik is successful in his bid to take over Emure, there will be a shift in power in the region that the United States cannot afford."

"There is another problem," the Secretary of Defense stated. "The discovery of the mines has not been publicized. Only the highest ranking officers and certain members of the royal family of Emure know of this. Someone in that group is working with Tarik."

The conversation he had with Zsa Zsa when this all began came to mind.

"There is still the task of determining who the solider was King Tochi befriended. It is conceivable that solider was given the information. That folder in the Asmere file needs to be opened. We need to find that solider." He held the Senator's stare as he waited for the response.

The Secretary of Defense slid a file his way. Joshua opened the file and began to read. He looked at the pictures, then at Senator Davenport. "You are the target?" Royce nodded. Joshua looked back down and continued to read. When he came to the end, there were more pictures in the back of the folder. There were pictures of King Tochi and Queen Maya. Then there was a picture of a woman with King Tochi with a child. The woman was not Maya. He held the picture up. He suppressed a groan. "Who is this?"

Royce smiled. "LaSheera Abdulrazaaq. She was King Tochi's lover and the mother of his only child.

Joshua threw the picture on the table and watched when Royce stopped it with his hand. "Tell me the story."

Royce frowned at the angry tone Joshua had taken. However, he respected the man enough to know he had a reason for the question. "Tochi was educated here, in the United States. We met at Howard University and became friends. When he returned home he married Queen Maya. As with most in that region, it was an arranged marriage. Tochi understood and accepted his responsibilities. As it turned out Maya could not bear children. Marriages in that region are different than here. The husbands are allowed to have other wives or concubines. Tochi turned to the daughter of one of his trusted servants, LaSheera Abdulrazaaq. As you can see, she was quite beautiful. Believe it or not, she was more beautiful on the inside. Tochi fell in love with her. When I went to visit him that last time, I met her and I believe she stole a piece of my heart as well. She was a very proud woman and fearless to a fault. Tochi warned that that pride of hers would get her killed one day. As it turned out, he was correct. Before I left, Tochi confided in me that he believed his brother was conspiring to take his throne. He gave me that picture of them and their child. We had the child finger printed and DNA tested to prove parentage. All of that information was filed and sealed to protect the child's identity." Royce tilted his head as he looked at Joshua. "You are under the impression that I was the child's father. Why?"

Joshua pulled out his handheld device, hit a few buttons then stared at the screen. He hesitated, but knew what he had to do.

"Gentlemen, meet Akande Ariana Aubree, better known to you as Sofiat Abdulrazaaq. The true Queen of Asmere."

Senator Davenport picked up the device, looked at the picture of a sleeping Akande and could not believe his eyes. He looked up at Joshua, then back at the picture. "Where has she been all this time? We searched Asmere and beyond."

"If what I think happened, she's been in the basement of the palace in Asmere. Joshua stood, his nerves would not allow him to sit any longer. "It all makes sense now." He looked at the Senator. "They don't care about the sanctions. They want to destroy any proof of her existence and anyone who knew of the proof. That's why they want you and Akande together in one place. They brainwashed her into believing you're her father. She was told you dishonored her mother during one of your visits to Asmere. When you were told her mother was with child you disowned the child, then convinced the powers to be in the United States that the leaders of Asmere were corrupted in some way." He picked up the device. "She has been an assassin in training for fifteen years. Like you, they could not find her for years. Once they did, they began to plot this revenge against you. Now that the diamond mines have been discovered, the timeframe to implement the plan changed. They don't care about sanctions. They want you and Akande in the same place to kill you which tells me one thing. You better beef up security. They are here."

Chapter Nineteen

The tea kettle whistled the moment she hung up the call from Royce. The situation he was working on was at a sensitive point. He had to stay in D.C. Shelly could not believe how this man had become such a part of her in just a week. But, he had. Royce Davenport had come in and rocked her world. One minute they would be sitting around talking world events and then the next minute he had her body feeling like it was in heaven.

Thinking of him, and the way he makes her feel, she decided against the tea. Instead she pulled out the bottle of wine Royce brought the last time he was there. She took a glass from the cabinet and filled it to the rim. She sat in the chair in the family room, pulled her feet up under her and stared at the sofa. They made out on the damn sofa like teenagers. She laughed out loud. As if on cue, her cell phone rang. She did not have to look at the caller ID to know it was Rocy calling. She picked it up from the table, laughing. "Hello, Rocy."

"Hello, Shelly. It's been a minute. How are things going?"

Shelly took a long drink of her wine, then sat the glass down. "I discovered something really important."

"What was that?"

"You know, I don't kiss and tell," she said sweetly. "But DAMN."

Rocy fell out laughing on the phone. "You gave up the cookies to Royce Davenport?"

Shelly held her arms out, animated with the story. "It just happened. It started the moment he walked in the door. I swear the heat in the house hit a hundred and fifty degrees before dinner was over. After dinner it was on. Everything came off."

Rocy was on the phone screaming as if she was there with them. "Okay, okay, okay, here's the question. Can he work it?"

Shelly laughed. "My body is still humming."

"From Tuesday? Damn, Shelly."

"Well, Tuesday, Wednesday, Thursday."

"Wait," Rocy paused. "Every night this week? He's coming again tonight?"

"No," she took a drink. "He asked me to come to his place in D.C. this weekend. I don't know if I can do that."

"Yes, you can," Rocy replied. "You deserve to have a man who knows how to make your body come alive. Just don't give the man a heart attack. Remember he is a little older than us."

Shelly took a drink of her wine. Calmer now, she resumed the conversation. "I think that's why we enjoyed last night so much. We are older. We knew what we wanted and there were no inhibitions on either part. He didn't hold back and neither did I." Shelly shook her head. "I have never experienced anything like this before."

"Enjoy it, Shelly. Make the most of whatever the Senator has to offer. Just be careful. I don't want you to get hurt."

She hesitated. She did have concerns about this relationship with Royce. She was a school teacher, he a politician. She liked him, more than liked him, but she just wasn't sure they were a good fit. "I told him I don't own pearls."

"I cannot believe you are letting something so trivial hold you back from a caring man." Rocy hesitated. "So what, we did not grow up with pearls like, Tammy Richardson. You are good people, Shelly. You are who you are. You can't change it and you shouldn't want to. I bet you Tammy is not getting her rocks off like you." The two laughed.

"You know Rocy, for the first time in my life, I just want to enjoy my sexuality. Royce seems to be at the same point. I'm not expecting anything from him. When this ends, it ends. For now, I'm going to enjoy the man and his body."

"Good for you, Shelly. Let me know how it goes. I'm living vicariously through you these days. Talk to you soon."

"Check you later, Rocy."

Shelly picked up her glass of wine, turned some Will Downing on the stereo, and went upstairs to run her a nice hot bath. Afterwards, she was going to pack an overnight bag and spend the weekend with Royce. To hell with the damn pearls.

**

Joshua appeared to be asleep when Akande came out of the shower. They had made love all afternoon. He looked so peaceful. Looking at his body, his back was so strong. She smiled at the way he even smiled in his sleep. Something buzzed. She looked around and saw his cell phone light was on. She didn't know much about cell phones, but it looked like a message was coming through. She gasped when she saw the name, Royce Davenport appear. He had contacted Senator Davenport. She sighed. He had kept his promise.

The reality of the moment sent chills up her spine. This would probably be the last time they would be together. Her mission was about to end. The mission driven Akande was about to re-emerge. The woman, Akande, wanted to hold him one last time. She took her robe off and laid her naked body on top of his. She just needed to feel his skin against hers.

Joshua did not move when she lay on his back. He could tell from the tears, flowing down his back she was battling with herself. Telling her what he knew would ease her fears. However, he was ordered not to reveal the information at this time. Senator Davenport was using his contacts to locate Tarik's people. They knew someone from Asmere was in the United States to destroy the information and kill Akande once her mission was complete. Before they set the trap, Joshua wanted to know where every player was on the chest board. He wanted to keep this woman in his life, now that it was a fact she was not the enemy. Very few things surprised him. When he pulled the picture from the file, and Akande's eyes looked back at him, the Senator could have stuffed him in an oven and called him done. For a second, only for a second, he thought not to reveal the discovery. Then he was angry. If the file had been released when it was first requested, this situation could have been solved before they left Asmere. If it had, then the cave would not have happened, and he would have never experienced the feelings he had for her. That was something he wasn't sure he would have changed. The time in the cave meant something to him. Hell, how many people get to play Adam and Eve? Now, all jokes aside, he could only pray when all was said and done, she would choose him over Asmere.

***

Royce had just hit send on his phone when Kathy buzzed his line indicating he had a visitor. He put the phone away and stood as JD walked into his office. "Governor," Royce extended his hand. "Always good to see you."

"Thank you for making the time, Senator." JD shook his hand then turned to LaVere. "Senator, I don't believe you have formally met Prince LaVere Ashro of Emure."

"No, we haven't met." Royce extended his hand. "Prince Ashro. Please have a seat."

LaVere shook his hand and took the offered seat.

JD began. "I'm here as an intermediary between Emure and the United States. We have a situation."

Royce knew this all too well, however, all parties had been sworn to secrecy until they could locate and contain the killers from Asmere. The statement confused him. "A situation?"

"Yes." JD shifted in his seat. "You are aware of the incident earlier today here, concerning Joshua Lassiter and a young woman from Asmere?"

Royce nodded. "I am."

"During that incident information was revealed concerning the kidnapping of Prince LaVere's sister, Princess Zsa Zsa. The information was investigated and we now have proof that a member of the royal family was involved. We also understand that the young woman rescued with the Princess was a ploy.

Her intent was to get to the United States to take your life."

"I am aware of that." Royce sat forward now intrigued with the information.

"The information given by this member of the royal family was a partial payment for the kidnapping. Another ten million dollars exchanged hands giving them financing needed to carry out your assassination. The person involved knows of the strong relationship between Prince LaVere and the Lassiter brothers. He also knew that Samuel and Joshua worked for the government. It was their intention that the kidnapping of a member of the royal family would bring one or two of the brothers to Emure. Which, it did. That brings us to the current situation." He turned to LaVere.

"Our family has no wish to cause you any harm or to be in disgrace with the United States by taking such action." LaVeré sat forward. "I am certain you are aware of the current partnership for protection of a certain parcel of land near the border of Emure and Asmere."

Royce agreed, "Yes, I am."

"For that reason and many others we wish to keep the good relations between your country and ours intact."

With a frown on his face Royce asked, "Do you know the reason for the traitorous act by your family member?"

"I do not." However, King Aswan has been notified of the situation. Once he arrives, it will be dealt with, swiftly.

Royce sat back, then glanced at JD. "It is your belief that they wanted the ransom to finance my assassination. I'm afraid it is much deeper than that. For your sake, he looked at LaVeré, I pray this family member was not aware of the true purpose of the ransom." Royce pulled a folder from his desk drawer. "I was working on this just before you came in." He put one of the pictures from the folder on the desk in front of LaVeré. He pointed to the picture. "This is Tarik only hours ago. This is the army he has financed from money gained from the kidnapping." He pulled out another picture. His plan is to attack the palace and take control of your country. I'm certain you know why."

"The diamond shafts."

JD looked at LaVeré. "Diamonds?"

"A strip of land between the borders of Asmere and Emure was recently excavated for a settlement during which time a substantial mine shaft of diamonds was discovered. No one other than members of the royal family and the United States knows of this."

"We have been protecting the area at Emure's request."

"This Tarik person is aware of this and is planning to take control of the area."

Royce shook his head. "The region. The discovery is so substantial that whoever controls it will control that region."

"Thus the U.S. intervention," JD nodded in understanding. "We do not want an unsavory leader with that much control in that region."

Royce sat back and sighed. "Greed never ceases to amaze me." He sat up with another question. "Something is still not clear. Why the attempt on Joshua and Akande's lives? They wanted her here to carry out the mission. Why try to kill her before that is done?"

"She saw the person at the Asmere palace." JD explained. "She recognized him at a hotel here in D.C.

The chase pursued and you know the outcome." JD shook his head. "I'm still not clear on why all the cloak and dagger? If they wanted to kill you, why send the girl? Why not a professional assassin or a member of their military?"

"That's where the plot gets a little deep." Royce stated. "We are speculating on some of this mind you, but here's what we believe. Akande has been brow whipped into believing it is her responsibility to restore her family's honor and stabilize the country for it was her mother and father, me, who brought this hardship on their country. Therefore, it was her duty to have the sanctions lifted and kill the man who dishonored her mother. The reason behind the plot was simple. They needed me to present the evidence given to me by King Tochi so it could be destroyed. Once the evidence was destroyed, then they could kill the only two people who could threaten their reign. The true leader and the person with the evidence, me."

"Why Akande?" LaVeré asked.

Royce smiled. "It has not been verified. But we believe Akande is King Tochi's daughter."

"The true ruler of Asmere." JD sat back as a smile began to form.

"Then why not kill the girl." LaVeré asked, still confused.

"We are told Queen Sermyera enjoys torture. We believe at first it was to torture her sister's child. I met her, years ago. She was very jealous of her sister. See, when King Tochi requested a daughter from his servant, Sermyera was the chosen one. The King discovered Sermyera wasn't pure and rejected her. He then turned to her sister LaSheera. King Tochi fell in love with LaSheera and loved the child even more. This only fueled Sermyera's jealousy."

"I remember when Tarik married Sermyera, many believed they conspired to kill King Tochi and his family." LaVeré added. "According to my father LaSheera escaped from the palace and hid the child."

"That is true. Her body was found outside the palace as was her father's." Royce acknowledged. "Tarik knew we were searching for the child and had been watching them closely. The girl never surfaced. How Sermyera found her, we don't know. Their fear was the United States would declare war if the body of the heir was ever discovered. They could not risk the child being discovered dead or alive, they would have been removed from the throne."

They both stopped talking and turned to the now quiet JD. "What are you thinking?" Royce asked.

JD stood. "Give me a minute." He walked over and stood in the middle of the office, put his hands in his pockets and just hung his head in thought. He sighed and looked up a minute later. "We may have a solution to stabilizing that region."

"I'm all ears," Royce said as LaVeré looked on.

"You may not like it, but the more I play it around in my head. It may be the perfect answer."

"Are you going to share your thoughts?" LaVeré asked.

"I'm thinking a merger between Emure and Asmere."

"We are enemies," LaVeré stated. "Have you not been listening for the last hour?"

JD walked back over and sat down. "You are enemies with Tarik and this Sermyera person. You are not enemies with the true Queen of Asmere."

Royce caught on. "A union would eliminate the threat in the area." He nodded in agreement. "It could work."

"What could work?" LaVeré frowned.

Both men stared at him.

Chapter Twenty

The train ride from Richmond to Union Station in D.C. was just the amount of time she needed to settle her nerves and prepare her mind mentally for the weekend. Naturally, she brought a romance novel to read on the way. The choice tonight, Deadly Sexy, by Beverly Jenkins. When Ms. Jenkins created that fine ass Reese Anthony, she out did herself. Shelly licked her lips just thinking about those black cherries. What better way to set the mood? She sat back crossed her legs, and began the story of the sexy truck driver.

An hour later, Shelly was humming as the taxi pulled up to the address Royce had given her. She was ready for what she was going to find behind that door. Walking through that door meant she was ready to accept the possibility of a permanent relationship with Royce. Her life would change, that was for sure. She was taking a chance accepting his offer. To her, Royce was worth whatever the consequences might be.

She put the key in the lock and turned it. Smiling as the door opened. Quickly she looked around for the alarm panel he told her about. "There it is," she smiled and walked towards it, but then it dawned on her, it hadn't gone off. *Hmm*, she thought, turned, took the handle of her little overnight bag and walked into what she supposed was the family room. Looking over her shoulder she was admiring the curving staircase, when she felt the impact of a cold metal object pressing against her head.

Maybe she wasn't ready for what was behind the door.

***

Monique hesitated at the door. After the angry words directed at her last night, she did not want to be the messenger again. Prince LaVeré eventually settled down once Uncle JD spoke to him, but for thirty minutes his wrath was directed at her. If it were any other man, she would have taken his ass out. From him, it hurt, deep. Now she had to tell Joshua who was trying to kill Akande. She took a deep breath. "He better not yell at me," she said, then opened the door.

"MacGyver? Really?"

Joshua looked over his shoulder. "Hey. Come join us while we watch a master at work." He was fully dressed in one of his signature suits, with Italian loafers. It was good to see the old Joshua back.

"I cannot believe a man as intelligent as yourself would look at such a show," Akande shook her head.

"What?" Joshua threw his hands up in the air. "MacGyver is the man."

"MacGyver don't have nothing on Jack Bauer." Monique waved him off, then picked up the remote.

Joshua nodded his head. "I'll give you that one. Bauer was the business. But MacGyver, he could blow up anything with a pen and a watch." He laughed, "That is talent."

"That is crap," Monique said as she turned the television off.

"Hey." Joshua pouted as he glared at her.

"We need to talk."

Akande stood. "I'll give you a few minutes."

"No, stay." Monique took a seat. "This concerns you."

Akande sat back down as Joshua sat forward. "What's up?"

Monique sat on the edge of the table. "Yesterday Akande recognized Prince Raheem Ashro. He was the man who met with her aunt in Asmere."

Joshua jumped up. "What?"

"Yes." Akande nodded. "He was there when I was taken to speak with my aunt."

"Prince Raheem? Are you sure?"

"Yes. I am certain."

"Why in the hell would he have his own sister kidnapped?"

"That we don't know." Monique stood. "I met with Prince LaVeré Ashro last night to verify information I found. The money trail was well hidden, but it led back to his brother. He also identified two of the men killed yesterday. The Prince is not happy, but he is convinced, Raheem is responsible for the kidnapping."

"His people were trying to kill us." Joshua was furious. "I rescued his sister and his people tried to kill me." He grabbed his device off the table. "I'm going to kill him with my bare hands."

Monique jumped up and grabbed him. "Not you. He wasn't trying to kill you. He was trying to kill Akande."

"It's one in the same." He looked at Akande. She deserved lazy mornings like this for the rest of her life. To have that, Tarik, Sermyera and Raheem had to die. He walked over, took her into his arms and kissed her long deep and passionately. He pulled away. "This has to end." He turned and walked out the door.

"Joshua, wait." Monique ran after him. She stopped at the door. "Stay here, Akande. Lock the door."

Akande did as she was told and then walked over to the window to see if Joshua would appear. A knock sounded at the door. She opened the door. "Did you catch..." A pinch in her neck and the world went black.

***

This was not what she had in mind for this weekend. A little bondage with role playing might have been interesting with Royce. However, it wasn't Royce standing next to her with a gun to her head. She put her hands up. "Okay, look. I don't live here. I have no idea where any valuables are, but I'm sure if you look around in some drawers, you'll find something."

"Where is Davenport?"

Screech. That was a female. Shelly turned to see a woman dressed in foreign clothes with a wrap around her head. There were two other men in the room, who looked to be of African descent.

"Answer her." The man next to her pushed her.

Shelly had a low tolerance for bullies. She was pushed around all through elementary school until her friend Rocy came along. Rocy showed her how to stand up for herself. She didn't know how to take a gun from an armed man, but she'd be damned if she was going to let him push her around. She raised her knee and with all the force she could gather kicked him in the balls.

"Argh," the man groaned as he fell to the floor.

The other men pulled their weapons and pointed them at her. She smirked at the man on the floor then looked up at the woman. "I don't know where he is, but I have a few choice words for him when he gets here. This isn't the way to treat a guest."

"Tie her up," the woman commanded. "We will wait for Akande to arrive."

Two men took her by the arms, dragged her into the dining room and sat her in one of the dining room chairs.

"Who are you?" Shelly asked as she frowned at the men.

The woman walked over and stood in front of her. "The person who will take your life if you do not do as I instruct."

The men tied her hands behind her back and her feet. "Somebody died and left you Queen for the day?"

A chilling laugh came from the woman. "Not yet, but they will soon." She took a seat. "We shall wait."

"And once this Akande person gets here, then what? I'm only asking because I had plans for the weekend."

"After you do what I ask, I will probably kill you anyway."

Shelly shook her head. "That doesn't really give me an incentive to cooperate."

***

Monique reached Joshua in the parking deck of the hotel. "Joshua." she ran to him and stood in front of his SUV. "Listen to me. I know you want to kill Raheem right now. But, think, is it the smart move?"

"Get the hell out of my way Monique."

"I can't because you are thinking with your dick and not your mind. You are too emotionally involved in this woman to think clearly. Raheem is no longer a threat to Akande. King Aswan has him in custody. The threat now is the contingency from Asmere. Locating them should be your priority. You will have your chance to confront Raheem. Just not now." Now that she had his attention, she exhaled. "You told me never to allow emotions to rule my actions." She shrugged her shoulders. "What are you doing?" She shook her head. "This thing is almost over. We know all the players. Don't lose it now."

She was right and Joshua knew it. He had let his anger interfere with the job. He slammed his fist on top of his vehicle then looked up at her. "They whipped her. Did you know that?"

Monique shook her head. "No. I didn't know that," she replied sympathetically.

"They brainwashed her, kept her in a basement and beat her into submission."

"People are cruel, Joshua. That's why the government hires people like us, to balance things."

He hung his head, then looked up at her. "You are learning well." He walked towards her.

"I have a good trainer." she smiled. "Let's go back up to Akande. She's probably looking out the window for you."

"I'm keeping her," Joshua said as they walked towards the elevator.

Monique laughed. "Does she have a say in that decision?"

"I'll let her think she does by asking. How's that?" he said as they entered the elevator.

"Think about what you are saying. Are you ready to give up the life?"

His cell phone rang. "Lassiter," he answered as he glared at Monique. "Slow down Davenport." Joshua jerked away from the elevator wall. "What? Which hotel?" He ran to the room as soon as the elevator door opened. "No."

Monique heard his gut wrenching yell before she reached the door. He had the look of a tortured man as he raced through the rooms. Monique pulled out her cell. "Ned, we need security tape on the hotel now."

"What's happened?"

"They snatched Akande."

Joshua walked from the back with his trench coat and did not say a word. She followed him out. "Send the footage to my device. Track their direction."

"Done. Have it to you in five."

***

A door in the back of the room opened and two more men carrying a woman walked in. They sat the woman in a chair next to her then tied her up as well. *The woman was asleep,* she thought. Shelly looked at the woman sitting across from her. "Akande, I presume."

The woman ignored Shelly and stood. "Wake her," she commanded.

One of the men who'd brought the woman in, pulled a syringe from his pocket, flipped the cap, then pushed the needle into the woman's arm. A few seconds later Shelly heard the woman moan. The woman who Shelly determined was the leader of this little troop stood, walked over to the young woman and smacked her across the face.

"Hey!" Shelly yelled. "Why did you do that?"

"You dare to question me? You American."

"You say that as if it's something dirty. Yes, I'm an American and damn proud of it, if for no other reason than it will be my American justice system that will crucify your ass when they catch you."

The woman raised her hand and backhanded Shelly so hard she almost tilted the chair over. "You Americans need to learn your place. You will lower your eyes when you speak to me."

"Oh, man." Shelly shook from the pain in her jaw. She shook her head back and forth, then licked her lips. "When I get free, oh, it's going to be on."

The woman was about to strike Shelly again when Akande's weak voice called out. "My Queen."

Sermyera, turned to her niece and snarled. "You had one mission in this life. That was to lead us to Davenport. He alone, holds the key to Tarik's future as the leader of Asmere. You have had days, yet you have not made contact with the Senator. Your purpose has ended."

"There is much I do not understand, my Queen." Akande looked around to glance at the woman sitting next to her. She did not know the woman, but had to do what she could to keep Sermyera's attention on her. Her focus returned to Sermyera. "Before you take my life, explain to me, why."

"It is no longer important." Sermyera smirked. "Once you are gone and I have what I need from Davenport, everything will be as it should." She nodded to one of the men, who pointed his weapon at Akande.

"Look," Shelly interjected trying to pull the woman's wrath. "I don't know you, don't want to at this point, but the Senator will not negotiate with you. He has no reason to."

Sermyera tilted her head and smiled at the other woman. "Of course he will. I have you, Mrs. Davenport."

Shelly laughed out loud, then laughed harder. The woman looked at the two men who were standing guard at the door. "Whew." Shelly sighed. "That was funny." She looked up at the woman and the man standing next to her with his weapon pointed at Akande. "Do you see any pearls around my neck? I'm not Mrs. Davenport."

The woman's head turned angrily to the man next to her. "What is the meaning of this? Is this not Davenport's wife?"

"She bedded him on several occasions. I assumed she was the wife."

"How do you know I bedded him?" Shelly sputtered. "I mean I did, and he is damn good. But how do you know?"

"We have been following him for months now," the man replied.

"You've been in my house?" Shelly asked angrily.

A hand came down hard across her face. "Silence," Sermyera growled. "Is she or is she not the wife? Without the wife, we have no leverage over Davenport."

"Woman, I swear you are asking for it." Shelly, groaned. "Look, I don't know what your game is here. I don't know why you want to kill this young woman. But if you are holding me to get something from Royce, you're barking up the wrong tree." She looked at Akande, then back at the woman she referred to as her Queen. "You may want to keep her alive."

Sermyera screamed furiously at her guard. "Is this Davenport's woman?"

The man nodded. "Yes, he cares for this woman. I have seen them together."

Sermyera turned narrow hate filled eyes back to Shelly. "You will call him."

"I will not." Shelly had the nerve to smile. "You people need to learn how to use the word please. I am not one of your subjects you can just command. You are not my Queen." Sermyera raised her hand. "Hit me one...more time and it will be the last thing you do."

Something in Shelly's look stopped the woman. "Go through her purse. Get her cell phone." She held Shelly's defiant glare. "You will call him or I will order Tobyn to kill Akande."

One man pointed a gun to the young woman's head. "I take it you are Tobyn." Shelly sighed. Another man emptied the contents of her purse on the table, pulled out her cell phone and placed it on the table next to her. Shelly just looked up at him. "What do you expect me to do with that Sherlock, my hands are tied?"

"It is going to give me much pleasure to kill you." Sermyera nodded to the man. He picked up the phone, searched through it and found the number for Royce Davenport. He pushed the button then put the phone to her ear.

Royce's voice came through the line. "Hello, beautiful."

Shelly almost cried when she heard his voice. He sounded tired, strained. "I'm here, at your house to surprise you. Imagine me throwing my hands up. Surprise."

"You're here, in D.C.?" She could hear the happiness in his voice. She closed her eyes. She would really rather die than set this trap for him. She swallowed hard, not knowing what would happen in the next minute. "You have visitors with guns," she said quickly. The man hit her with the butt of the gun breaking her nose on impact. Shelly screamed.

"Sermyera picked up the phone. "Good evening, Senator Davenport. It has been a while."

He recognized the accent and assumed it was the person they had just discovered was staying at the same hotel as Joshua. "Sermyera."

"You have one hour to bring me what I need or your woman and Akande will die." She hung up the telephone.

Akande had to find a way to keep the woman alive. She had nothing to do with the situation. She had to keep Sermyera's attention on her. She prayed Joshua or Monique knew she was missing.

"Please do not antagonize them more. They will kill you," Akande said to the woman.

"They are going to kill us anyway," Shelly replied with blood running from her nose.

"I will do what I can to keep them from killing you."

"The Senator will be here soon," Sermyera stated, interrupting their brief conversation.

"What does my father have that you would kill for?"

"He is not your father," Sermyera shrieked and laughed sarcastically. "You are truly your mother's daughter. You are as gullible as she was before I killed her."

"What?" A shocked Akande murmured, forgetting about the woman. "What do you mean, he's not my father?" Her voice began to rise. "You told me he was. Raised me to hate him because of what he did to our family. You told me our grandfather killed my mother because she allowed the American to have his way with her. You told me this all my life." She pulled at her restraints as she yelled at her aunt. Tobyn pressed the gun against her temple.

Sermyera, pulled his arm away. "No. She wants to know the truth." The woman's smirk was menacing. "Royce Davenport is not your father," she hesitated with a smirk. "Your father is King Tochi of Asmere, my dear niece. My sister had his only child." She smirked. "That's right, enjoy this moment. You are

Queen Sofiat Abdulrazaaq of Asmere. Well, at least for the next few minutes."

Sermyera laughed, as she returned to the chair and sat. "You see King Tochi befriended the American Davenport while in college. The fool believed he could trust the man with everything," she snarled. "Upon his return to Asmere he was forced to marry Queen Maya. She could not bear him any children. Therefore, he was allowed to step outside the marriage. I was the King's choice. Me!" She screamed. "My father, you see, had other plans. Somehow he found out about Tarik, the King's brother and I. He knew I was not pure and the King would doubt his bloodline. He then decided to place your mother, LaSheera before him instead of me. Like a fool Tochi fell in love with her. My sister and her damn innocence, won him over. Soon she was with child. All was kept secret only a few trusted servants in the palace knew. Even that Queen Maya liked LaSheera." She frowned with hatred for her sister clearly etched on her face. "It was an insult to me to watch her carry the heir to the throne. Yes, a true insult. It should have been me. However," her menacing smile appeared again, "My love, Tarik and I planned to make all of them pay. Tarik and his men took over the palace and killed them all. But not before your mother escaped with you. We searched and searched, but were unable to locate you. Tarik declared there was no heir, leaving him next in line to be King. Because of Davenport, the United States refused to accept him as the rightful leader of Asmere and placed sanctions against our country. It was then we learned of Tochi giving the proof to the American from one of the servants. For years he continuously protested the right of Tarik to sit on the throne. He always had the threat of exposing us with the documents about you. Once we discovered where you

were, we killed the woman your mother chose to keep
you safe and took you. We knew we could never tell
you the truth of your birth. Davenport would not stop
looking for you, nor with his relentless declarations
about Tarik not being the rightful holder of the
throne. Tarik thought to kill you and be done with it,
but I could not bring myself to do it. I knew that
Davenport would somehow find your body and take
the throne away. For he was determined to avenge his
friend's death As Davenport's popularity strengthened
we feared him more." She smiled at her own cunning.
"What better way to get the information then to use
the child Davenport has been searching for. Once he
saw you, I knew he would recognize you to be
LaSheera's daughter, for you are the very image of
her. Davenport would do all within his power to
convince you of your true heritage. He would present
you with the proof. Once the two of you were together,
we could kill you both and destroy the proof. It was a
good plan, was it not?" She released a wicked laugh.
"Now Asmere and all that she has to offer will be
ours."

Akande's world had just been turned upside down.
"Asmere is poor. It has nothing to offer." Akande
blatantly corrected her aunt.

"It will not be for long. That is the glorious part of
the entire story. Asmere will prosper again."

"It will never prosper as long as evil rules. You and
Tarik will never be the true rulers of Asmere. Never."

Sermyera moved quickly. "Tarik is Asmere," She
slapped Akande across the face.

The anger was so deep that Akande did not feel the
assault from her aunt. The hurt and anger of her
words had already killed her. All she could do at this
point was give Joshua the time to find them. How, she
did not know, but she did trust that he would.

"It was all a strategic move." She smiled down at Akande. "You have to admit, the plan worked perfectly." She sighed happily at her antics, then spread her arms out. "Here we are." The men snickered with her. "As the Americans would say, you were played."

"Your hand must really be killing you. You slap her, you slap me. What do you do all day, go around slapping people?" The woman turned to her. "I mean, really. You have to be sorely disappointed for you went through all of that for nothing." Shelly shook her head. "Senator Davenport will never let you walk out of here alive."

Sermyera sneered at Shelly. "You have balls for a woman. I like that. But in my country you would die for speaking to me in such an insolent manner."

"Then it's a good thing we are not in your country. For this would certainly get me killed." She kicked out, knocking Sermyera's feet from under her. Akande, kicked out at the same moment, knocking the man in front of her to the floor. Before they could do more damage, the third man was at them with his gun pointed directly at Akande's head.

Sermyera stood slowly. "You are right. You will die first."

"I wonder," Akande spoke urgently, "Why isn't Tarik here?" She waited for Sermyera to turn towards her. "Why did he not come to claim the document?"

"He has a country to run, you fool."

Shrugging her shoulders, "If it were me, and my country was at stake, I would have come, if for no other reason than to ensure the death of my enemy. That's what I did. I came here to kill the man who you claimed to be my enemy. Could it be he knows this was a fool's mission and chose to send you instead?"

"Are you trying to get me to kill you now by infuriating me with your words?"

"You might as well kill me for I have lost the desire to harm Senator Davenport and have nothing more to live for."

"Akande, you are wrong," Shelly spoke. "If what she says is true, you now have a country that is going to need you to lift the cloud from these monsters." She glared at Sermyera. "Please be sure to invite me to the execution."

Sermyera smirked. "I tire of this foolishness. Kill the woman."

***

Parked in a black SUV two houses down from Senator Davenport's townhouse, Monique turned to Joshua. "How do you want to handle this?" He had not said a word since leaving the hotel. Her only indication that his mind was on the situation was him studying his handheld. Sitting there she could still feel the anger radiating from him each time he changed the screen.

The device indicated there were seven people in the room. One he was certain was Akande. From his position he could see two men near the door, one standing behind Sermyera then another next to Akande with a gun pointed to her head. There was another woman tied up who had not been identified yet. Joshua signaled to Monique."We are going to enter here." He pointed to a basement window. "At the top of the steps you go left, I'll go right. There are three sitting. I believe the one sitting here with a larger body mass behind them is Sermyera," he growled at her. "She is mine. One of these is Akande. Until we have eyes in that room, we will not know for sure. The other person in there is an unknown. We will make that call once we are inside."

"Joshua." Monique pointed. "Two heat sources are on the move.

They looked up to see two men walk out of Davenport's house. "They are setting up a perimeter. Just means they will die first."

"Will we question them first?"

"In the movies, the bad guy always get a jump on the good guys when we waste time asking questions. Kill them, then figure out why. You'll live longer." Joshua put the silencer on his gun, got out of the SUV, raised his gun and fired twice in quick succession. Both men dropped to the ground. Neither one had an opportunity to pull their weapons.

Monique had barely made it out of the vehicle as she watched the back of his coat flapping from the slight breeze. He pulled one man by the leg and threw his body behind the hedges. If the bullet had not killed him, his body slamming against the brick house would have from the impact. He picked up the other man and threw him so that he lay in a pile with his partner. He looked over at her.

"You coming?" he asked, then walked to the back of the house.

She grinned. "Hell, yeah. I want to see a master at work."

"Let's go."

At the small basement window, Joshua used his device to determine if any security feature was activated. There wasn't. From his coat he pulled out a flat round item. He pushed a button and it inflated into a small suction cup. He stuck it to the window then checked to ensure it was secure. He then pulled out his laser, pointed it, and seared through the outside of the rectangular shaped glass. He put the laser away, bent down and pulled the glass out then laid it to the side. Monique slipped in first. She winced from the pain in her left arm, but landed firmly on the carpeted floor of the basement, pulling her weapon to secure the area. Joshua followed doing the same. They walked the lower level ensuring the area was clear. They did not want anyone walking up behind them. They followed the plan, easily reaching the main level of the home. Monique went to the left, Joshua forged straight ahead.

The men were unprepared. Their weapons were down, not raised and ready to fire. That had proven to be a fatal mistake. Two head shots and both were down before a weapon was fired. He hit the floor and rolled as the man standing near the window fired once, then went silent. Joshua pointed his weapon at Sermyera, who was now standing with her hands on Akande's shoulder and a knife to her throat.

"Ahh, you must be this Absolute I have heard about," Sermyera taunted. "Well, do you think your bullet can reach me before I slit her throat?" The menacing laugh filled the room.

"The only thing keeping you alive is your niece. All she has to do is blink her eyes one time and I will put a pretty red mark right between your eyes."

"I don't think..."

The bullet hit her right between her eyes so fast her body had not registered she was dead. Monique grabbed the knife from the women's hand before she hit the floor.

"You don't waste much time talking, do you? Shelly asked, with blood streaming down her face.

Joshua stood there, grinning at Akande as Monique cut her loose. "You blinked four times."

"I wanted to be certain you received the message." She ran into his arms the moment she was free.

Monique was cutting the other woman loose when they heard a sound behind them. She jumped in front of the woman and Joshua pushed Akande behind him. They both pulled their weapons ready to fire.

"Hold up. Don't shoot!" Shelly yelled, then ran towards the man. "This one is mine."

They lowered their weapons when they recognized Royce coming from the back. He lowered his weapon just as Shelly flung herself into his arms.

"Senator, tell me you did not come here alone." Monique sighed.

Before he could reply, his front door was kicked in. "Secret service. Everybody on the floor."

Monique and Joshua groaned. "Late as usual."

Shelly looked up at Royce. "Surprise," she threw her arms up in the air. "I don't think we will be eating in the dining room tonight, dear."

They all looked around and laughed. Bodies were everywhere.

Royce kissed her. "This isn't what I had in mind for the weekend."

"Not my idea of a good time." Shelly smiled, with blood dripping from her nose. "I must say it was interesting."

Royce kissed the tip of her nose.

"Ouch."

He frowned. "Let's get that nose looked at." He stopped and looked at Joshua, then at the woman in his arms. "Akande." He smiled. "They were right to keep you hidden. You are the spitting image of your mother." He exhaled. "I am not your father."

Akande took a step towards the man she had hated most of her life. Now, she did not know what to think or believe. "I was told many things, that I now know are false. While I have no desire to harm him you, I do not know who to trust or believe." She looked at

Joshua, then back to Royce. "Joshua believes you to be a good man, an honorable man. Then I will believe it as well, for I trust him. You have this proof my aunt so desperately wanted to destroy?"

"I do," Royce replied.

"Then we must confirm the information before we go any further."

"I will have Secret Service escort you back to your hotel."

"We'll take care of that." Joshua took Akande's hand, then looked over his shoulder at Monique. "Let's get out of here."

Monique looked at the Secret Service agents. "You guys can clean this up, right?" She grinned then followed Joshua and the Senator out of the room.

Chapter Twenty-one

The tension in the room was thicker than a dense fog on a stormy night. No one knew how this confrontation was going to end up. While all in the room believed a viable solution was on the table, it was anyone's guess if the guilty party would accept or reject the offer.

Monique watched as Prince LaVeré stood at the window with his back to the others essentially blocking everyone from his thoughts. She could feel the anger radiating from him. As he said, to him, the offer was rewarding treason. The alternative was far worse. His family would be ripped apart if the information went public. His mother and father would be devastated and his sister, well, it's unclear how all of this would finally impact her. However, it was his brother, King Aswan who would have the most difficult task. He would have to order the punishment for treason, death, against his own brother. Monique did not envy what LaVere' would have to endure in the next hour. If it were at all in her power, she would take the pain for him by simply putting a bullet in his brother Raheem's head.

A knock at the door prompted Monique into action. She pulled her weapon before opening the door. Taking the note from security, she glanced at it, thanked the gentleman and proceeded to close the door. She walked over to where Prince LaVeré stood. "Senator Davenport and Governor Harrison are on their way up. Would you like to talk a minute before they arrive?"

LaVeré turned to her. His facial expression was unreadable. "I believe all has been said Ms. Day," He looked at her arm in the sling. "Men trained under my tutelage caused you harm. For that please accept my apology on behalf of my country."

The sincerity in his eyes sent shivers through her. She looked away. "It will heal."

"I'm certain the flesh will heal. But there are the underlying wounds that do not reach the surface."

"Are we talking about me, or your sister?"

A feeling of sadness came over him. His features became unreadable, but the anger and concern were clear. "I cannot trust my brother to make wise decisions. I love them, both of them however, their concern is for country first. I made the mistake once of putting my country before my happiness and that of someone I once cared about. I know now that was a foolish move. Now, I must put Zsa Zsa's future and safety before all else. It is going to be difficult to convince my parents to allow her to move to the United States with me, without disclosing my reasons why. I must try. For Zsa Zsa is innocent in all of this. I cannot allow her to be used as a pawn again." He looked up at Monique. "Do you agree with my assessment?"

"I'm not certain I'm qualified to answer that question," Monique replied. "It's a family matter."

He held her eyes with his. "I see wisdom in your eyes. Wisdom that is much deeper than your years reflect. You know the situation. I seek your advice."

"You really want to know what I think?"

"I do."

"If it was up to me, your brother would be dead. I don't know the reasons for his actions. But, as my father says, blood is blood. He would never have done anything to put his sister's life in danger. Blood is supposed to protect blood."

LaVere' stared at the young woman. She was as beautiful as he thought the first night they met. She was young, but wise. "Your father should be very proud of you. I'm not certain I would allow a daughter of mine to be in your line of business."

"Allow?" Monique raised an eyebrow. "Prince LaVere' we are in the United States of America. You...do not allow. I do and you accept."

LaVere' braced his legs apart and stood with his arms folded across his chest. She reminded him of Cynthia Thornton with her feisty ways and smart mouth. The fact that she was standing there daring him with her eyes, to disagree almost made him smile. "I think your father may have given you too much liberty. An attitude such as yours could lead to trouble."

"My middle name is trouble." Monique smirked. "You should know, there's good trouble, and there's better trouble. It doesn't necessarily have to be bad."

He took a step towards her. "Trouble is trouble; I don't care how you look at it."

Monique didn't cower at his menacing stance. "Some men find trouble enticing."

A knock sounded at the door. Neither one moved as they stood a breath away from each other. The knock sounded again.

"I think you need to get that," LaVere' stated as he stared at the woman who barely reached his chin.

Monique grinned. "Trouble is a dangerous game, Prince LaVere'. Don't start a game you can't finish." She walked by him towards the door.

"LaVere'."

She stopped to look over her shoulder at him.

"My name is LaVere' and there are few games I am not a champion of, Ms. Day."

She began walking towards the door again. "Monique is the name. Your play."

She swung it open. JD, Royce and Samuel entered the room.

Monique hugged her uncle. "Hello, Uncle JD," she kissed him on the cheek. "I'll be outside."

"No, you should stay," LaVeré stated.

Monique looked around the room. No one seemed to have objections. She nodded, then stepped back near the door. "Very well."

"The President has signed off on the agreement," Royce stated. "With stipulations."

LaVeré nodded. "Understood. King Aswan will be advised."

"Until the new leadership demonstrates they have Asmere's best interests at heart, certain sanctions will remain in place," JD added. "If there is any sign of unrest, the United States will consider it an act of war and we will respond accordingly."

LaVeré looked up at JD. "I cannot believe our countries have come to this."

"Your brother's actions have put Emure in a difficult position," Senator Davenport stated. "It has blemished the reputation of the royal family."

"You have not gained the agreement of all parties. This deal is null and void without it." Samuel added, clearly angry about the situation.

"The alternative is to leave the new ruler and the country unprotected for any of Tarik' s men to take over," Senator Davenport stated. "Which would you prefer?"

"People are going to be hurt," Samuel replied.

"One broken heart for the stability of a country," LaVeré countered.

"Two," Samuel corrected. "Two broken hearts."

"As you said, Samuel," JD added, "All of this is null and void if both parties do not agree."

LaVeré stood. "I will present this to my King. We will have a response within an hour." He looked at Monique, "Is everyone in place?"

She nodded. "Yes, Your Highness."

He nodded then left the room.

***

Akande had been moved to a lavish suite with Secret Service agents surrounding the entire wing of the hotel. The DNA testing had proved that she was indeed Sofiat Abdulrazaaq, Queen of Asmere.

"Your Highness, you almost look as good as me." Joshua grinned at the woman dressed in a royal blue top and skirt set, with gold trim and long dangling earrings, that made her face sparkle.

She turned in her new outfit, giving him a full view. Her smile was so alive when she turned back to face him, he had to kiss her one more time before they left for the meeting with the President.

Seeing the intent in his eyes, she opened her arms wide to him and welcomed his loving embrace. His lips scorched hers as their tongues tangled freely, without fear, of danger or death between them. It tasted of the life to come, free to love each other. His cell phone rang.

"Argh," he growled as his lips left hers, then kissed her neck. "Hold that thought." he smiled at her displaying those tempting dimples. "Lassiter," he said into the phone as Akande dipped her tongue inside one.

"We're ready." He closed the phone and held out his hand. "Your Highness, the President of the United States awaits. Shall we go?"

"By all means," Akande took his arm. "The sooner we go, the sooner we may return."

"My thoughts exactly; there's something we desperately need to discuss."

She looked sideways at him. "You have something up your sleeve, Joshua. That's the same look you had before you threw me in the river."

He opened the door. "I did not throw you in the river. We jumped in together."

There was something in the way he said together that made her tingle.

Secret Service agents surrounded the two and escorted them to the White House.

They were shown into the Roosevelt Room where Senator Davenport and Samuel were seated.

"Your Highness," Senator Davenport bowed his head, as did Samuel.

"Please, you were once my father. Akande will suffice. Hello again, Samuel."

"Your Highness."

"Sammy." Joshua held his arms out to his brother and hugged him. "I'm glad you are here."

Samuel had never seen his brother like this and it killed him to know it could end within the hour.

"Mr. Lassiter," one of the Secret Service agents called out. "The President would like a word with you."

Joshua started to remove his trench coat, but then remembered the small box he'd received from Lucy inside and decided against it. He kissed Akande. "I'll be right back."

"Don't forget me, Joshua."

"How can I," he smiled and walked out of the room.

Samuel gave Royce a hard look and followed his brother.

"Mr. President," Joshua extended his hand. He proudly served this man he admired for he was a gentle leader. When actions had to be taken, he was direct and firm with his decisions and proved to be a formidable Commander-in-Chief.

"Agent Lassiter," He shook Joshua's hand. "Please have a seat."

"I want to thank you for securing this region for the country. Your actions were courageous, your decisions decisive. It is due to your bravery we were able to avoid a war that would have cost us many lives."

"Anything for my country, sir."

The President nodded. "I'm sad and pleased to hear you say that, for we do have to ask more of you."

Curious, Joshua sat forward, rested his elbows on his knees. "If it is within my power, sir, it is yours."

"Joshua, I need you to listen to a story. At the end I am asking you to stand down."

"I'm not sure I understand, sir."

"It will come to light, son. Please know, if there were any other way, I would not ask this of you." the President stood. Naturally, Joshua did as well, still not clear on what the President needed from him.

"I am going to meet with Queen Abdulrazaaq. When you are ready to talk, my door will be open."

He was being dismissed. "Yes, sir," Joshua said then walked out the door he came through. Samuel was standing outside the door. Two agents stood outside the door and he noticed a heavier presence along the hallway. The look on his face was murderous. "Care to tell me what in the hell is going on?"

"What did the President say?"

"He wants me to make a sacrifice for my country."

"Son of a bitch." To men like Samuel and Joshua that was the same as a direct order.

"Agent Lassiter, would you come with me please?" the same agent as before asked.

Joshua looked at Samuel, then the two agents behind him, then back to the two in front. "Do I have a choice?"

The men did not respond as Joshua followed them to another room. The agent opened the door. Joshua stood looking at King Aswan, Prince LaVeré', and Prince Raheem, with a security team surrounding him. Joshua looked over his shoulder to see Samuel and Brian Thompson behind him. They were not facing him, but the men at the door. He knew the maneuver. He'd done it several times himself. They were letting the men know, to get to him, they had to come through them. LaVeré' stood, then walked to take a position next to him.

Joshua scanned the room, turned to his brother and asked. "Where is Akande?"

Samuel never turned. "With the President."

"Please, have a seat Joshua," King Aswan motioned toward the chair at the head of the table. Joshua, pulled the chair out, flipped the tail of his coat out, then sat as requested. "Your President trusts your judgment above all of ours. Before Emure can move forward from this unfortunate incident, he has requested you to hear what Raheem has to say. If you believe him to be no threat to Emure or Asmere, then and only then will we move forward."

Joshua's father always told him, there was a time
to speak and a time to listen. This was the latter. He
sat back.

Prince LaVeré' picked up a chair and sat next to
him. Joshua looked at LaVere'. "You are not
concerned I will kill your brother?"

"I would help you if it were up to me."

"LaVere'," King Aswan warned.

Prince LaVere' nodded. "Respectfully, my King."

King Aswan nodded to Raheem.

Prince Raheem sat forward and spoke for the first
time. "I am a man who loves his country. It was
because of my patriotism that I believed something
had to be done to ensure our borders were safe.
Before King Ahmed stepped down, he summoned me
to his office. He shared his concerns with the changes
we as a country were about to undertake. He knew
there would be unrest, as did I." He narrowed his eyes
at his brother. "He stated we must ensure our borders
were secure for unrest within our country would make
us appear to be weak. I agreed with his estimation. I
pleaded with him to name me as his successor for
Aswan would be weak on defense. He refused for one
reason and one reason only. The throne was to go to
the eldest. It did not matter that he was the weakest of
the three of us. I even implored him to place LaVere'
on the throne. It was our ancestor's way and my father
would not be deterred.

Once Aswan was named his successor, a number
of our enemies within the country formed a union and
began to build armies to strike against the monarchy.
I came to Aswan to tell him of my findings. He refused
to listen. He believed the people would come to accept
the change without bloodshed. I did not believe he
was right then and I still believe there will be
bloodshed in our country. I was compelled to do

something that would make Aswan see reason. See that we were not secure under his rule. A small attack would be easily handled and explained away, by Aswan's diplomatic words. I had to make my father and Aswan see the danger. Therefore, I had Zsa Zsa kidnapped. At no time was she in danger, for I arranged for Queen Sermyera's niece to be there with her. I swear on my country I never ordered Akande or you killed. However, my men were loyal to me and they believed in my cause. The actions taken were done out of a sense of duty to me. Therefore, I am responsible for their actions. Make no mistake, I love my country and my family. I did what a leader must do to protect his land and his people. I made a tactical decision. I would do it again to protect my country."

Joshua listened. Never once did he feel Raheem was lying. He did feel the passion he felt for his country. "Are you sure this wasn't about greed?"

"We are wealthy beyond reason. I have no need for money. I do have a need for my country and its citizens to be safe."

"Were you aware, Tarik used the funds from the kidnapping to finance an army to attack Emure?

The look on Raheem's face clearly indicated he knew nothing of this. "No."

"Your judgment was questionable, not only in the conspirators you chose, but also in the control of your men. No one under your rule should ever act without your knowledge. Tell me, what would you have done if the men holding your baby sister had raped her? Would you believe that was an acceptable sacrifice?"

"The woman was placed with her to prevent any such occurrence. I also promised to withhold payment if any harm were to come to Princess Zsa Zsa."

"That would have been after the fact." Joshua shook his head. "Your judgment is lacking. This could be what your father saw when he made the decision to place King Aswan on the throne. I believe you meant no harm to your country. However, you did irrevocable harm to Zsa Zsa. To lead, it takes more than a strong army, it takes compassion and diplomacy. Your actions demonstrate you have neither."

"Do you, Joshua forgive Raheem's attempts on your life?" King Aswan asked.

"I'm still here. I'm cool. You would have to ask Akande's forgiveness, Zsa Zsa, and your parents when they learn of this. As for Prince Raheem, he is your country's problem to deal with, not mine."

"You have not heard all." LaVere' glared at his brother.

"Remove Raheem from the room," King Aswan ordered.

LaVere' stood. "Raheem, you are my brother whom I love. However, this man who you are about to injure risked his life for your country. You are indebted to him for as long as you shall live. If you ever dishonor his sacrifice, I will take your life myself."

Raheem held his brother's glare, then walked briskly from the room.

The room grew quiet. Joshua had a feeling the other shoe was about to drop.

Samuel came to sit at the table. "May we have the room?"

King Aswan bowed his head, and stood. "With the right guidance Raheem will do well as a leader."

Joshua watched as King Aswan and his men left the room.

"I'm staying," LaVere' stated.

"I'm staying too," Brian said as he stood behind Joshua.

"Okay, everybody is staying." Joshua huffed. "That's good, because I will be leaving in about five. I have a lady waiting for me and a ring to put on her finger."

Samuel dropped his head. "Joshua." He sat back, closed his eyes and exhaled. Minutes ticked by without anyone saying a word.

"Will somebody say something damn it?" Joshua hit the table.

No one in the room reacted.

***

In another room next to the oval office, Akande sat with the President of the United States and Senator Davenport. Monique had just entered the room and stood quietly by the door. Akande quickly motioned to her.

"Monique, please have a seat here with me."

Monique waited until she received a nod from the President, then sat next to Akande. She knew the woman was going to need her support.

"Queen Abduzalraaq."

She reached out and touched his hand. "Akande, please." she smiled.

The President returned her smile then covered her hand with his. "At this moment, I need to speak with Queen Abduzalraaq. I pray after this conversation you will still give me the honor of calling you Akande."

Akande slowly sat back, glanced at Monique, who looked nervous. "Very well." She returned to look at the President.

"This has been quite an ordeal for you and I'm afraid it is not over," The President began. "In the last twenty-four hours we have taken control of your palace. Tarik and a few of his men escaped. He knows his plans to take over Emure failed. An announcement was made, on your behalf stating the rightful heir to the throne has been found and certified by our government. Your people are anxious to have you home."

Nervously, Akande wiped the palms of her hands against her dress. "I must say, I don't know much about running a country." She paused with a shaky smile. "Only a month ago all I had to run was a small room. This is a bit overwhelming."

Royce smiled. He liked the young woman. "You have demonstrated bravery and loyalty towards your country. In most cases, that is all that it will take to rule a country." He sat forward. "You have a little more to contend with."

"I'm not sure I understand." She looked from one man to the next. Monique reached over, took her hand and smiled reassuringly. Akande looked at the joined hands, then up at Monique. She tried to let the feeling of dread slip away, but it stayed. "Where is Joshua? Shouldn't he be here?"

"He is being briefed on this conversation as we speak," The President replied then nodded to Royce to continue.

"There is a situation we'd like to make you aware of. Your country is about to become one of the wealthiest in the region. It is for that reason, we have to take steps to ensure the leader is protected and understands the responsibility along with the power."

"Emure is actually the wealthiest country in our region. Asmere is very poor. Believe me, I've lived there all my life. I know."

"That's about to change," Royce interjected. He pulled out his computer and placed it on the table sitting between them. He turned it on. "These are pictures of the southwestern border between Asmere and Emure."

Akande nodded. "I know the area."

"What you don't know is it happens to be the location of several diamond mines recently discovered."

"Diamonds?" Akande inhaled as she squeezed Monique's hand, she turned to her and smiled. "My country has a diamond mine?"

"Yes," Royce replied. "It is the reason Tarik planned to attack Emure, to control the land and the region."

The smile faded from Akande's face. "There was a plan to attack Emure?"

"Yes. With Tarik and some of his men still at large, we feel it is imperative to stabilize the area with due haste," the President replied. "It is going to take a sacrifice of a great personal magnitude on your part to accomplish this."

Akande stood. "I will do anything, anything to secure the safety of my country. We do not have an army, not really. However, I am certain with military assistance from you, we have men who would be willing to fight for their country as well. No sacrifice is too great for one's country."

The President and Royce shared a look. "Then we appeal to your sense of honor and duty when we ask you to wed Prince Raheem Ashro to secure the border between Asmere and Emure." When the President looked up at her, Akande was white as a sheet.

"You are asking me to marry the man who tried to kill me?"

Monique pulled her back down to her seat. "There are circumstances you are not aware of yet, Akande. Joshua is listening to Prince Raheem's reasons for the attempt on your life. If he accepts the Prince reasons and believes you are not in danger, only then will the United States ask this of you." She gave a stern look towards the President. "You do have a choice here."

"Joshua will never agree to this. I know he will not."

"Agent Lassiter does not have a country to consider, Queen Abduzalraaq," The President stated.

"This is all new and coming at you fast," Royce softened the statement. "However, you are not Akande anymore. You are Queen Abduzalraaq. Your duty, your responsibility, right or wrong is with your country."

Akande looked to Monique. The anguish on the woman's face almost tore at her heart. But then she remembered what her mentor told her. We serve at the pleasure of the President of the United States of America. Whether we agree or not, we do as they request. Monique held Akande's hand tight. "Joshua loves you."

"Agent Day," the President cautioned.

Monique gave him a side eye. "Allow me to do my job, sir." She turned back to Akande then continued, "He has not said those words, but I believe he does. He is a patriot to the United States. His family is here, his home is here. His President is here. You are the Queen of Asmere. Your countrymen are depending on you to make the right decision. They have no one else. Akande, you must choose between Asmere and Joshua."

***

Samuel stood, bracing his hands on the back of the chair he'd vacated. He began to explain. "An agreement has been offered to the Queen of Asmere that the President and others believe will stabilize that region. If she accepts, there will be a union between Prince Raheem Ashro of Emure and Queen Sofiat Abduzalraaq of Asmere. The countries of Emure and Asmere along with the United States for the security of the borders."

Joshua laughed. Then he looked at Samuel, and laughed again. "Like hell it will." He stood. "Like hell it will," he said now fully understanding what they were saying.

Samuel stood in front of the door blocking Joshua's way.

"Don't do it, Sammy. Get the hell out of my way."

"I don't like it, not one damn bit. But your President asked you to stand down." Samuel ran his hands down his face as he watched his brother's eyes turn to fury.

Joshua grabbed his brother's shirt at his chest, lifted him and threw him against the wall. He pulled open the door to see the hallway filled with Secret Service Agents. Samuel grabbed him from behind, trapping Joshua's arms to his side and swung him onto the table face down. Brian and LaVere' stood between them and the agents in the hallway. "Get the hell off of me, Samuel!"

"Joshua listen to me. You have to let her go."

"No!" Joshua struggled to escape Samuel's grasp. "I will not, cannot do that Sammy!"

"It's her choice, Joshua. It's her choice." Samuel held his brother, feeling every ounce of his pain.

"I don't believe that, Sammy!" he continued to struggle. "Where is she? Where is Akande?"

"I am here, Joshua." The serene voice wasn't loud, but the impact froze everyone in the room.

Samuel released Joshua, but stood there restraining him from moving.

There was no light in her eyes. That was the first sign he noticed. Tears streamed down her face. The President, Senator Davenport and Monique stood behind her.

"Akande don't," He shook his head in disbelief. "You are free now. To love and live as you choose. You do not have to do this," he whimpered.

She held her head high. "I am Sofiat Abduzalraaq, Queen of Asmere." Tears flowed. "I must do all that is in my power to protect and defend my country. As I know you would do for yours."

He yanked away from Samuel and slowly walked towards her. He wanted to reach out, to touch her face, her lips one last time, but he stopped himself. "You have the right and the freedom to refuse the offer." He inhaled, his chest heaving from the pressure of his heart about to explode.

The hurt in his eyes was too much. Her heart was breaking. But what choice did she have? The people in her country were depending on her. "The union between Emure and Asmere will bring peace and prosperity to my country, Joshua. Please, understand. This is my duty."

"Duty?" He stepped back as if he had been slapped in his face. He swiped his hands down his face, removing any trace of tears. "What about your duty to me? See when I gave you my heart, it became your duty to protect it." The anger was oozing through his pores. "I trusted you to protect it."

He looked around the room, shaking his head not believing this was happening. "You said to me several times. You were no man's whore. Yet you are going to marry a man you do not love and lay with him in the name of duty."

"Joshua," Akande softly called out. "You gave me the freedom to make my own decisions. I choose my country."

For a long while the room was quiet. Not a soul moved. It wasn't clear if anyone was breathing. Joshua held her eyes and knew he had lost. He exhaled with a chuckle. "The price of freedom...right, Mr. President?"

"It is the price son," the President replied.

"Yeah, well..." He looked at Akande for the last time. "The hell with you, your choice and your country." He turned and walked out of the room.

Samuel, Brian and LaVere' followed.

Agents looked to the President. "Stand down." The President said in a warning tone. "If you value your life, stand down."

Chapter Twenty-two

Royce lay in Shelly's embrace as he told her of the situation with Akande and Joshua. His heart hurt for them. For nights he had prayed that the two would find a way to heal.

"In time they will." Shelly held his head to her breast. "That poor girl...all her life she had to deal with that evil woman. Now, she has to spend her life with a man she does not love all because she is a Queen. What kind of sense does that make?" She sighed. "I don't know what kind of world we live in, but somebody better make it better soon."

"I'm trying." He kissed her between her breasts. "It's times like this I want to say, the hell with the country. Let the crazies have it. But, then I think about you and what those crazies did to you and I know I can't let them have control. I will do all that's in my power to keep this country safe." Royce sighed. "We sacrificed Joshua, but he still understands his duty to his country. I admire that young man and pray in time he will accept why we asked this of him."

"I don't know, Royce." She leisurely rubbed his head. "It's one thing to serve your country, but another to lose your heart. I only saw them together for a few minutes, but I think he loved her."

"I know he did," Royce replied. "I think Akande's heart belongs to her country. As Queen, it should. Joshua, well, he fell hard, just for the wrong woman."

"Most players do." Shelly exhaled. "The next woman to capture his heart is going to catch hell."

"I know that's true. But with everything, that's happened, he's still protecting her. Today, Tarik's body was delivered on the doorstep of the palace. The palace is surrounded by our people, our security. No one saw anyone drop it off. Joshua is the only man I know who can pull something like that off. He knew as long as Tarik was alive, Akande would be in danger and the border would not be secure."

"Wow that is powerful love. She broke his heart and he is still protecting her from her enemies."

"I'm certain he is not finished yet. It would not surprise me to find Raheem's body one day. If the man died falling off a horse, I would swear Joshua was behind it."

"Do you think he will be at the wedding?"

"Which wedding?"

"Akande and the Prince's?"

"No. He will be near, but he will not come."

"Hmm," She rubbed his arm as she thought of Akande. "She found love, only to have to let it go. "When you find that right person, you have to grab on to them and never let them go. She's going to wish she had made a different decision."

"No, she made the right decision," Royce said as he sat up. "Joshua would never leave the life to be the husband Akande would need. He is a patriot. Whenever his country calls on him to serve, he would be there. Where would that leave Asmere?" He reached down to the floor for his pants. "Joshua will realize that once the pain goes away." He sat back up, placed a long black velvet box on her stomach, then kissed her navel.

"What is this?"

He kissed below her navel then looked up. "Open it." He spread her thighs.

"How in the hell am I supposed to concentrate with you down there eating my cookies?"

He looked up and licked his lips. "Okay, I'll wait." He inhaled her heat rising with anticipation.

Shelly, opened the box and fell out laughing. "Oh hell-to-the-no! I don't care if you bring me the oysters with pearls inside and string them yourself, I am not going back to your place in D.C."

"Not even for this?" He held his finger out, with a solitaire diamond ring dangling from it."

Shelly sat up in bed so fast she almost knocked him on the floor. "Royce." Her breath caught as she touched the ring. "It is beautiful."

"Will you do me the honor of being my wife? You have pearls now."

Epilogue

Samuel sat at one end of the table, his parents Sally and Joe, at the other end. All of his brothers and sisters except Joshua were seated around him. His wife Cynthia and his baby girl Samantha were there, along with his sister Diamond's husband Zack. It was his duty to explain Joshua's situation to his family.

"JD said Joshua was very brave and accepted the President's decision in a way that would make any man proud, Daddy," Pearl, one of the Lassiter sisters said nodding to her brother. "Isn't that true, Samuel?"

"Why hasn't he come home?" Phire, their baby sister asked. "It's been weeks, Sammy."

"I know, Phire." Sammy, put his daughter in her mother's arms and sat forward. "Joshua was hurt by Akande's decision. It's going to take him a little while to come to terms with it. He has asked the President to assign him to an undercover operation. It may be years before we see him again. The President granted his request."

"Is she safe," Sally asked?

"Who?"

"The woman who broke Joshua's heart? He would want her to be safe. I know this in my heart."

"Yes," Samuel replied. Only his mother would care about the woman's safety. "Akande is safe."

"But, married to a man she does not love." Adam shook his head. "According to you a man who tried to kill her. Ain't life grand?"

"It was her choice," Ruby the oldest sister stated. "I'm sure if Joshua were here he would tell all of us, there are other women out there that want him."

"Yes, he would say that," Mathew, one of the younger brothers added with a smirk. "We Lassiter men always have a honey waiting in the wings." The other brothers joined in the chorus, and smiled.

"It's different when you meet the right woman," Zack stated, as he pulled Diamond close. "My Uncle Royce said he believes Joshua was in love with Akande, but he wasn't sure of her commitment to him."

"Senator Royce Davenport is your uncle?" Pearl asked.

"Yes, my father's brother."

"Why did he let this happen to Joshua?" Phire asked. "Why did he and the President allow this to happen? Joshua is faithful to his country. But his country turned their back on him what kind of sh....crap is that?"

"It's not their fault, Phire," Jade, another sister added. "Love happens, sometimes it works out, like with Sammy and Diamond and sometimes it hurts. Joshua is going to make it through this. Right now, he needs us to pray for his soul." She held out her hands to her brothers and sisters.

Everyone around the table bowed their heads and joined hands, as Jade nudged her twin Timothy to begin the family prayer.

An hour later, once everyone had dispersed back to their college dorms, and homes, Pearl, Samuel, Cynthia and their parents sat in the family room.

"On Memorial Day, Governor Harrison is going to announce he is running for President."

"That is wonderful news." Joe smiled. "He's a good man."

"Yes, he is," Samuel stated. "He was also the brain behind this deal between Asmere and Emure."

"What?" Cynthia asked, surprised. "I can't believe JD would do anything to interfere with two people in love."

"I don't think he knew." Samuel rubbed his wife's shoulder. "Let's be real, Joshua runs through women like water through a faucet. None of us knew until he was in too deep to recognize the warning signs."

"I knew," Sally spoke softly.

Joe looked at his wife. "How did you know?"

"He came to see me and told me about her. He wanted to know about trust." she smiled remembering the conversation. I told him about you and Sofia."

Cynthia sat up. "Sofia who? My mother Sofia?" She looked from Sally to Joe.

Sally looked up at her husband, who sat next to her. Joe shook his head. "That was a long time ago woman."

"It was." Sally nodded.

"You and my mother?" Cynthia stared at Joe."

He nodded. "When we were younger."

"Is that why she hates the Lassiters?"

"Probably," Sally replied.

"Daddy," Pearl chimed in. "You and the Queen of Ice?"

"Let it go, Pearl," Joe warned.

Pearl looked over at Cynthia. "I am so sorry I hated you as much as I did, now that I know about your mother. I understand why you were such a whore in high school."

"I wasn't a whore," Cynthia defended. "You may not believe this, but I did not lose my virginity until I was in college." Pearl looked at her in disbelief. "It's true."

Sally laughed at the two women. Happy to see they could now at least joke with each other. "Anyway, I told him about Sofia and how she betrayed your trust. You can never fully love another without trust. To my way of thinking Governor Harrison may have saved Joshua from a mistake. For you see, Joshua never really gave his heart to her, because he did not fully trust her." She lowered her eyes, as tears flowed. "There are times when there is a facade of love. It feels real, it looks real, sometimes, it acts real, but it's just a facade. We make a choice based on what feels good rather than waiting for God to put the right person into our lives. You see, He gave us free will, to make choices, but He also asks us to trust in Him."

"Trust in the Lord with all your heart, and lean not on your own understanding." Proverbs chapter 3 verse 5," Samuel quoted.

"In all your ways acknowledge Him and He shall direct your path, Proverbs chapter 3 verse 5," Sally added.

"I fear Joshua has lost his way," Joe said.

Sally was visibly shaken, with tears streaming down her face. "I need to see my son Samuel. I need to know my child is all right. You make it happen."

This was the first time Samuel had ever seen his mother's tears. He looked at his father for help. There was none there.

"Your mother made a request of you, son. I expect you to honor it. This family comes before your President."

Samuel looked to Pearl, but she too, had tears in her eyes.

***

A week later, Sally opened the envelope lying on her nightstand. Inside was a cross. The one she had given her second son the day he told her he was joining the military like his big brother. Tears sprang to her eyes. Emotions were tugging at her heart. It had been weeks since Joshua walked out of Royce Davenport's condo in Georgetown, or since anyone had heard from him. She read the passage he had written.

Joshua 1:8

> *"Do not let this Book of the Law depart from your mouth; meditate on it day and night, so that you may be careful to do everything written in it. Then you will be prosperous and successful."* (NIV)

> *I lived by the law. I meditated on his words day and night. Put my trust in GOD, yet I was betrayed. Why hast thou forsaken me?*

The passage was the one he selected when he was sworn in as a CIA operative. The one he swore he would take into his heart and live by. He told her, he would keep the cross near his heart as well. The removal of the cross frightened her. For she knew her son had lost faith.

Joe walked into the room to see the tears streaming down his wife's face. She couldn't speak. She held the cross to her heart and leaned into her husband. Joe read the note. "He will find his way." He comforted his wife. "He will find his way."

As he did, Joe said a silent prayer for his son's safety. For the first time in his life, he feared for his son's life. He cleared his throat of the sob trapped there and quietly called out his son's name. "Joshua."

***

An unshaven Joshua, dressed in black jeans, black tee shirt, army boots, and his trench coat, sat in the corner of the cave where he and Akande made love for the first time. This was where the false hope of a normal life emerged. This place made him think it was possible for him to have a life like Samuel, a beautiful wife, a daughter or son who loved him unconditionally. Even now he wondered if Akande could be carrying his child.

All of his life he believed in God's words. Love Him above all else. People often wondered why he wore suits all the time. It wasn't because he was arrogant about his looks. He wore suits because when he was a little boy, every Sunday his mother would dress him in his one suit and off to church they went. It was the way he was presented to God on Sundays. He felt good, reverent and loved. Wearing suits was his way of honoring God every day, not just on Sundays. Every day he opened his eyes he would thank God for allowing him to see one more day. Then he would ask God to be with him throughout that day. At night he would thank God for allowing him to make it through that day and ask God to watch over him through the night. He never missed the feeling of God's presence in his life. Until today.

Today Sofiat, his Akande, married Raheem. Asmere now had its true ruler. The country was celebrating. Deep down, he was happy for her. She was a true patriot of Asmere. She would have given her life so her country would prosper again. Well, she didn't have to give her life after all. She only had to give him up. He could not bring himself to look upon her again. He had never felt so alone or forsaken.

He thought of his mother. She was the one he feared for more than any other. For he knew she had a deep trust and belief in God and in him. He promised her he would not allow harm to come to himself. It was the one promise he may have to break. He didn't want to feel any more. He wanted to destroy any and everything that came into his path. They say a wild animal is more dangerous when it is hurt. Well, he hurt like hell and he had a license to kill.

Joshua stood and looked around the cave. From his pocket he pulled out the box he received from Lucy. He opened the box to take one last look at the object inside. Leaving the top open, he placed the solitaire diamond ring on a fern leaf.

"Good bye, Akande."

Joshua climbed the rocks to the top of the hill. He boarded his chopper then pulled off. He looked down on the waterfall one last time, then pushed a button on the panel. BOOM.

Never looking back, he heard the explosion that sealed the cave forever.

THE BOOK OF JOSHUA II

Believe

IRIS BOLLING

Gems & Gents Series

The Book of Joshua II - BELIEVE

Prologue

Joshua pulled the paper from the sealed container. There were several on the same letterhead. It had the seal of the United States at the bottom. It wasn't the Presidential Seal. He knew the seal well, for he had several of them himself. He took a quick glance at the signatures. The Vice President and the Secretary of Defense. Joshua shook his head not wanting to believe what he was reading. Pulling out his handheld, which he affectionately called Sally, after his mother, he scanned the document then sent it to Ned, his handler, for review. He knew he had to have the original to authenticate, but this would at least let him know what evidence they'd found. Before putting Sally away, he held the document up and shined his black light over it. There were certain security features in the paper used by the President's office that could not be seen with the naked eye. The features were there. Someone from the White House gave immunity to this man. Joshua looked around at the weapons of mass destruction. Who in the hell would allow these weapons on U.S. soil?

He folded the paper and placed it inside a covert section of his coat pocket, near the small GPS button. If something happened to him, Ned would be able to locate the coat using the GPS. The document would be found. He quickly scanned through the other five documents in the file, sending a copy of each to Ned, then placed them back.

This was not his mission. He was in Mexico City to deliver a secure message to the President of Mexico without being detected. Afterwards, he stopped in Monterey to see an old friend, Alejandro Mateo. Yes, he was the head of the Mexican Cartel, but from time to time, he had proven to be a friend to him and the

United States. Never hurt to have friends on both sides of the law in his line of work. It would not serve him or Mateo any good if he was seen leaving, so he used a back way to return to his chopper, which he'd landed at the tail end of Mateo's property some ten miles away. He was about to turn into the densely wooded area where his chopper was, when he heard gun shots, then loud cheers. Turning away from the chopper, he walked towards the sounds and found men taking target practice with M2 Browning machine guns. Sitting next to them on the ground, was an open case of weapons. He heard the men talking and knew this was an arms deal going down. For a minute he thought this was Mateo's doing, but then he heard the man say, Mateo would have him killed if he knew about this. Joshua was about to leave, hell Mateo was ruthless, he would handle this, but the man turned. A face from the past stood not fifty feet away from him. The last time he saw the man was outside a window in Richmond, Virginia.

Jonas Gray. What in the hell was he doing here?

He listened a little longer. When they mentioned documents assuring immunity from the highest level in the U.S. in his safe, Joshua was shocked.

"I'll take all you have. Come with me," Gray said as he turned toward the building.

Using the trees as cover, Joshua followed the men to a log cabin style house, with a building to the left. The man placed his hand on a panel, to the right of the door, to unlock the building, another man backed a truck up to the door. Using Sally, he took pictures of the men, the weapons being moved, then made himself comfortable next to a tree. He wanted to see what was in that building.

It was hours later, when he deactivated the sophisticated alarm system, then walked through the door at the back of the building. He couldn't believe his eyes at the stock pile of weapons of mass destruction. The M2s were only the tip of the iceberg. He sent Ned a message. We have an issue. He sent pictures of semi-automatic rifles, AK-47s, AR-70s, Uzis, AR-15s, MAC 11s, even his favorites, grenade launchers. There were crates and crates stacked almost to the ceiling. He walked through the building and found an office towards the front. He deactivated the alarm on the office door and entered. The office wasn't large, maybe twelve by twelve. There was a desk with two chairs in front of it, against the wall, a file cabinet on another wall, a glass case with an assortment of rifles displayed. On the fourth wall, there were pictures and that was what caught his attention. Jonas Gray was in each shaking hands with several people he recognized. Two in particular: Vice President of the United States, Jerry McClintock, and Admiral Mark McGary.

"What were they doing in a picture with a man like Gray?" His curiosity was peaked. He looked around. He sifted through the file cabinet, which wasn't locked. Not much, records of sales mostly. Not what he was looking for. The man mentioned a safe. Using Sally, he activated the sensor. If there was a metal safe, Sally would find it. And she did. It was in the floor under the two chairs and carpet in front of the desk. That's where he found the papers.

Now, standing with his arms folded over his chest, he knew there was no way he could allow these weapons to move from this location. Not with the destination being the United States. Smiling, he nodded his head. "Why the hell not?"

He took the walk back to his chopper, activated the sleuth mode, then took off in the direction of the building. Using night vision glasses, he flew in the dark. Before emerging from the trees, he saw activity on the ground. Something must have alerted the occupants of the house, for two men were standing outside of the building and another was running back into the house.

"Oh hell, sorry about this guys. I just wanted to get rid of the weapons."

Just when Joshua was about to fire a missile to destroy the weapons below, the sensor on the chopper panel went off. A missile had locked on to him. "No you did not fire at me."

He swung the chopper around, dropped the missile, then flew away from the explosion that was about to occur.

He flew in the direction of the Mexico and Texas border, using every evasion maneuver he knew, but the missile had locked on him, he could not shake it. The only thing he could do was find a dense area with no population and go low. He heard the explosion from below, but could not celebrate, for he still had a missile on his tail. He flew towards a mountainous area, headed towards one, then pulled up right before hitting it. The missile nipped the tail end of the chopper sending it into a tail spin, before exploding into the mountain.

The chopper was out of control. Joshua sent a message to Ned. *Going down.* He was still in Mexico, not far from the first explosion. The monitor on the dashboard of the chopper indicated his location was close to Laredo, Texas, just not close enough. He knew the men on the ground would get to him before anyone from the U.S. could. Just before the chopper crashed, his last thought was, he never gave his mother grandchildren. Sally was going to be pissed.

Made in the USA
Monee, IL
02 January 2023

24004870R00157